Having previously worked as a journalist and then a psychotherapist, Caroline Dunford enjoyed many years helping other people shape their personal life stories before taking the plunge and writing her own stories. She has now published almost thirty books in genres ranging from historical crime to thrillers and romance, including her much-loved Euphemia Martins mysteries and a brand-new series set around WWII featuring Euphemia's perceptive daughter Hope Stapleford. Caroline also teaches creative writing courses part-time at the University of Edinburgh.

Praise for Caroline Dunford:

'A sparkling and witty crime debut with a female protagonist to challenge Miss Marple' Lin Anderson

'Impeccable historical detail with a light touch' Lesley Cookman

'Euphemia Martins is feisty, funny and completely adorable' Colette McCormick

'A rattlingly good dose of Edwardian country house intrigue with plenty of twists and turns and clues to puzzle through' Booklore.co.uk

A DEATH
IN THE
HOSPITAL

A EUPHEMIA MARTINS MYSTERY

CAROLINE DUNFORD

ACCENT

First published in 2020 by Headline Accent
An imprint of HEADLINE PUBLISHING GROUP

1

Cataloguing in Publication Data is available from the British Library

ISBN 978 1 7861 5796 6

Typeset in 10.5/13pt Bembo Std by Jouve (UK), Milton Keynes

Printed and bound in Great Britain by Clays Ltd, Elcograf S.p.A.

HEADLINE PUBLISHING GROUP
An Hachette UK Company
Carmelite House
50 Victoria Embankment
London
EC4Y 0DZ

www.headline.co.uk
www.hachette.co.uk

The theme and title of this book were chosen over
two years ago. I had always intended to dedicate this
story to the NHS who have, at various times, saved
the lives of every member of my family, and who gave
such kind and gentle care to my dying mother.

At the time of writing, we are in the midst of a pandemic
and such thanks have never seemed more appropriate.
The NHS is simply wonderful, as are the people who
work within it. My hope for the future is that we remember
how priceless both are, and we treat them accordingly.

I'd also like to dedicate this book to Harold Floate,
my maternal grandfather, who died long before I was born.
He was a spotter in WWI. Gassed, buried alive, and
shell-shocked, he eventually made it home, but never
fully recovered; a small man of great strength.

Chapter One

A turning out and sorting of things

The day was dull, with the kind of white sky that bears down on you and leaves you restless and feeling out of sorts. The apple trees outside the morning room dripped steadily with fat raindrops. I couldn't hear them through the glass, but watching them, it felt as if I could. The ground outside was turning to mud, and all I could think of was the young men from the estate we had so recently sent off to war.

'Mrs Stapleford?'

Our housekeeper, Mrs Templeton, a widowed lady of a mellowed age, who had fallen on hard times, tried valiantly once more to turn my attention to the bed linen we were inspecting.

'I'm sure you are right, Mrs Templeton.'

'About what, Mrs Stapleford?'

'Everything,' I said hopefully.

Mrs Templeton pinched the bridge of her nose with the fingers of her right hand. 'I fear I shall have to get eyeglasses,' she said. 'I keep getting the most annoying headaches.' She gave a small, ladylike sigh.

Guilt pinched at me. 'Mrs T,' I said, directing my full attention to her, 'I am aware I appear pre-occupied. I very much need to get back to my study. I employed you because I have confidence in you and your decisions. If you feel all this linen needs replacing, then do it. Turn out the cupboards to your heart's content. I expect there are even ones that we have not opened since we settled here. I leave it entirely to you.'

'Madam, if I may say so, this is a very strange way to run a household.'

'I am afraid, Mrs T, I will always be a strange mistress. I have had my fill of running houses. I am content to issue the most general of orders, although I will continue to approve the daily menus. That, and the occasional conversation with our new factor, will be my only concession to the day-to-day housekeeping routine.'

'But won't Mr Stapleford wish to talk to the factor?'

'Probably, but afterwards Mr McArthur will generally wish to see me. He doesn't like to bother my husband with the more trouble-some details. His heart, you know.'

'Of course.'

'Now, if you will excuse me, I have some urgent letters to attend to.' I nodded briefly to her and did my best to sweep out of the room as my mother would have done, but with a touch less haughtiness. I liked Mrs Templeton. I knew she would be good at her job. I only wished she would leave me alone.

The small room off the morning room is my office. We call it my writing room, so the staff don't find it too unusual. It's really a remote occupational base. It's bad enough that I have my own tele-phone apparatus in there that none of them are allowed to answer. I closed the door and went to sit at my desk. I stared at the wretched new-fangled device and willed it to ring.

All I could hear was the sound of the rain falling steadily and relentless against the windows of White Orchards.

The truth was, I had no new letters to write. I took some papers out of a locked drawer and again read my copy of the notes I had presented to my masters in London. News had reached me yesterday that one of the supply lines I had advised the army to use had been compromised. I went over my information and my report. I could find no flaw in either. The British Expeditionary Force had begun to land in France three days ago, on 7th August. A small force, but all of them hardened veterans, they were there to help the French and Belgians repel German invasion.

What was not generally known to the public was that there had been an earlier landing. Spotters, or scouts, as they were sometimes known, had gone in to check the lie of the land. Sending back information to analysts like myself, on the terrain, population, roads, etc, they also looked for places to engage of the enemy, locations for bases, and everything an advancing army might need. The very best of them had gone forward to scout the enemy lines – or as close as they could get. That's where my partner, the spymaster Fitzroy, currently was. He likes to think of himself as my superior officer, but as my standing is still in debate in the Service I have said I will only work with him if he considers me his partner. I have admittedly also said I will respect his experience. It's a stand off.

Our last mission had seen us travelling back through France and Germany in February and March. Fitzroy had been recovering from a knife wound in his side, so we had been meandering back in a leisurely manner, pretending to be a newly married couple, but in reality scoping out the environment in anticipation of the war that we both feared was imminent.

As soon as we were back on British soil, he had been transferred to train the spotters. I had been drafted to do the analysis of their work as I had so recently driven through much of the landscape. I agreed I had no place training army veterans as spotters. Fitzroy had a lot of experience and I was a newish recruit. It also meant that I got to stay at home with my long-suffering husband, Bertram. Yet I had been unprepared for the levels of anxiety that would suddenly seize me with Fitzroy away in the heart of the action. He had been working successfully for ten years without my concern – as he would have happily pointed out. Although, last time, I had saved his life at least twice. However, he was with men he had trained and trusted – and that's the best you can hope for in the field. It was just that with that food supply line becoming compromised, I had this nagging doubt in my mind that something had gone very wrong.

At this point I hadn't heard from Fitzroy by post or official communication for two weeks. I hesitated to telephone head office. That

I was a female spy was bad enough. That I had previously worked exclusively with Fitzroy had started extensive rumours. I believe, before he left, Fitzroy had punched two junior officers, who had made inappropriate comments about our partnership. If I called Head Office about his welfare, I would undo all his 'good' work. I presumed – I hoped – they would tell me if he wasn't going to come back.

I sat in my office for the rest of the afternoon, until it was time to change for dinner. We keep things informal here in many ways, but both Bertram and I agree one should, at the very least, smarten up for dinner. He likes the ritual of it. I need something to break up the endless monotony of body and soul into which I appear to have fallen.

Dinner proved to go down very well with Bertram. Our game-keeper had supplied some fresh duck, of which he is very fond. I find it a dark and fatty meat, but with little pleasing me, I could at least do my best to please my husband.

Bertram smiled at me from his end of the shortened dining table. The candlelight we prefer at dinner caught in his deep brown eyes, so that they shone with happiness. 'Jolly fine dinner, darling,' he said. 'Fancy a game of chess afterwards? I've read the ruddy papers three times. Nothing in them but ridiculous speculation. I dashed off a couple of letters to the editors. Ones I hope that will quite spoil their digestive systems.' He took a swig of claret. 'But other than that, my day's been rather dull. How's yours been?'

I pondered on which question to address first. Bertram tends now to deliver his thoughts in bunches. Almost as if he is saving them up to avoid diminishing his energy during the day.

'In order, dearest: I am glad you like your dinner. I will happily play chess with you, but I will beat you, as I always do. The papers are speculating wildly to gain a better readership and because no one yet knows what will happen.'

'Be over by Christmas,' muttered Bertram.

'I applaud you writing to the papers. As I have said before, you write very well, and I think you should offer yourself as a consultant correspondent. My day has been spent in various ways, from looking at linen with Mrs T to trawling through some work documents for information.'

'Which you can't tell me about?' said my husband, his voice losing much of its pleasantness.

'No,' I said. 'Besides, I believe you would find it of little interest.'

'All for old Fitz-bang, is it?'

It was on the tip of my tongue to state that I could neither confirm nor deny, but the servants had left us, so I threw him a crumb. 'My reports are going to Head Office.'

My husband's shoulders descended from being near his ears and he leant back in his seat. 'Ah, well, I see. One must do one's duty and all that. Especially in these times. I don't suppose I . . .'

Bertram has, in the past, acted as an asset for the Crown.

'I will ask Head Office next time I call,' I said, knowing that would not be any time soon.

'After all, I do have experience,' said Bertram. 'I want to do my bit.'

'Absolutely,' I said. 'But you have a weak heart and must be accommodated accordingly.' I levelled a firm gaze at him. 'You will not be going off to war. Why, we haven't even been married a year!'

'The third gardener, that young chap Bobby, married two days before he volunteered,' said my husband. 'I don't want to be an exception.'

I stood up. 'I wish to retire. It's been a ghastly day. Would you be so kind as to escort me up the stairs, husband?'

'Damn it, Euphemia it's not even seven p.m. I know we're keeping country hours, but there is no way I will be able to sleep. I will end up staring at the ceiling for hours. There's nothing to do in bed . . .' He caught my expression. 'Unless you were thinking . . .'

I tilted my head very slightly.

'You don't mean . . .? Why, the sun isn't even down!'

'How outrageous,' I quipped. 'Whatever would the staff think?'

'They are not employed to dictate our actions.'

'Exactly.'

'My goodness,' said Bertram, standing up and trailing his napkin

5

from his waistcoat. 'And skipping pudding too. You are a rascal, Euphemia.'

'But I'm *your* rascal,' I said, coming over and kissing him lightly on the mouth.

'To think I would ever have married such a goer,' said my husband with an enormous grin.

At breakfast the next morning Bertram read the papers while humming softly and discordantly to himself. We had not yet been married long enough for me to find this any less than charming, and I fussed around him with the coffee pot. I did not prevent the maid from bringing up second helpings of all the dishes. Bertram had lost a second waistcoat button yesterday. He was spreading. With the weather so bad, the opportunity for exercise waned. Our poor horses, wearing weather blankets, congregated under the elms and regarded the house miserably as if we had the power to turn back the rain.

In truth I could have screamed with the boredom and anxiety of it all – despite the lovely evening I had only just spent with Bertram. I had always loathed White Orchards and the Fens, where it was situated. Bertram loved country living. I, who had grown up in the country, constantly longed for something different. However, I had known of my husband's heart condition before I married him, and I wished us to have a long life together. If only there could be a little more to it . . .

The telephone rang loudly in my study. I excused myself and ran to answer it. For it to ring outside office hours was abnormal, and significant. I picked up the receiver while I was still an arm's length from my desk. 'Hello!' I said breathlessly.

'Mrs Stapleford?' said a male voice.

'This is Alice,' I said, giving my code name and confirming no one was within earshot.

'We thought you should know. There have been further complications arising from your information.'

'Another supply line?' I said, my heart sinking.

'No, this concerns the report you wrote when you returned from France. In particular, about the German border.'

'Can you say who is speaking, please?' I asked. I needed to know what his rank was because I had an overwhelming urge to tell him *to damn well spit it out.*

'No, but I can tell you Captain Fitzroy is missing. We believe he and his group of spotters were caught in an ambush.'

I sat down heavily in my chair. 'Can you tell me . . . no, you said, missing. You must know the Captain co-authored that report with me.'

'I am aware he signed off on it. He said you had done the bulk of the work.'

I closed my eyes. Fitzroy often tried to give me more credit than I was due. He was constantly trying to bolster my importance to the Service. This time it might well have backfired. Although the words hadn't been spoken, I could hear the suspicion in the nameless voice. Twice now my data had led to failures – possibly captures or deaths. My throat tightened.

'Alice? Do you have anything to say that could be of help?'

'Such as what?' I said.

'Could you or your material have been compromised?'

I didn't snap back the response I wanted to. I owed the lives of the men involved more than that. 'I have not been compromised,' I said in a level voice. 'I have followed all the set protocols for delivering information.'

'Have you spoken to your husband about your work? We are aware he has also signed the Official Secrets Act.'

'No. I was expressly told he did not have clearance.'

'That must make things difficult for you.'

I did not make the mistake of thinking the voice was empathising with me. 'I know my duty,' I said curtly.

'Then you will agree, we have a problem.'

'It would certainly appear Captain Fitzroy does,' I said, struggling to maintain my temper. 'Would you notify me at once when you hear from him, please?'

7

'We will follow all normal protocols. Until you hear from us again, consider yourself stood down, Alice.'

The voice rang off.

I stormed back to the breakfast room. 'I don't bloody believe it,' I yelled at Bertram. 'I've been stood down!' Then, without warning, I burst into involuntary tears.

Chapter Two

The unexpected

It is very difficult for a husband to console his wife when she cannot tell him the better part of what is distressing her. However, Bertram did his best. He has always been the kindest, gentlest man I have known. He is passionate about right and wrong, abhors injustice, and has always supported me in my suffragette ideals. He was so concerned for me that he even suggested, three days later, days which I had spent in misery and unable to eat properly, we might have a party. 'I know it's not the bally thing to enjoy oneself right now,' he said. 'But I've been giving it some thought. Why don't we have some kind of event to raise morale and even funds, or . . . socks, or something for the boys going away and the families left behind?'

I quietly untangled this suggestion. 'I do think that is an excellent idea. Many women must feel helpless with their men away at the war.'

'Has all this – your mood – got something to do with *that man*,' said Bertram, a scowl marring his face. 'If it's he who has upset you, I'll damn well punch his lights out, dicky heart or not. I won't have him upsetting you.'

'No, Fitzroy hasn't done anything,' I said. *Only disappear. Possibly die,* I thought. I came closer and buried my head in Bertram's shoulder, sniffing a bit. How could I possibly tell him about my anxiety for my partner without him reading more into it? Only partners who have shared life and death experiences in the field could understand the bond of camaraderie that builds up between you. No agent would dispute it. Except when it involved partners of opposite sexes.

9

It didn't help, of course, that Fitzroy had something of a reputation with the ladies. None of them seemed to understand the man was a consummate professional and would never have entangled himself romantically with me, even if I had wanted him to.

'I think people may have died as a result of information I sent to Head Office.' I sniffed louder. 'And they seem to think it might be my fault.'

I looked up into Bertram's horrified face. 'I shouldn't have told you,' I said quickly. 'They already think I've been careless with secrets.'

'My dear girl,' said my husband, 'I appreciate, under the circumstances, I cannot set about these rotters with a large stick, but I know you. You always do your duty with the utmost care. Even if they don't know that now, they'll work it out. Cannot Fitzroy speak for you?'

I shook my head. 'He's in the field.'

Bertram huffed. 'Should have known the bloody man would never be around when you need him. When you don't want to see him, like when you've returned from your honeymoon by a few hours, the damned man turns up like a ruddy bad penny.'

I straightened up. 'He is rather like that,' I agreed. 'I will speak to Mrs T about your party. Perhaps we could involve the vicar and do a sort of fete in support of the troops and their families. Involving the church would make it seem less frivolous.'

'That's a damn good idea,' said Bertram. 'We could have candy cotton stalls, and coconut shies, guess the weight of the cake and all those jolly kinds of things. But no clowns. Clowns wouldn't be appropriate.'

'No,' I said, smiling very slightly. 'They wouldn't. Besides, you still have nightmares about your brother popping out of your wardrobe wearing a clown costume.'

'Reckon that's what did it for my heart,' said Bertram. 'I know one shouldn't speak ill of the dead, but Richard was a rotter, through and through.'

'You'll get no argument from me,' I said. 'Let's convene a

meeting with the vicar, McArthur, Mrs Templeton, and even Merry. We'll make it a tea-time affair with cake.'

Bertram's eyes misted with tears. 'You are the very best sort of a wife,' he said, and grabbed me in a rib-crushing embrace. Fortunately, after years of trying, Bertram has given up attempting to grow a beard, and so there was no impediment to kissing him after breakfast.

'Now, you must let me go, so I can arrange a meeting of the fete committee. Is this afternoon too soon?'

'Not at all,' said Bertram. 'May I take it upon myself to visit Cook and speak to her about the cakes required?'

I knew this meant we would end up with far too many cakes, which the household would be forced to finish off – in other words, Bertram. 'Of course, my dear,' I said.

I sent my old friend Merry a note offering, if necessary, the attention of our cook to mind her baby. I rather hoped she wouldn't agree to this as I knew Cook, who loved babies, would completely desert her preparations for dinner and Bertram would end the day in a most grumpy mood when he received some hastily scrambled eggs and cold cuts for his supper.

I then wrote notes for the vicar and rang for Mrs T. I explained the plan and asked her to get the boot boy to deliver my notes. Having done all this, I sat back in my chair, feeling very much like the wife of a country squire. It was not an unpleasant feeling and I felt the fete could lift all our spirits. It would give me an excuse to spend more time with Merry, who, unless she was invited, would not make the journey from her cottage to our house for fear of overstepping boundaries. I had given up trying to persuade her otherwise.

I then had the thought that it would be rather a good idea to include our local doctor, an intelligent man, who often joined us for dinner when the evenings were long. Dr Samuel Butcher, who was fully aware of the irony of his name, possessed a wry wit that often had Bertram and I in stitches. Although only in his thirties, he was a widower. Neither Bertram nor I had ever enquired into the details of this tragedy and he had never offered up his history. However, he

11

was a good, sensible doctor, who displayed empathy and understanding to all his patients, regardless of status. His tongue could be sharp, as anyone who had called him out in the middle of the night for a trivial reason could attest, but when his patients were in need, he would do all within his power. The birth of Merry's son had not been easy and, unlike most doctors, he had stayed with her the whole time. Merry was so grateful she had given her son the middle name of Sam. Michael Sam was a hearty baby who had appeared several months before his father had departed for war and was already showing signs of becoming a most determined child. I had no doubt that caring for the baby had been a comfort to Merry, as well as extremely hard work.

I sent the note off to Dr Butcher with the addition of suggesting, if he wished, that he could refer patients to our house during the meeting if an emergency arose.

I had written my notes at a small desk in the morning room. I had shut the door to my office and did not intend to open it until I was called to duty. If I was called, that is. I rang the bell for our butler, Giles, who in the politest terms, and with the most nuanced of expressions, always subtly managed to convey his disappointment at his master having such an outlandish wife. To be fair, I did, on the evening of our first acquaintance, run off into the night after another man's vehicle calling for him to return. The scrapes *that man* has got me into.

I pulled out a fresh sheet of paper and began to make notes on what we might feasibly do for the fete in a short time, and with limited resources, and most importantly, where we would be able to move the festivities if the Fens proved to be dour and rainy for the rest of time. Anything to drive thoughts of the Department and Fitzroy from my mind. There was nothing I could do – and it was a feeling I deplored.

However, I was soon distracted by the fussing of Mrs T, who was unsure if she should sit down with the doctor, being a servant. We settled that we should all stay in the morning room, so the meeting would be as informal as possible, while remaining civilised.

Merry sent a note saying she would attend and that her elder sister was currently staying with her and would mind the baby. It was the first I had heard of her sharing the cottage with a relative. I guessed this sister might also have seen her husband march off to war. I was glad she had company. If a little jealous. We were close, but we were not blood.

The time until the meeting passed while I wrestled with thoughts of pop-guns, peppermint sticks (could we get enough sugar?), bunting, and how many balloons was enough. Might we hold a dance? (Were there still enough men?) Bertram wandered in at some point mooing about lunch, but I sustained myself with a sandwich at my desk in the morning room. I believe he muttered something about eating in the kitchen, but I merely smiled and nodded. I wanted to have some cogent ideas and a proper agenda for our meeting.

In the end I should not have worried. Our small group could not have gelled better. Dr Butcher's open manner and friendliness bypassed Mrs T's worries. Although Merry did blush on first meeting him. I realised he would have seen in her ways not usual in polite society. However, the doctor pretended not to notice, and Merry quickly settled down. I was delighted that she had no qualms at embracing me when she first entered, and quickly chatted away like her normal lively self. Bertram too threw himself wholeheartedly into the meeting. His long acquaintanceship with Merry, as well as the fact he and I both suspected she might be his half-sibling, ensured there were no clumsy barriers of class. The vicar posed a small obstacle in that he wanted the fete to orientate entirely around the church, including his giving a short sermon. Reverend MacKay is a worthy soul with fluffy white hair and a deceptively soft demeanour, but put him in the pulpit and he becomes all vinegar and fire. Decidedly not someone I wanted speaking at our fete.

Bertram had the grand idea of supplying him with a surfeit of ginger cake, which he adores, and we gradually talked him out of the sermon, but accepted the offer of the church hall for the stands if the weather proved inclement.

Mrs T proved so practical, I wondered inwardly if I should draw on her knowledge of foodstuffs and their preservation when next

13

perusing potential supply lines. Then I remembered I was currently stood down, and I sat back and let the conversation wash over me until Bertram asked me if I was quite well. I reassured him and accepted the offer of ginger cake, which the vicar was now extolling as the nearest thing to the manna of heaven here on earth.

I smiled and made plenty of notes on what was said. Inwardly I had the strangest feeling, as if I was being sucked down into quicksand. I felt heat throughout my body in an unpleasant manner, and although I knew the room was well ventilated, it felt terribly close and stuffy.

As we neared the end of the meeting, I paused the discussion and reminded people of what we had agreed. I also mentioned the tasks that people had allocated for themselves and the ones yet to be assigned.

'Good heavens,' said Samuel Butcher, 'I had no idea you were paying such close attention, Mrs Stapleford.'

'I had no idea we had come up with such organised and complete plans,' said Merry, looking at me very hard. 'I'll take it upon myself to talk to the schoolteacher and see how best she thinks we involve the children.'

'I shall have to consider you for taking the church committee minutes, Mrs Stapleford. We haven't seen you there for quite some time,' said Reverend MacKay. 'It appears you have been hiding your light under a bushel.' He leant forward and tapped me lightly on the knee. I imagine he had no idea that the tightening of my knuckles around my pen was a sign of my supreme effort of will not to plunge the pen into his carotid artery.

Bertram cast a worried look at me, but it was our factor who loudly claimed that if anyone was to have my time as secretary, it should be him, as the estate trumped the church in terms of importance. At this point a bit of an argument broke out. I was well aware what he meant – that without the support of the estate there would be no people, and no church, but MacKay looked upon it as putting the secular before God. I sat back and let them wrangle. I could not find the energy to intervene.

There was a crunching and slewing of gravel, followed by a screech of brakes. 'You have a visitor, ma'am, sir,' said Mrs T, who was now standing uncomfortably while the two men argued.

'I'm sure Giles will attend to it,' I said. 'Are you expecting anyone, my dear?'

Bertram shook his head. He was a little red in the face. I gathered he was working himself up to try and settle the argument.

I heard the front door slam. This was most unlike Giles. I sat up and paid attention to the door. A man in the dull khaki of the army strode in. He carried his cap under his arm and his gloves in his left hand, as his right arm was in a sling. He stopped a pace into the room and surveyed the crowd. His strong presence completely quelled the argument. In the sudden silence we heard the quick footsteps of Giles hurrying after him, obviously annoyed and wanting to explain, or possibly eject, our visitor. He stalled when a commanding palm was thrust in his direction. The soldier was dark-haired, tall, and of wiry build, but with dark hollows in his cheeks and around his eyes that indicated recent suffering. His face had thinned so much it was only when he sought out my gaze among the crowd and our eyes met that I recognised him.

Bertram was quicker. His eyes swept over the man's uniform. 'My dear chap,' he said. 'Congratulations!'

Fitzroy stepped forward to take Bertram's hand. 'Terribly sorry to intrude like this.' He stopped and offered no further explanation. Bertram goggled slightly.

'There is no intrusion,' I said, standing, 'We had just finished our meeting. Thank you so much for your time, ladies and gentlemen. I will send copies of what we have agreed to each of you by tomorrow lunchtime. I think we have made excellent progress and I am sure it will be a great success.'

The others, clearly curious about our intruder, slowly gathered their things and began to depart. Fitzroy went to the still open door and made a show of holding it open for them. Our guests speeded up their departure. 'Some tea, sandwiches, and fresh cake, please, Mrs T,' I said.

'Better put out a decanter and a couple of glasses along with that,' said Bertram.

'If we could take it in Bertram's library?' asked Fitzroy.

'Of course. Please also see the fire is lit, Mrs T.'

Fitzroy closed the door after the housekeeper, leaving the irate Giles still standing in the hallway. Then, displaying all the manners of a man very much at home, he threw himself down on the settee and put his boots up on the coffee table. I was about to protest in no uncertain terms when I noticed how much he was drooping. Now there was only we three in the room, he looked as if all the stuffing had come out of him. I found myself still standing and looking down on him in horror.

'Thank you,' said Fitzroy. 'I could eat a horse. May even have done so in the last month, thinking about it. I have a ton of favours to ask you both and I really am quite extraordinarily tired.'

Bertram sat down again in his armchair. His face was a picture of concern. 'I say, old chap, are you all right?'

Fitzroy gave a small crack of laughter and smiled up at me. 'I must look ruddy awful. Euphemia's as pale as a ghost, and her husband's expressing concern for my welfare!'

'I say . . .' said Bertram indignantly.

Fitzroy sat up slowly and swung his feet down onto the carpet. 'I would not claim to be A1 health-wise. But I'm not going to drop dead on you. In fact, compared to how I looked a week ago, our quack said I had made a remarkable recovery.'

I sank down to my seat. 'Dear God, is this all my fault?' I said.

Fitzroy glanced at Bertram, indicating I should say no more. 'I've told him I've been stood down,' I said. 'He can know that much, can't he?'

Fitzroy put his hand up to where he normally had a moustache and brought it away again from his face hurriedly. He was completely clean-shaven. 'Yes, of course,' he said. 'I'd trust Bertram with the best of them.'

My husband's eyes sprang open in a startled manner, but he also

16

puffed out his chest a little like a proud pheasant. 'Nice of you to say so, old chap.'

'Can we have less of the old?' said Fitzroy mildly. 'I am feeling my age today. Hence the lack of 'tache. Takes years off me, don't you think? Do you think they will have the fire and food in the library yet?'

'Let us go and see,' I said.

The library fire roared in welcome. The shades had been drawn and the lamps lowered to the ambient lighting we both preferred when not actually reading. Fitzroy found his favourite wing-backed chair and sunk into it, rather like a boat coming into its moorings. He then proceeded to make massive inroads on the sandwiches. I poured tea and Bertram topped up his and Fitzroy's cups with brandy.

'So, you're a major now,' said Bertram.

Fitzroy frowned, 'Oh yes, I keep forgetting. I am.'

'Any particular reason you were promoted that you can tell us about?' asked Bertram. I winced.

Fitzroy brushed off the question. 'The usual,' he said. 'Staying alive.'

It was not until he reached the cake section of what can only be described as his gorge that I realised his eyelids were flickering. 'Perhaps we should speak at dinner?' I suggested. 'I expect the housekeeper will have prepared a room for you. There's really nowhere else to drive to at this time of day – for a normal person,' I added.

'How did you drive with one hand?' asked Bertram.

Fitzroy held out his cup for Bertram to add more brandy. 'With ingenuity,' he said, 'and sheer bloody-mindedness – as usual.'

'Griffin isn't with you?'

Fitzroy shook his head. 'No, I've left him sorting some things out in London.' He looked a Bertram. 'I've got a new man. Takes a lot of the day-to-day organisation off my back. Good chap. Completely loyal.'

At this point, from somewhere below us in the house, we heard a signal bark. Bertram, who has an ingrained dislike of dogs, stiffened.

'Oh, that would be the other being totally loyal to me,' said Fitzroy. 'My dog, Jack. Gentle creature. You'll like him. I expect he's found the kitchen.'

'There's an unsupervised dog running around my house?' queried Bertram.

'He's extremely well trained,' I said hurriedly.

Fitzroy set his cup down on the edge of his saucer and only by some miracle prevented the whole thing from turning over. 'Euphemia, do you think you could show me to my room? It might be an idea for me to freshen up before we talk. Besides, Jack will be looking for me.'

'Of course.'

Fitzroy rose to his feet. To my horror, he had to catch himself on the arm of the chair, but I knew better than to offer help in front of someone else, even if it was only Bertram. In the hallway he said, using my code name, 'It's all right, Alice. I'm a bit knocked up, but I will live to fight another day.'

I half turned on the stairs. 'I hate to think this is all my fault.'

'Of course it bloody isn't,' growled Fitzroy. 'I didn't half give them a seeing to when they said they'd stood you down. Bloody desk jockeys. You're brighter than the lot of them. You didn't make any mistakes.' His chin dropped suddenly. 'For God's sake, woman, show me a bed before I collapse where I stand.'

Chapter Three

Fitzroy back on form

I came back down into the library. 'Good God, Euphemia,' said Bertram. 'It's a long time since I've seen any man look that rough and remain standing.'

'He was asleep before I closed the door. Practically dropped where he stood,' I said. 'But, you'll be pleased to know, Jack made it through the door just as I was closing it.'

'What is it? Some great muddy hound, I expect.'

'He wasn't even slightly muddy. Although I fear he has eaten all the sausages for tonight, if Cook's comments are anything to go by. He's a white bull terrier. A medium-sized dog, very sleek fur. Utterly adores his master. It's quite sweet really.'

'Sweet,' said Bertram in tones of utter disgust. 'I don't want some smelly creature sniffing and pilfering our food.'

'Oh no, Cook gave them to him. She was apologising to me. She's taken quite a shine to him.'

Bertram poured a large dollop of brandy into his empty teacup. 'Of course she would. I should have known Fitzroy's dog would be an ingratiating beast, just like his wretched master.'

When Giles sounded the final gong for dinner, Fitzroy came into the drawing room freshly shaved, smelling of cologne and wearing a dinner suit. 'I didn't know if you dressed for dinner, but I see I made the right choice.' Bertram scowled and wordlessly handed him a pre-prandial drink. 'What did I say?' said the spy, looking at me.

'Oh, you didn't say it,' said my husband, 'but the implication was that we yokels dress for dinner as it's the only entertainment out here in the midst of nowhere. You heard it too, did you, Euphemia?'

I became rather interested in the lace of my sleeve.

'Well, I wouldn't say such a thing for two reasons,' said Fitzroy taking a large swig. 'No, make that three. Firstly, I wouldn't be so rude . . .'

Bertram interrupted him with a 'Bah!' but the spy continued,

'When I am coming to ask so many favours of you.'

At this point Bertram made an 'Aha!' noise.

'Secondly, I grew up in the country and have no distain for rural living.'

'Bah!'

'Thirdly, if ever I *were* to utter such a sentiment, I would do so more eloquently.'

'Bah!' said Bertram again, and added a short snort.

'Has your husband entirely given up using language in the evenings, or is this merely a treat for me?'

At this point Bertram almost choked on his drink and we both ended up patting him on the back. Before further hostilities could be declared Giles called us into dinner.

It was an excellent dinner. One of Cook's very best, despite the amount she had lost to the dog. And it worked its magic, as a good meal will. Bertram, in either a spirit of pride or generosity, had got Giles to decant an excellent red. We all ate in silence until the meat course. Fitzroy had got about halfway through his steak when he sat back in his seat and sighed. 'You cannot imagine how many weeks I dreamt of food like this. Your cook is a delight, Euphemia. You should hamstring her, like olden lords did with their blacksmiths to prevent them running away.'

Bertram's loaded fork paused halfway to his face. 'Only you, Fitzroy, could give a compliment with one hand and throw in such nastiness with the other.'

Fitzroy raised his glass. 'Thank you.'

Bertram's face scrunched into a grimace, but I heard him inhale deeply and his fork resumed its journey.

20

'Did you have a very bad time?' I asked

Fitzroy dropped his gaze. 'It got a bit ticklish. I don't think of myself as old, but for the first time I truly appreciated why the army prefers recruits to be between eighteen and twenty. You have so much more stamina at that age.'

'Some of our younger men on the estate have already joined up,' I said.

Fitzroy gave me an odd look. 'I'm sorry.'

'They'll all be home by Christmas,' said Bertram. 'This whole debacle is ridiculous. The old Queen adored him, and he her.'

'Yes,' said Fitzroy, 'but Queen Victoria is dead. The Kaiser may have been her favourite grandchild, but that bond is over. He hates the English. Always did.'

'His mother was English!' said Bertram.

'And she was attended by English doctors, who he believes were negligent in his delivery – causing his withered arm.'

'He must have been in line for the British throne when he was born,' I said.

'Sixth,' said Bertram and Fitzroy in unison – and glared at each other.

'Perhaps he feels he is entitled to it.'

'I imagine he likes the idea of a joined Germany and Britain ruling a large part of the globe,' said Fitzroy. 'Men with physical disadvantages, especially when it comes to appearance, too often feel they have something to make up for in their manliness. Military action becomes all too attractive to them.'

'Not a problem you share,' said Bertram in rather a tight voice.

'No,' said Fitzroy. 'I acquit you of it also, Bertram. You've far too much sense.'

I rang the bell for the pudding to be served. Once more Cook had excelled. Although I knew Fitzroy had a large appetite, he tended not to indulge in cakes and the like. But not tonight. He loaded his plate repeatedly. He caught me watching him and grinned. 'I think I can afford to put on a little weight. I've had to pull my belt in by an additional three notches in order to keep my trousers up.'

I didn't respond. In the field, Fitzroy and I often spoke frankly. There was no time for anything else. However, at dinner with my husband, I felt rather awkward about discussing another man's trousers.'

'So, what do you want from us?' said Bertram, taking another three large spoonfuls of trifle. He turned to me before Fitzroy could answer. 'Did you taste the ginger, Euphemia? I do believe our clever witch of a cook used what was left of the ginger cake in this. Ruddy marvellous.'

Fitzroy waited politely to see if I would respond, and when I didn't, said, 'I would give almost anything to believe this debacle will be over by Christmas, but I rather fear it won't be. I was over there . . .' he paused. 'I think we will be in it for a long haul. I'm very much afraid this will be a war of attrition.'

'That sounds bad,' I said.

'For once I would dearly like to be wrong – and you know how I feel about being wrong.' He gave me a wry smile. 'Naturally, I would not ask Euphemia to work overseas at this time.'

'Well, thank God for that,' said Bertram.

'But I did wonder . . . you have some unused buildings here, don't you?'

'Yes,' said Bertram, gripping his spoon.

'Don't worry, it's nothing sinister. I was simply wondering, if we do end up with a lot of casualties, if you might be prepared to host a recovery centre. Not a hospital, but a place where, once the quacks have finished with them, the men can come and rest up before either going back or being invalided out.' He looked past Bertram out of the window. The nightly extravaganza of a summer sunset was beginning. 'It is remarkably beautiful here. A wonderful place to watch the sun rise and set, I would imagine, for most of the year. It's tranquil. Calm. The kind of place one craves after being in engagement in the field.' With obvious effort, he brought his attention back to us. 'You'd be paid expenses, of course. We can specify only officers, if you wish and, of course, they'd have attendant staff. You wouldn't have to do anything – in the main.'

Bertram and I exchanged glances. 'I can't see any objections in principle,' said Bertram. 'I want to do my bit, of course. I'm more than prepared to sign up if needed.'

'Bertram . . .' I began.

'You wouldn't pass the fitness test,' said Fitzroy bluntly. 'However, as you have signed the Official Secrets Act, there will always be ways you can help.'

'Grubbing around for other people's secrets,' said Bertram. 'And all that filthy business.'

I flinched.

'I'm sure I could find something more in your line,' said Fitzroy peaceably.

I found myself blinking back tears. Was this how my husband viewed my professional life? Fitzroy glanced over at me and gave me a tiny shake of his head. I hung my head and pushed the remains of my trifle around my plate. Bertram continued to give full voice to his views on spies and spying. I don't care to remember all he said, but I recall being surprised that my spymaster didn't contradict him. Instead, when Giles came in with coffee, he merely said, 'I don't suppose we could retire to your excellent library, could we? I do find myself rather susceptible to the cold at present, and that room has a wonderful fire.'

'Excellent idea,' said Bertram. 'I shall go and check the decanters are full.'

'Some of that brandy I gave you at Christmas would not go amiss,' said Fitzroy.

Bertram grunted and left us.

'He doesn't mean it,' I said.

'Oh, he does,' said Fitzroy, 'but only as pertains to my actions, not yours. He adores you and sees you as always honourable.'

'Then it's as well he doesn't come into the field with us,' I said.

Fitzroy stood and came to pull out my chair. 'My dear, even I call you my moral compass, and while I will never admit as much to Bertram, I do need some guidance in that area.' He opened the door for me. 'Besides, I am about to send you away from him again.'

'We're going into the field together? I thought you said you wouldn't take me overseas. I was quite insulted . . .'

'Shhh, Alice, a battleground is no place for a woman. There is nothing that could force me to send you into such conflict. It's men at their most ugly, most bestial. If women knew how men could act in times of war, well, they'd never have anything to do with us again.'

He placed a hand in the small of my back and gave me a push. He didn't shove me, but he left me with no option but to go through the door ahead of him. I went forward, but I said quietly over my shoulder, 'If you ever try to shove me again, I will strike you.' He gave a slight chuckle but made no comment. I considered stepping backwards into him. 'You're fortunate you're in recovery,' I said.

As we drew side by side in the hall, he stopped and, eyes twinkling, said, 'Oh Alice, have at it if you dare. I ask for no quarter.'

'You're ridiculous,' I snapped. 'As if I would do anything so unladylike here.' I stormed off to the library, not caring if he followed or not. Bertram looked up when I entered.

'Do you want a snifter too, Euphemia? It's been a horrible day.'

'Made no better by my arrival,' said Fitzroy, coming in.

Bertram handed him a glass. 'You've yet to ask for anything outrageous, so I presume you have not finished your wish-list of favours.'

Fitzroy took one of the seats near the fire. The firelight illuminated his face, exposing the hollowness of his cheeks and how very drawn he looked. 'Well, I was wondering if I might spend a few days here. I could do with a short break away from things. There's Euphemia's telephone, if anyone desperately needs me, but otherwise I'd rather like to have some time away from business.'

'What would you do?' said Bertram. His eyes narrowed in suspicion.

'Oh, read, play chess, if you wished, perhaps ride, if there was a compliant enough horse. Long time since I tried to ride with only one functioning arm.'

'I suppose the dog would have to stay too.'

'I'll keep him well away from you. He rather likes Euphemia, and she him, I think?'

'The dog is a perfectly amiable companion,' I said.

'Then there's this mission I should be going on . . .' said Fitzroy. He swirled his drink around in his glass and looked deep into it. 'It's in France. Not combative. But it needs a gentleman who speaks French well enough that he can pass for a native. I'm sure we have someone, somewhere. The last two I tried spoke well enough, but they had the vocabulary of a child. Can't risk it with anyone who isn't absolutely fluent.' He looked up and directly at Bertram.

'No,' I said.

'So, you're looking for someone to go with you?' said Bertram, frowning.

'No, there's no passable reason why I – the French me – would be in this state.'

'You need someone to *be* you?' said Bertram.

'Not as hard to do as you might think,' said Fitzroy. 'No one at the meeting has met me in person. They don't even know what I look like. To be honest, you're much more believable as me than I am. You've got the bone structure, and the frame. And you don't look half dead.'

'Well,' said Bertram. 'I do want to do my bit. I'd need to know more about it before I decided.'

'Of course,' said Fitzroy. 'We can discuss it later. It's better if Euphemia doesn't know. We like to keep things compartmentalised.'

'Fitzroy!' I exploded.

'Alice,' said my superior officer. The tone of voice brooked no argument. I hated him for it, but my oath to the Service meant I couldn't disobey, or cross, him when he pulled rank on me. 'I will give your husband all the information he needs to make a decision,' he said in a more moderate tone. He turned back to Bertram. 'I wouldn't ask if we didn't need this. The meeting is almost upon us. However, there should be no physical risk to you. I'd be sending you in as an asset, not training you as a field agent. It's a simple enough job.'

Emotions traversed across Bertram's face. He glanced at me in the manner of a worried hound, wide eyes and raised brows, and then he turned his focus on Fitzroy. The change was marked. He inhaled and straightened his shoulders, raised his chin – all these movements were tiny, but I knew him well enough to know that whatever he said, he was pleased and proud that Fitzroy would think of entrusting him with a mission. 'What about Euphemia,' he said. 'Would you be staying here with her?'

Fitzroy shook his head. 'I don't think that would do at all. I rather thought it would be a good idea for Euphemia to get some basic nursing training at one of our receiving hospitals here in England. If you were to agree to the recovery unit, it would be helpful to have someone who understood such things on the estate. Not that we'd expect Euphemia to work as a nurse here, but it would be worthwhile her knowing the basics anyway. We're training a lot of young women at present. She could take Merry with her and she could work at the recovery unit. I believe it's good to link in the community with the recovery homes.

'So, she wouldn't be battling enemy spies?' said Bertram.

Fitzroy gave a laugh and held out his glass to Bertram for a refill. 'I think Euphemia can best help the war effort at present by learning about nursing. She'll be able to set up the basics of the recovery site before we send people up. I rather fear it won't be long before we are feeling the stretches on our medical personnel.'

'Would she run the recovery thingy here?'

'Call it more of a watching brief,' said Fitzroy. 'Merry could be on staff. I imagine she's missing her husband. Having been in the military previously he will have gone straight into the BEF and will be one of the first into action. No matter how much faith one puts in the British army, it's got to worry a wife. Besides, he's not exactly young is he? This will distract her.'

'She has a baby,' I said.

Fitzroy glanced up at me. 'I know. She also has her sister staying with her, who I am sure would be able to look after the infant for a few months. He's weaned, isn't he?'

Bertram blushed at this, but I merely nodded. 'So that would be fine. You can ask her. It would be good for your wife, don't you think, Bertram? Much better than driving around with me, what? You never liked us working together so closely, did you? Don't blame you. If I had a wife, I wouldn't like her popping off with another chap – even if it was purely professional.'

Bertram made a coughing noise then said, 'Good of you to appreciate that, old man. I wasn't happy at all. I didn't want to stop her from doing her duty and all that, but I'd be much happier seeing her play her part as a nurse.'

'Is anyone in the least bit interested in what I want to do?' I slammed my drink down on a small table. 'Or is it to be decided between you as if I am some kind of chattel?'

'Euphemia!' said Bertram in horrified tones.

Fitzroy tilted his head and drew a monocle out of his pocket which he screwed into his left eye. 'Mrs Stapleford, which part of our oath to King and Country did you believe allowed you to decide how you contributed?' His voice was coldly dispassionate.

'I say, that's a bit strong,' said Bertram.

Fitzroy turned his attention back to my husband. 'We are a military department, Bertram. We must all obey orders. While your wife has an aptitude for the Service, she is a woman and we are at war. War is dealt with by men, don't you agree? It is not a woman's place to be combative.'

'No, I suppose not,' said Bertram. 'I'm sorry, Euphemia, but I would rather you were a nurse.'

'I see,' I said. 'So, it is decided. In which case, gentlemen, there is nothing more to say. I wish you good night.'

I walked out of the door. I heard Bertram call after me, but I ignored him.

Chapter Four

Lies, lies, and more lies

I rather dreaded seeing either my husband or my spymaster at breakfast, but I came down to an empty table. I enquired of Giles, who insisted on standing by the breakfast buffet like a stuffed kipper each morning, where the men were. 'They breakfasted early, madam, and are, I believe, now engaged in taking a walk about the estate.'

I longed to ask when they might be back, but I feared I would seem even more of an incompetent wife to Giles, so I merely nodded and thanked him. Then I got on with my breakfast.

'I believe they took the dog with them,' added Giles.

'Mr Stapleford cannot have liked that.'

'On the contrary, madam, he seemed quite taken with the little beast, as are we all below stairs.'

'All the ingratiating tricks of his master,' I muttered to myself. Giles pretended not to hear.

I spent the morning continuing the plans for the fete. Although, not knowing if I would still be present made things more complicated. What if both Bertram and I were away? I supposed, if necessary, Dr Butcher could stand in for us. I stopped writing midsentence. Why wasn't Dr Butcher being made the liaison person to the recovery centre? He was the clear choice. I removed the tip of the pen from my mouth as I clenched my jaw. Fitzroy. Damn the man. I needed to talk to him.

However, at luncheon only my husband joined me. 'He's gone off to beard Merry in her den and talk her into his plan,' he said as soon as I entered the room.

I sat down at the table. 'It will be pleasant to have luncheon with only the two of us,' I said. 'After all, we have no real idea how long he is staying.'

'Not that long,' said Bertram. 'At least, I hope not. You're cross with me, are you? I won't do anything foolish, but I would like to play my part.'

'I know that,' I said, adding in my thoughts, *and so does Fitzroy.* 'I understand.'

'And you can't blame me for wanting you somewhere safe,' said Bertram. 'You always worry about me. And having the hospital here would mean nothing bad could happen. I mean, the enemy isn't allowed to do bad things to wounded men, is it?'

'I rather doubt that the Germans will be able to do anything to us in the Fens,' I said.

'I hope so. Talking to Fitzroy, it's all sounding a lot hairier than I imagined. Mind you, this thing he's asked me to do could help. Sorry,' he said, crumbling a bread roll into pieces on his side plate. 'I'm not allowed to tell you anything else.'

I smiled at him. 'That, I understand. If you must do this mission, listen carefully to Fitzroy, and ask as many questions as you want, however silly you might think them. Whatever else he is, he's a good trainer and he won't think less of you for asking them. Now, shall I ring for some more bread?'

I didn't see Fitzroy until three days later. He breakfasted early and spent a lot of time cloistered with my husband. Otherwise he was an almost invisible houseguest. Cook told me he'd requested a sandwich lunch, which he always took on a walk with him in the afternoon. Supper he took in his room, and while Bertram said he had asked to borrow books from the library, I never saw him.

Then, on the morning I knew Bertram had gone to a nearby town to see about some first editions, Fitzroy joined me in the breakfast room as I was finishing an omelette.

'I'm about to go riding,' he said. 'Bertram kindly arranged for a couple of horses to be tacked up. Normally, I wouldn't mind doing that myself, but . . .' he raised his arm. 'Could I bother you to come with me? Just as a precaution. If I fall off and brain myself, you can tell the undertakers where to find me.' He smiled. It was a completely artificial smile that didn't touch his eyes.

'I will have to change,' I said. 'Can you wait?'

'Of course.'

A short while later I found him pacing up and down the hall. 'I've just heard,' he said, 'they haven't used a side saddle for you.' Then he focused in on what I was wearing. 'Bertram lets you ride around like that?' he said, genuine astonishment in his voice as he took in my trousers.

I walked past him. 'There's rough land round here, as well as the marshes. He wouldn't expect me to risk my life for the sake of a skirt.'

Fitzroy said nothing but walked behind me all the way to the stables. Once we were inside, he mounted his horse with ease. 'Is your arm hurting at all?' I said.

'It needs rest,' said Fitzroy. 'I wrenched it hard from the shoulder socket. If I don't take care, I might not regain full use. I haven't been lying.'

I clicked my tongue and urged my horse forward. 'Oh yes, you have,' I said. 'You've positively outdone yourself this time.'

I didn't let him catch up with me for a few miles. It transpired he could do no more than trot, which suited Bertram's gentle mare well enough. My steed, however, enjoyed a good gallop before I dropped back to ride alongside him.

'So, you know the nursing role is a cover?' he said.

'Where are we really going?'

'You misunderstand,' said Fitzroy. 'I'll be on the other end of a telephone if you need me, but I'm not going with you. And you *will* be undergoing nursing training.'

'This is what I am going to do for the war?'

'Don't be stupid, Alice, of course not. I won't waste your talents on sponge baths and bed pans.'

'But you said . . .'

'I thought you didn't believe me?'

'You mix your lies with the truth so well.'

'As I have taught you to do,' said Fitzroy. 'I told Bertram a lot of what he needed to hear, to feel better about himself.'

'I'm surprised you care.'

Fitzroy didn't blink. 'Until you learn to manage your husband, it appears I must do it for you.'

I flinched but recovered. 'Is his mission even real?'

'Very much so.'

'Will he be in great danger?'

'I've said repeatedly, it's not a combative mission. I have no intention of making you a widow.'

'So why am I learning to be a nurse?'

'Do you recall that we suspected there could be a leak at HQ?'

'I thought you had ruled that out?' I said.

'Let's say I rather hoped it was impossible. But when I went across . . .'

'With the BEF?'

'I and my men were among them, but we weren't part of them. Look, do you mind if we stop for a bit? I'm getting a little winded. Will the horses stay, or do they need to be tied?'

'The worst that could happen is they would walk back to the stable. There's a group of trees down there. The ground should be drier.'

Fitzroy nodded and set his horse in that direction. I found a low branch and looped my reins over it. My horse immediately started to graze. Fitzroy dismounted with obvious effort. I pretended not to notice. He dropped his reins and sat down, his back to one of the larger trees. I say sat, but it was more of a collapse.

'Are you going to be able to ride back?'

'I just need a little time and I'll be right as rain.' He took a packet of cigarettes from his top pocket and lit one. I noticed his hand shook slightly as he put the match to the end. He offered the packet to me.

'No thanks. I didn't know you smoked.'

'I don't usually. A slight indulgence while I'm recuperating. I'll drop the habit when I'm back on duty.'

31

I sat down near him; my legs crossed in a most unladylike manner that only trousers made possible. I raised my eyebrows at him.

'Yes,' he said. 'I'm not on active duty. The Department knows I'm here to get Bertram up to speed. That mission has been sanctioned. But yours . . .'

'Is a bit more off book?'

He took a drag on the cigarette and blew smoke into the air above my head. 'You could say that.' His eyes focused past me at some point in the distance. 'My group were ambushed because the enemy had been fed our location and because someone on the ground helped them. I believe it was coordinated from HQ and that one of my men had been compromised by our leak there.' He grimaced. 'In other words, I had a traitor in our midst.'

'What do we do? Who do we tell?'

Fitzroy sighed. 'That's the thing. You saw all the information that was leaked . . .'

'I am under suspicion?'

'Not by me, I swear. Besides, so far, they're only worried about the supply line – that you might have accidentally let that slip. But if I pass on my suspicions, it is you they will look at for what happened to my team. All of them were the very best, above suspicion, and anyone higher up the chain is . . .'

'Unthinkable,' I finished for him. 'Even I would consider myself the most likely to be guilty.'

'More than possible, I'm afraid. They might even look at me. After all, I got out – and I recruited you. We could be in it together. My reporting it could be a double bluff. That's the way the minds of the Department generally work.'

'What do we do?'

'I can't let it lie. The ambush was a bloodbath. Good men died.'

'I'm sorry,' I said.

His attention turned to my face and he smiled slightly. 'Thank you. I don't care so much about the danger this fellow put me in, but I'm damned if I'll let him get away with murdering people under my care.'

'Your command,' I corrected gently. 'It's not like they were Department trainees you were schooling. They were all veterans, weren't they?'

'Veterans, yes, but I was the one training them as spotters – scouts. The men I had with me were the very best of the lot. By the time we were at the barn, I only had a core troop left. Fifteen men. My elite. We had one critical mission close to Germany's border . . .'

'You mean past it, don't you?'

'The less you know about the exact location the better. I'll only say we were bunked overnight in a barn of a friendly native. You know I'm something of an insomniac, so although it wasn't my watch, I was awake when it happened. That's the only reason I got out. If I'd been asleep, none of us would have made it.'

His attention flickered away from me and into the distance again. 'I should have known something was wrong. There'd been too many cock-ups. Not only with the supply lines, but other things too. Timings for meetings were off. The route we were supposed to take was too exposed. I did catch that one. We would have been sitting ducks. A fox got in among our camp supplies, that should never have happened, but no one could figure out how it did. The whole time I was out there I was on tenterhooks. Even training them, as we moved through France, I felt on edge. That damages your focus. That's why I thought at first it was all my fault.'

'But it was no more your fault than mine.'

He reached over and patted my leg in much the way I'd seen him pet Jack. 'No, Alice. I was there. I should have trusted my intuition. I should have turned back. Never taken my group forward.'

'You can't think like that,' I said. 'You know you can't. We can only go forward.'

He gave me a wry smile. 'Surprisingly, having one's own training maxims turned back on one isn't as comforting as you might think.'

I looked down at the ground. He patted me again in a consoling sort of way.

'It's on me, and the only way I can make any of it right is to catch the bastard that set us up.'

33

'You said there was someone on the ground. Did you mean one of your team?'

'Ah, so you *were* listening. My exit from the barn was hurried and confused. We were under fire and the greater part of the building had caught alight. I'd just seen one of my best men throw himself on top of a grenade, sacrificing himself to save us. Ghastly death. I can't say I was at my best. But I am damned sure I saw a lit lantern hanging in the window of the hayloft. No one in their right mind would have done that. Unless they wanted to signal to someone where to attack.'

'Doesn't that mean that person would be at risk too?'

'I imagine they had some kind of identifying code – as well as knowledge of where the enemy was going to breach the walls.'

'Still risky.'

'If someone is prepared to actively betray his comrades and his country, I can only assume that their motivator is powerful, and that an element of risk is acceptable.'

He fell silent. The weak sunlight slipped behind a cloud throwing us into shade. Fitzroy looked smaller than I remembered, not so much less tall as less present. He was diminished. I wondered if another man might have been broken by what had happened. A man, one he had hand-picked and personally trained, had betrayed not only him but men under his command. He must feel doubly responsible. The fact that his own loyalty to his King, his country, and his men was unassailable must make it all the worse. Fitzroy knew of the duplicity of mankind. He'd rooted out traitors before and he knew better than me how low a man could go. But I guessed that he had never been betrayed by one of his own, until now. It had hit him like a felling blow, and he was still reeling from it.

'You're very quiet,' he said suddenly.

'I was thinking,' I said. 'Would I be wrong in thinking that the men who survived were all injured and are all now in hospital?'

'All of us who got away from the barn were injured to varying degrees at the time, or as we made our way back across the lines. We split into groups to give us a better chance of getting back. None of the injuries were life-threatening at the time. But some groups came

34

under fire twice more on our way to the port. They lost men. Those that got to the shore were all rather banged up by that time. Somewhat unfairly, I think I got the least of it.'

'Another betrayal?'

'I don't think so. I hope not. From what I've read in the others' reports, they weren't a hundred per cent and the situation was too extreme. Not so much betrayed as genuine casualties of war. That some men survived at all is a credit to their skills.'

'Skills you gave them,' I said.

Fitzroy angled his head sharply at me. 'You're neither my mother nor my nurse, Alice. I'd appreciate if you would stop trying to make me feel better. It isn't helping. What I need from you is to identify which of the surviving four men is the traitor. Then when you've handed him over to me, he will tell me who he is working for at HQ.' The last part of this was said between gritted teeth.

I nodded. 'What can I tell Bertram?'

'Nothing,' said Fitzroy. 'Nothing at all. I won't have him worrying about you while he's on his mission. He's to think you're safe and well, learning to be a nurse.'

'And what of me worrying about him?' I said, standing up and brushing myself down so he wouldn't see the anger in my face. He was forcing me to lie to my husband again.

'You're a professional,' said my training officer. 'Besides, you were an agent first. You didn't have to marry him.'

'But I became an agent so I could marry him!' I said.

'You became an agent so you wouldn't hang for a murder you didn't commit. That you decided to marry Bertram afterwards, knowing you would be an active agent during your marriage, was your decision. And not a wise one, I might add.'

'You encouraged me to get married. You'd been pushing me towards marriage for years, almost from the moment I became one of your assets.'

Fitzroy leaned hard against the tree with his good arm and got to his feet. 'Are you mad?' he said. 'What's it to me – other than the sheer bloody inconvenience of it – if you're married or not?'

35

I put out a hand to steady myself against the tree. The bark felt rough beneath my fingers. I tried to focus on that to turn my thoughts away from Fitzroy, but it was useless. My anger was too intense.

Why had I ever thought anything could touch this man? He never told me the truth, yet he effortlessly twisted others, including me, to his whims. He wasn't weakened and diminished by his experience. His body had suffered, but inside he was burning with white hot revenge. As ever, nothing mattered to him but getting the job done. I had to remember what he was.

'No, of course it wouldn't matter to you,' I said, keeping my tone polite. 'Will you be all right getting back to the house alone? I've not ridden out for days. I could do with the exercise.'

Fitzroy flicked his cigarette to the floor and ground it with his heel. 'No, you go on. I need more hours with your husband. He's coming on, but we have a long way to go.'

The way he said it made me feel as if I should have a married a more suitable husband. I nodded to him, and mounted my horse, glad I had lived long enough in the country that I needed no help. Then I rode off. I didn't look back. For some ridiculous reason I found myself crying – and I didn't want him to see.

Chapter Five

A long journey during which I
discover how distant is my own shore

Merry and I caught an early train to the south coast. Bertram had given me a lavish supper and seen me off with a cheery smile. He had no idea I was going on a mission. Fitzroy had politely wished me a good journey in a suitably indifferent manner, but he had palmed me a slip of paper on the platform. I had tucked it into my reticule without anyone seeing and had yet to read it. Now Merry and I sat in a carriage across from one another as around us the countryside slid away at an unnatural pace. Despite my friend's smiling demeanour, I felt low and desperately lonely. I hated that my farewell to Bertram had been filled with lies. Damn Fitzroy. If something happened to my husband. If the last words I ever spoke to him were lying ones . . . I realised Merry was speaking.

'So do you think they will manage without us?'

I blinked rapidly. 'Your sister and the baby?'

'No,' said Merry, her jaunty expression fading somewhat. 'Michael adores my sister. He's too young to realise I'm gone.'

'Oh, I don't believe that.'

'No really, as long as a mummy object is around and feeding him he'll thrive. Even Dr Butcher agreed. As long as I'm back before he says his first word. I want to be there for that.' Her eyes brimmed with sudden tears. 'We will be, won't we?'

'I should think so,' I said. 'We're only learning the basics of supporting nursing staff, I believe. It takes years to become a real nurse.'

'Major Fitzroy said they'd be teaching us enough to be confident we'd do no harm. Then we'd be learning on the job.' She paused. 'He seems a nice man.'

I suppressed an explosive declaration of opposition with difficulty.

'He's said he'll try and get me details of where Merrit is stationed. He said he's old enough he wouldn't be going abroad in any of the early waves. Who knows, it might even be over before he gets to the Channel.'

'Did Fitzroy say that it might be over?'

Merry shook her head. 'But I can hope, can't I? Merrit's ten years older than me, you know. I used to think that was romantic. Now I realise the older men get the more pig-headed they become. Even the prospect of leaving little Michael behind wouldn't stop him.' Her eyes welled up again.

'I'm sure Fitzroy was right,' I said. 'The army wouldn't send older men to the front. They want young energetic men to help them defeat the enemy.'

'I don't know how I feel about that either,' said Merry. 'I'm the mother of a son now and I couldn't bear the thought of Michael being sent off to war.'

'Then you had better see that he grows up to be a doctor, or a farmer or a policeman or some such other profession that will be necessary at home and therefore unlikely to be sent to war.'

'Is that an option?'

'I've no idea, but it should be. The services are quite sensible about these things. Now, we're turning a larger part of the estate over to farming, Bertram believes McArthur won't be called up. He'll be needed to help feed the nation during wartime.'

Merry looked at me oddly. 'Shall we talk about something brighter?'

'Absolutely,' I agreed. 'What were we talking about before this?'

'The fete and whether they will be able to manage without us.'

'You know I've been compiling lists, and ordering stuff for the catering, but I'd almost forgotten in doing all the little things that it was actually going to be a thing in itself.'

Merry nodded. 'Dr Samuel and I . . .'

'Dr Samuel?'

'That's Dr Butcher's first name. We've become rather good friends. He suggested I call him by his first name, but I didn't think that was appropriate for a married woman so we compromised – anyway, he's terribly organised in, well, everything. He's drawn up a timetable for the whole thing. He's even roped your Fitzroy in to running the air rifle stall.'

'Really? The mind boggles. I didn't even know he would still be around.'

'He's been talking as if he might mind the house while Bertram goes off for some cure. He seems determined to make himself useful. I can't say I quite understand his relationship with you both.'

Merry's bright brown eyes sparkled with intelligence and curiosity. I'd forgotten how inquisitive Merry could be. 'Didn't he explain when he convinced you to come with me to train?'

'He offered to pay me,' said Merry bluntly. 'Of course I want to help the wounded in any way I can, but with Merrit on a private's wages and my sister living with us, and I think I'm going to need help with our vegetable garden, that was pretty strong inducement.'

'You know you only have to ask if you need anything . . .'

'That's kind of you, Euphemia, but I'd rather pay my way. It's hard enough being friends with the Lady of the Big House without accepting your charity.'

'Merry, you practically grew up with Bertram, you went into service with his family as a child. He's always considered you family.'

Merry stood up and pulled her carpet bag down from the overhead rack. She placed it on the seat. 'I'm sure I packed them. She scrabbled in the bag like a dog looking for a bone. 'Aha!' She pulled out a battered set of cards. 'Let's play Old Maid until it's time for lunch. We get to go down to the dining car, don't we?'

I nodded. Merry dealt the cards. 'I'm sure you're used to travelling first class, but it's a great treat for me.'

39

I didn't respond. Obviously Merry noticed my absences from White Orchards. I could hardly tell her that Fitzroy and I were more likely to be travelling in the belly of a fishing trawler. The opportunity to 'live it up' rarely happened on missions I had undertaken – and when it did, it usually put one or other of us in dire peril. When I was merely one of his assets who he called on from time to time Fitzroy had made his life as a spy seem glamorous and mysterious. As an agent, the further back the curtain was drawn the more I realised how difficult a life it was. It suited him as a man and as a bachelor.

'Euphemia, where do you keep going?'

'I am sorry. I have a lot on my mind.'

'Did I get too close to the mark with my comments about the major? Are you romantically entangled with him? I thought you and Bertram . . .'

She broke off because I was, as my little brother would so elegantly have put it, laughing like a drain. I wiped tears from the corner of my eyes. 'Oh, Merry, you couldn't be more wrong. I would never think of Fitzroy like that – and you wouldn't suggest it if you ever got to know him.'

In the nature of things, the day on which we travelled was fine. The train ran perfectly to time and the food in the dining car was bearable. To Merry, the food was a revelation. She'd never eaten quail. The wine-based jus and delicacy of the finely turned vegetables bemused her. 'Carrots never look like this when they come out of my garden,' she said wonderingly as she held up a tiny, perfectly shaped baby carrot on her fork. 'Why didn't they let it grow more? It's hardly a mouthful.'

Bertram and I did our best on an estate that constantly demanded investment. We ensured the people on our estate were paid a decent rate and that the tied cottages were kept in excellent order; we had opened a school for the local children, and we had enticed Dr Butcher to live locally and tend to their needs. We paid his fees. However, despite all our bills for falling chimneys and collapsing floors, I lived a very different life to Merry in her cottage. My mother had trained me to run a large household, hoping one day I would marry back into the aristocracy that had birthed her. The closest I had come before marrying Bertram was to run a substantial residence as a housekeeper. Indeed, Merry and I had met when I first became a maid, and she had taken me under her wing. I had no idea how to clean and sweep, but I knew how to arrange to perfection the seating plan at a political dinner.

When I had married Bertram I had far too easily adapted to having servants and running my own household. The time spent as a companion to Bertram's sister, Richenda, had doubtless helped my transition, but more often than not I had been coaching her on how to run the home of her long-suffering husband, Hans. I had lost my perspective. No wonder Merry only visited me when I sent explicit invitations. In her eyes I had become a Lady and she remained very much of the working class. I determined to ensure I got to know her all over again during this mission. As far as she would be concerned, we would once more be on an equal footing, and that could be nothing but a good thing. I had become far too high and mighty for my own good. My father would have been appalled.

We had to be almost at the end of our journey when Merry said, 'What is the name of the hospital we're going to?'

'I never thought to ask,' I said, thinking what a rubbish agent I was. 'Wait a minute, I think I scribbled it down.' I rooted in my reticule and found the piece of folded paper Fitzroy had slipped me. I opened it and read in Fitzroy's distinctive slanting handwriting:

> *Dwyer*
> *Hobson*
> *Wilkins*
> *Lecky*

These must be the names of the men I needed to investigate. 'Rats,' I said aloud. 'I picked up Mrs T's list for the dairy order.'

'Oh,' said Merry, her eyes wide. 'I hope someone is waiting for us at the station.'

'I shouldn't worry. If the worst comes to the worst we can find somewhere with a telephone and call up Bertram at Stapleford Hall. He can ask Fitzroy for us.'

'I suppose so,' said Merry, still looking worried.

It occurred to me that Merry hadn't travelled very much in her life, whereas my last mission had seen me careering across the Continent. The fact that we were still in England and that everyone spoke the same language as me made me feel comfortably at home. Merry, with her husband in one direction and her baby in the other, was more likely to be distressed by our lack of knowledge. I tried to think of something helpful to say.

'Really, it's fine. I've done a bit of travelling now. I'm confident I can sort things out.'

'With Major Fitzroy?' asked Merry.

'Why do you keep coming back to *that man*?' I snapped.

Merry winced. 'I only meant that it must be much easier with an officer to sort things out for you.'

'I am referring to matters I sorted myself, without the major,' I said. 'You may have seen me set out with him, but we rarely remained together for any length of time.' This was too often true, but usually because one of us had been stabbed, or fallen off a bridge or been kidnapped or some other absurd thing.

'You're very different from when we first met,' said Merry. 'You've had so many experiences. You must have so many stories to tell, but you don't.'

'I always think other people's travel stories are a bit of a bore, don't you?' The carriage gave a slight jolt. 'I think we're stopping,' I said. 'We must have been slowing down and not noticed.' I got up to look out of the window. Although I didn't make the mistake of opening it. I had no desire to inhale the smut and smoke that came from the engine. 'Yes, look! If you press your face against the glass, you can see we're pulling into a siding. It doesn't look like there is a station though.'

'Perhaps another train is going to pass us?' said Merry.

'Possibly.'

Our train drew to a complete stop. Merry and I sat and waited to see what would happen. We heard doors up and down the train slamming. 'What do you think we should do?' asked Merry, biting her lip.

'I'm sure someone will tell us.'

Our carriage door was flung open and a small man in army uniform said, 'Bleedin' 'ell, we didn't expect no volunteers to be sitting in first class. Grab your bags and 'op out girls, the bleedin' charabanc is about to leave. You'll 'ave to 'ot-foot it.'

I grabbed my bag and jumped out. Fortunately there was a temporary platform, for jumping down beside the track would have been difficult in my clothing. Merry followed more slowly behind me. 'Come on, girls. You don't want to be stranded out here at night. No nice London cabbies to pick you up here.'

I noticed the man was a corporal and if I'd not been undercover I'd have given him a piece of my mind. However, it seemed Merry and I had been cast as rather helpless upper-class women come to do their bit. It seemed something of a long shot to me. No one who heard Merry speak would think she was other than of the serving classes. I supposed she could pose as my maid – and I, a very generous employer. But then I had no idea what Fitzroy had told Merry about the trip. If he hadn't briefed her she'd be as likely to give our real names away the moment we got there. I kicked myself for always closing her down when she'd mentioned the spy. She might have been building up to ask about – well, whatever he'd said to her. He certainly hadn't said a word to me, but then after our conversation under the trees I'd not made it easy for him to see me.

The corporal brushed my shoulder as he ran past. 'Pick up the pace, girls. I can 'ear the driver starting his engine!'

I ran after him, easily keeping pace. I could hear Merry puffing behind me. It surprised me a little, but then I'd been given some tough physical training. I had assumed that Merry's life was as active. It appeared not.

43

We ran along the makeshift platform, which was no more than boards raised to the level of the track in the siding. Either side of us rose high grass banks. I lifted my skirt above my ankles and lengthened my stride as the corporal dived off up the bank along a shallow green path. I came to the top on his heels. In front was a large pale blue charabanc that had seen better days. Through its wide windows I saw a number of women, a quick estimate made it around twelve, all sitting in their seats, clutching their bags on their laps. I quickly lowered my skirts again. All of them sat ramrod-straight, either, I assumed, by training or by breeding. Certainly, no one would have mistaken them for a holiday outing. All of them positively radiated tension.

The charabanc stood in the middle of an open area that was part sand, part gravel. The ground sloped away from it on all sides with a narrow lane leading out of the clearing. I got a glimpse of countryside with no visible landmarks, but I thought I could definitely smell the sea.

The corporal wrenched open the door of the vehicle. The whole thing was shuddering with vibrations from what must have been a more powerful engine than had been originally installed. I didn't wait for him to step in, but fairly flew up the interior steps. I sank down into a seat that was part uncomfortably hot leather and part rough carpet-like material. Merry staggered on to the bus, one hand holding on to her hat and the other clutching her bag. Her face shone with sweat. The door closed with no sign of the corporal getting on and the driver pulled away. Merry lost her balance and landed flat on the floor.

There were both gasps and giggles as hands rushed to help her to her feet. She appeared more shaken than hurt, I thought. Someone helped her into a seat. A red-haired girl moved to sit by me. She had a heart-shaped face, freckles, and the kind of turned-up nose that some men find utterly adorable. 'I'm Ruth,' she said, thrusting a gloveless hand at me. 'You're lucky you made it. Old grumpy in the front was moaning about not getting home for his tea. He didn't want to wait for you, but the woman at the front, I think she must be a matron – the one with a nose like a cross between a Roman emperor and a witch – she made him wait. She didn't half give him a telling off. Went on and on about his dinner being of no importance in our fight against the Kaiser, but that the girls were of utmost importance to the war effort.'

'The girls?'

'Why, us, silly.'

Chapter Six

To do no harm

The journey to the training hospital was extremely bumpy. Whoever had refurbished the engine had not paid any attention to the comfort of the passengers. Either that or the driver was deliberately taking us by the roughest route in revenge for missing his dinner. I had the sense not to ask questions of Ruth. Within a few minutes of her acquaintance I not only learned about all her family and how they were contributing to the war – her brothers had signed up, and her mother along with her younger sister was leading a group in the local village hall who were knitting socks for soldiers – she also told me all she had picked up about the other girls. It came out at quite a pace, but I managed to retain that 'Mary', small, dark-haired, and from the West Country, had been so desperate when she'd got off the train that she'd had to wee on the grass. 'She'd been too afraid to ask the conductor where the facilities were, silly goose.

'And that Elsie, fat as a house, that matron will have her down on the floor scrubbing, you mark my words. They asked for young, fit women to volunteer, not ruddy great marshmallows.

'And that Margaret, why I sat down next to her and introduced myself as polite as you like and she hooked her nose in the air and said, "No gloves?" I'm going to see to it everyone calls her Maggie. She'll hate that. I was awfully glad when your friend fell over. It gave me a chance to move.'

I listened with half an ear. I knew a valuable source of information when I heard it. I even offered her some of my small supply of toffees, given to me on departure by the efficient Mrs T. It did stem the flow of information, but only slightly.

The view from the window was all high hedges, broken by the occasional gate through which I could see livestock. Usually sheep, although I spotted a few cows and once a goat. The road eventually wound down the side of a hill, and I saw the glitter of the sea ahead. Along the shore was a mid-sized town. It didn't look like anywhere I had been before. Then to my annoyance the charabanc diverted through yet more country lanes to bypass the town. I judged us to be about five miles from it when we eventually pulled up outside a large grey building. I only knew this must be the hospital because there were ambulances stationed outside it and uniformed hospital staff moving among them. The building itself looked more like somewhere a great many important papers and files would be kept, where men in suits would spend all day shuffling them back and forth. Either that, or somewhere one would come to register important events like births or deaths.

I got off the bus with everyone else. There were several shallow steps up to a double-height, double-width door. This, if nothing else, told me this place was never intended to be a hospital. Either side of the doors stood two very large and very naked statues, one male and one female. The woman was definitely on the voluptuous side, whereas the man appeared to me to be somewhat under-equipped. Ruth, who had followed my gaze, nudged me and said, 'Probably a Greek. Not used to our cold weather.' Then she gave a low and quite disgusting laugh. I found it the most appealing thing she had done since I met her.

I noticed Merry looking up at the statues in awe and fascination. Maggie ignored them far too obviously. Poor Fat Elsie blushed as red as a beetroot and little Mary was engaged in studying her shoes.

'Come along now, girls,' said the Emperor Witch. She marched up the steps and we all followed like a lot of obedient little ducklings. No one appeared to have packed lightly, so we were all lopsided with luggage and did indeed waddle. I realised how very tired I was. Merry and I had spent all day travelling. I, at least, had been suppressing a tumult of emotions, and exhaustion was hitting.

We lined up in a bare white room so that we could be assessed. The Matron went through a list of names, calling both Merry and I by our real monikers. 'You will be referred to only by your surname on duty. The doctors will address you as Nurse Whatever, as a courtesy. It will be a long time before you can call yourself a nurse and I tell you now, not all of you will have what it takes. However, if we can get a little learning into you then you will be of more use. There will always be a need for fetchers and carriers – and ones that know the correct names of medicinal instruments are most useful. I also tell you now, girls, that I do not put up with any squeamishness. You all volunteered and you will all be expected to deal with it. Yes, blood and bodily fluids can be smelly and unpleasant, but we all have them within us. There is nothing horrible about them. In time you will get used to the things you see on the wards and I tell you now, that in time you will not even notice a missing limb or an absent eye.'

This seemed rather too much to believe to me, but I schooled my expression to one of rapt, if somewhat dull, obedience.

'I see only one of you is qualified to work on Ward D.' She gave a huge sigh. 'Step forward, Stapleford.'

I did so.

'So, what do you know about nursing?'

'Not very much, ma'am.'

'How much cocaine hydrochloride would you give a patient who was distressed enough to be sedated, but was not due to be operated upon?'

I noticed at this point that the matron, who had still not introduced herself, had rather hard grey eyes. She was doing her best to intimidate me – and to generally assert her authority over the group. She clearly had no idea of what kind of training I had really had. I found her no more troubling than the ancient goose that lurked around the back of the big barn, honking in a threatening manner, but who never actually managed to summon up the gumption to bite anyone.

'As much as the doctor told me, ma'am,' I said.

'Are you trying to be clever, Stapleford?' She stepped up close to me. I lowered my gaze so as not to challenge her.

'Ma'am, I don't know very much about nursing, so I thought the best thing to do would be to carry out the doctor's instructions to the best of my ability. Obviously, if I didn't understand I would have to ask another nurse what to do.'

'Why wouldn't you ask the doctor?'

'Unless the doctor had been assigned to training I would believe him to have other more important tasks to do. But I would not risk harming a patient.'

'Yes, well. I suppose that will do. I can see why they put you forward for Ward D. You've clearly had some preliminary training, though not in medicine, am I right?'

I wished with all my heart I had buried the hatchet with Fitzroy and spoken in more depth about this mission. I could almost hear Merry's ears straining to hear my answer. I had an inkling of what Ward D might be. I racked my brains and came up with the best half-truth I could think of, 'I have had some basic first aid training, ma'am. It's useful when one lives on a farm.'

She leaned forward and peered so closely at me that I could feel her breath on my face. I also learned she liked peppermints. Then she stepped back smartly. 'Good enough. I like your attitude,' she said. 'Now, girls, one of our three-month auxiliaries will show you to your dorm. Then supper is in the refectory at seven. Follow everyone else. Be up ready for duty at five a.m. You will be collected from your dorm on the first day.'

Merry managed to bag the bed next to me. The dorm beds were simple and the mattresses thin, but the sheets were clean and separated one's person from the itchy wool blanket on the top. I noticed some of the women looking around in dismay. I wondered which discomforted them most; the lack of privacy or the lack of comfort. Fitzroy and I had both endured far worse and the fact there were regular meals on tap made the whole situation seem luxurious for a mission.

The girl who had shown us to the room left quickly without sharing any information. All twelve of us were in the same room. I supposed I would get to know the others, but after Ruth's introduction I felt I had a more than good enough basis to start. After all, I wasn't here to make friends with these women, but neither did I want to stand out as unfriendly.

'It's all a bit odd, isn't it?' said Merry. 'I feel rather like I did when I started at Stapleford Hall.'

'Out of your depth?'

'Homesick and small.'

'In age or height?' I asked. 'Because I am afraid both of those are non-negotiable statistics. Time moves on and you're not going to get any taller.'

Merry punched me gently on the arm. I grinned.

'Hey, girls,' called Ruth. 'There's a uniform tucked under the pillow and what looks like a shroud.'

We all immediately began to unmake our tidy beds. 'Night attire,' said Margaret. 'It is a respectable nightgown. I am not surprised you did not recognise, Miss Blackwell.'

'That's Nurse Blackwell to you, Maggie. It's a shroud as far I'm concerned. The one way I'll be seen in it is dead.'

'I think we should get into the uniforms. The matron will be cross if we don't.'

'Who said that?' someone asked.

'Wee-wee Mary,' came back Ruth's voice.

Mary gave a small gasp, but it was clear Ruth's nicknames were sticking. 'I wonder if this is what it was like to be at a girls' boarding school,' I said softly to Merry. 'Because if it was I am very glad I didn't go.'

Merry didn't respond. Her bright eyes were watching the interactions of the women around us. Certainly this was nothing like the camaraderie I had found at Stapleford Hall below stairs. The atmosphere here seemed confrontational and tinged with bitterness. Yet everyone here had volunteered. Was this how women without their men were going to behave? If so, I worried for the war effort – or was there something different at work? Did we have a deliberate agitator in our midst? Or was I looking for enemies among a pack of very ordinary women who suddenly found themselves displaced and disadvantaged? The matron had not set a welcoming tone. I wouldn't be surprised if a lot of our company were having second thoughts.

'What do you think of them?' I whispered to Merry.

'That if we whisper together they'll turn on us like a pack of wild cats,' said Merry. 'Ladies,' she said in a louder voice. 'Who's up for wearing the uniforms? I reckon if we all stick together they can't very well punish us. Hands up for votes for wearing it?'

Nine of the twelve women raised their hands, including myself. I had every intention of remaining right in the middle of the lot of them in all senses.

'Uniforms it is then,' said Merry.

A murmur went around the room as the women began to disrobe. Maggie was the last to submit to the general will. She uttered a number of 'I don't think we shoulds' and 'Shouldn't we wait untils'. Finally, Ruth said, 'Oh do stop bleating, Maggie, do. One of the reasons I volunteered was to get away from livestock.'

One girl tittered loudly in respond. 'Rose Channing,' said Merry in my ear. The rest of the women attempted to ignore the confrontation, although I saw many of them hiding sly smiles. Clearly lines were already being drawn. I felt a surge of annoyance. I didn't have time for this sort of bickering. I had a job to do.

If Fitzroy had been among a group of men he'd have either taken them to his club or a local hostelry and wormed all their secrets out of them while telling jokes, buying drinks, and being thought a generally good fellow. I couldn't imagine what the equivalent would be here. Neither could I imagine Fitzroy dressed up as a nurse. His legs were far too hairy for stockings.

A knock at the door revealed a commanding and stocky young woman with a large mole on her cheek and the shadow of a moustache. 'Dinner,' she said curtly. 'Follow me.' We all trailed after her as she walked away quickly and quietly on her rubber soled shoes. Now, that part of our uniform might be useful, I thought. It was a shame the rest of it crackled with starch. 'Remember the way, ladies,' she called over her shoulder. 'You'll only be shown it once. We're all too busy. Tomorrow head down for breakfast when the bell goes at five a.m. sharp.' So much for our escort on the first day, I thought.

The refectory was on the same level as the dorms, further along our corridor, past many other doors, and following the corridor that swept around in a slow arc. We walked a long enough way for me to think that the house was very much bigger than I had imagined. When we reached it the dining room was overwhelmingly full and loud with voices. Taking Merry's advice I sat between Rose and Maggie, so I could appear to be between the two forming loyalties. Dinner was simple. A greenish soup was followed by chicken, gravy, peas, and boiled potatoes. The sweet was an apple pie without cream. Large bowls of food were set on the long trestle tables and diners helped themselves. I ate more than I talked. I was one of the first to head up to the dorm.

Once I was sure the rest of them were asleep, I felt my way to my bag at the end of my bed. The curtains were drawn, but moonlight spilled around the edges. By the time I had found the right items my eyes had adapted to the dark. I donned a black high-necked jumper and trousers. Then I slipped on my new rubber-soled shoes. I rumpled my bed. Anyone noticing it empty would think I had gone to the lavatory along the corridor. I doubted anyone would stay awake to see when I came back. Now, it was time for me to get the lay of the land.

Chapter Seven

Old Enemies

The door to the dorm proved heavy enough that it took me some effort to hold it ajar and slip through. Dim lights illuminated the corridor and I didn't want a single ray to sneak into the dark dorm. Being missed was one thing, being caught in this clothing quite another. I tried to stay in the shadows but although this was obviously meant to be night lighting it felt far too bright to me. The air was sharp with the smell of polish. The floors gleamed and I was glad of the grip of my new shoes.

The moonlight did allow me to see the outline of the doors and the plaster coving that ran along the edges of the ceiling. The corridor arched round the central building. The outline had to be a large oval, unless other parts had been added on. The coving was the odd cup and egg pattern that was so popular a few hundred years ago in larger country houses. From what I had seen of this building so far I thought it must be well under one hundred years old. Possibly much less. So the coving must have been added to make the building seem more impressive, but by whom, and what had been its purpose? What was clear was that it had never been intended as a hospital. My best guess was that it had been some kind of municipal building. But for where?

I hugged the wall, rather uselessly, as I crept past a number of sturdy brown doors. Offices of some kind – or possibly other dorms. I still had no sense of how the building spread. Plus, the curving of the corridor was confusing my sense of direction.

I had no desire to peek into any of these rooms. My sole purpose tonight was to understand the layout of the building and where Ward D might be. The matron's comments at our arrival had sparked a thought in me about Ward D patients and who was allowed to see them. Fitzroy would never have pulled an obvious string, but he would take full advantage of any avenue open to him.

Again I cursed myself for not seeking him out. Although, if there had been things I needed to know, as my handler he had a duty to make me aware. Previously when he had been angry with me, usually totally unwontedly, he had avoided me or at the least avoided conversation. However, I didn't believe that he would deliberately put me in danger – that he would be negligent. But then he had had a bad time overseas and this was an unsanctioned operation. Was it possible that the traitor was the imaginary figment of a man overworked and sunk into paranoia? Losing your perspective after periods of extended stress had been a danger of spying raised more than once during my training. We weren't schooled how to spot it in ourselves, so much as how to spot it in others. 'You'll never know when it's you' had been one of the maxims drummed into us. Had I given Fitzroy too much credit? At least his mission with Bertram had been sanctioned, so he'd have the full back-up of the Department on that.

A door behind me opened. By now I was at the bottom of the stairs. I slipped behind a large pillar and held my breath. A man in a white coat hurried down towards me. He passed me with a quick step. I didn't dare breathe until I heard his footsteps clacking across the tiled lobby. If he had looked intently in my direction I have no doubt he would have seen me, but one of the first rules of stealth is that people do not look for people or things out of place. If you are as unobtrusive as possible you will be ignored if not in a direct line of sight. (If you are in direct sight, then you must behave as if you have every right to be wherever you are. This works more often than one might think.)

I crept down in the same direction. The dorm was on the first floor, but the corridor started on the ground floor and curved upwards. This meant there was a wedge of building beneath the dorm. One that I had seen no access to – unless one of the upper doors concealed the entrance to a staircase. I came into the lobby, which was also still lit. The large central light had been extinguished but around the walls every other sconce still glowed. Near to the front door was a desk. A telephone stood on it, but there was no sign of a night porter. Behind the desk was a normal-sized wooden door. It would lead into the wedge part of the building, but I doubted it was more than a cupboard. I wondered uncomfortably if the porter patrolled the building. The two enormous doors were closed. In the dimness I couldn't see how they were fastened, but then if I wanted a quick exit this would not be the way.

In the corners of the lobby stood pots of large leafy plants the height of an average-sized man. The corridor up towards the dorm was flanked by pillars, but the side directly opposite this was a wood and glass partition. The glass was obscured with thick curtains. Not a speck of light shone through. Again I couldn't tell if part of it opened out as a door.

The wall opposite the main entrance was broken by two new-looking wood and glass doors. They didn't fit with the building in any way, and must have been introduced when it was turned into a hospital. Through them I could see a long corridor that stretched into the distance with further glass doors leading off. I crept behind a stunted potted tree, meaning to look along the corridor. I thought I might be able to see into the side rooms or if I felt braver perhaps continue onwards. However, I quickly found myself entangled with the plant.

Except it didn't feel like a plant. I fumbled in the darkness. I had chosen a pot furthest from a light, and couldn't make out a thing. My fingertips found the end of a sleeve. My heart thudded in my ear. Had I found a person? A body?

I tugged on the sleeve. No one squeaked in alarm. Tentatively I let my fingers run around the edge of the sleeve and up inside it. Only seconds were passing, but when one is expecting to encounter the icy touch of dead flesh at any moment it can seem like a lifetime.

The sleeve was empty. Gingerly I pulled on it. The garment

55

remained tangled in the branches, but the force to move it was light. No body. I pulled on the sleeve once more. Harder this time. More of it came free. I checked all around, even above my head (only ceiling). I stepped back out into the lobby and pulled hard. It shifted a bit more. I pulled again. The coat flew free. I let it go past me. The whole damned thing was coming down on top of me.

I caught it in my outstretched arms. What the hell where these leaves made from? Bronze? I staggered under the weight of it. The branches sank past my face and onto my chest, engulfing me. The sharp ends of the leaves poked into my face. I quickly realised it was real. The plant wasn't exactly weightless, but the real issue was the extremely heavy pot filled with earth and goodness knows what that my pulling had urged onto its edge.

My movements were beyond conscious thought as I wobbled to and fro trying to get the wretched thing steady. I knew I couldn't hold it for long, but letting it go was not an option. There would be an almighty crash and I would be discovered. My mind went from Fitzroy being overtaken by paranoia to me being accused of acting traitorous on his behalf, and my last moments in front of a firing squad, when my final words would be to curse all potted vegetation.

I was on the verge of losing when I thought what Fitzroy would have said. The thought was so loud in my head it seemed to come from right beside me.

'For heaven's sake, Alice, stop waltzing with that damned thing and get on with the job. It's a damned plant. You've taken down killers and you're letting an oversized cabbage get the better of you.'

'It's a tree,' I said under my breath. But with a supreme effort I got the thing back onto its base. I prevented the thump of the base landing by holding tightly onto its leaves. Several came off in my hand as it juddered into place. I stuffed them in the base, trying to make it look as if they had fallen naturally. They didn't, but it was the best I could do.

Then I went over to cause of all this: the coat. It was a white coat, like the man who had passed me had worn. Could it have been his? But why stuff it in here? And was he coming back for it?

56

The coat, in this light, seemed clean enough. I put it on. My hair had spent the summer growing back, so I put the collar over the top of it, with the length then concealed by the coat. I knew how to walk as if I was a man, and if the light level stayed like this, someone might just mistake me for a doctor hurrying by.

I automatically checked the pockets. A key. About three inches long. Cold, metal. I slipped it into my trousers. I smoothed my hair back from my face, tucking it as far back as I could. The corridor ahead lay empty. It was a huge risk. I didn't even know if what I would find out would be worth it, but I'd feel a coward if I walked away.

I put my hand on the door handle. It turned easily. I closed it softly behind me and took three steps. The smell of disinfectant hit me like a wall. On either side of the corridor were windows and doors that led into small rooms. Through the windows I could see men sleeping in beds. I judged there to be about six to a room. Even from this distance I could tell their wounds were serious. In one room all the men had coverings over their eyes. In the opposite I saw men with heads almost entirely hidden by bandages. I didn't want to think about what lay underneath. Everyone seemed to be asleep. There was no sign of any staff. I thought this odd, but then they had been desperate for volunteers.

I moved on as quietly as I could. There was absolutely nowhere to hide. I listened so hard for the sound of approaching footsteps that I felt as if my ears were straining out beyond the sides of my head like some strange bat wings.

Again, I heard Fitzroy's voice scolding in my head. 'What is the purpose of this foray, Alice? Beyond that of your curiosity?'

I moved on past another two sets of rooms. This made six in all and a total of thirty-six patients. Ahead of me stood a T-junction. I could see no signage. Presumably everyone who worked here knew exactly where everything was. 'At least *they* know what they're doing,' muttered my imaginary internal Fitzroy. 'When have I ever suggested it was a good idea to wander around in the middle of the night in hostile territory without a scrap of a plan, Alice?'

It's not hostile, I thought. Mind you, it would quickly become so if they caught me. I chose right and headed down the corridor. I saw two open, tiled rooms with gurneys in them. Both had white chests of drawers that were locked. (Yes, I did try.) I decided they were recovery rooms. That meant the operating rooms would be nearby, but would there also be surgical wards here? Or even the infamous Ward D?

I hadn't gone more than another twenty feet before I heard voices. I froze. The voices stayed where they were. I leant back against the wall, so I could have a clear view of the corridor, and listened.

At first all I could hear was my heartbeat thudding in my ears.

'Those poor lads,' said a woman. It was a strong and sturdy voice, the kind you'd hear calling across a field rather than a ballroom. 'The state of some of them. I'm not entirely convinced it is right to keep them alive. Not like that. Not when we can't make them any better. I mean they're hardly likely to go back and fight are they? Some of them quite lost their minds.'

A low male voice murmured in answer. Clearly, this was someone who was more cautious about this conversation.

'I mean,' continued the woman, 'the one they had in here last night? He'd lost half his jaw. Oh, they can patch him up so he can feed himself, but who's going to want to sit at the table with a living nightmare like that? More than even a devoted wife would bear – and as for his kiddies, it'll give them the screaming ab-dabs. Why not let them remember there dear old da as he was?'

Another low murmur.

'Oh no, it is. Hun soldier fired right into his face. Took the side of it right off and a good chunk of jaw. Lucky to have kept his eye – or maybe not, bearing in mind what he'll see in the mirror every morning.'

'I need to get on,' the man said. It was followed by more urgent mumbling.

'There you go. Wait for me to leave. I don't want to know anything about it.'

I heard footsteps. She was leaving. I crept away as fast as I could. The glass-sided recovery rooms offered no escape. I padded as fast as

I dared back the way I had come. Behind me I heard the woman's footsteps pause and she began speaking again. I didn't wait to hear. I reached the T-junction. This time I saw one of the ward doors was open. There was a trolley covered in bottles and little cups in the middle of the corridor.

'Time for your medicine, Private . . .'

I couldn't risk it. I retreated back to the T-junction. Pressing my face to the wall I peered round. This left my back exposed should the nurse come back to her corridor. I blocked out the vitriolic comments from my imaginary Fitzroy.

Up to the right, the way I had been, I could now see a woman standing half in and half out of a doorway. Her attention was turned in on the room she was leaving. I quickly assessed her as middle-aged, blue checked coat or overall, stockings that had seen better days. A cleaner or an orderly. I might be able to bluff my way past her. What about whoever she was talking to? I'd heard enough to know he was up to no good, but was what he was involved in serious enough he might try to permanently silence me?

'Oh, Doctor?' called a light feminine voice behind me. I raised my right hand, in a gesture meant to indicate I couldn't stop, and marched quickly down the left side of the T-junction. I heard a frustrated sigh from the nurse, but no following footsteps from her.

If only the same could have been said of my cleaner. 'Night,' I heard her call and then sturdy stumping footsteps headed my way.

I didn't turn but kept going. This way lay more wards, but they were increasingly bigger in size. The corridor was also widening. It also curved slightly so I couldn't see straight ahead. I only hoped that it led to another exit. I reached the point where I was prepared to run out into the night in my white coat, which I would then ditch before very carefully finding a way to sneak back into the building.

The more I thought about it – which wasn't that long in real terms – the better this plan seemed. If I was spotted I would be thought to be a male medical person, possibly a doctor, and as long as I could elude pursuit long enough to ditch the coat, I'd have a chance of making it back to the dorm without being spotted.

Of course, once I actually had a plan it unravelled very quickly. I finally saw an exit at the end of the corridor, but as I passed the second to last ward the door opened and two men came out. They were lost in deep conversation over a clip board one was carrying, but it was too much to hope one of them wouldn't look up and spot me at any moment. Accordingly, I opened a ward door at random and walked in.

Only to see a nurse bending tenderly over a man in the far bed. Behind me, the doctors also seemed to be coming this way. To the left I could see one bed had the screens around it. For once I hoped the occupant was dead. I slipped through the screen only for the man in bed to sit up with a start. The darkest moments of the night had passed, so I saw his face. But more than that I saw the familiar green eyes that seemed to glow from within. His mouth opened in shock, but before he could speak I ran to his side and clapped my hand over the mouth of my ex-fiancé, Rory McLeod.

Chapter Eight

Secrets, confusion, and spiders

I admit I half expected him to bite me.

What he did was prise my hand off with his left and indicate that I should sit on the bed, raising my feet off the floor. I did as he bid. He put his finger to his lips.

The last I had seen of Rory he had been determined to see me hanged for the murder of Richard Stapleford. He had also been working in the special police force attached to the Service and was fully aware that Fitzroy had removed me from that crime for the price of my oath as an agent. I hadn't been guilty of murder, as at least Fitzroy knew. However, I had every reason to believe Rory still thought me a murderess, so I accepted his invitation to hide between the screen with him with a great deal of caution.

In the ward beyond I heard the nurse and doctors conferring over their charges. 'Why are you behind the screens?' I asked very quietly. Rory only put his finger to lips again.

Eventually we heard the voices quieten and then the retreating of two pairs of footsteps. Another set of footsteps moved past us to the back of the ward.

'It's about time,' said Rory in a low voice to me. 'I thought nobody was going to figure it out. Is that wretched man with you or do you have other back-up on the ground. I take it you're a full agent now?'

'Why are there screens around your bed?' I countered. It seemed slightly too convenient.

'The surgeon at the clearing station was a butcher. By the time I got here I had gangrene. They wanted to take my leg off, but I insisted they try an alternative. I managed to convince the head man it was worth the experiment. Especially if or when more men start coming in. But they don't want the others to see. It's rather disgusting.'

'You were going to lose your leg,' I said blankly.

'I took two bullets to the thigh and one to the shoulder when I was carrying another man back to the lines. No idea how I kept going, but I did. Didn't even notice I'd been hit at the time.'

'How are you now?' I said, among memories of dancing with Rory, walking over the hills with him, and running away from or after enemies when we'd both been assets together. But more than anything I remembered his tall handsome figure – and how I had once been in love with this man, whose love for me had turned to hatred.

'Oh, I'm mending nicely. I think I'm safe because these flimsy screens have effectively sequestered me from the rest of the ward. No one had been able to get to me, yet.'

I frowned. 'You were expecting me?'

'Not you, but someone. I just hoped to hell it wasn't bloody Fitzroy. If I never see *that man* again it will be too soon.'

'He can have that effect on people,' I said lightly.

'So, do you know who is doing it?'

'Doing what?' I said.

'Killing us off,' said Rory. 'The patients.'

'Is this Ward D?' I asked.

'Never heard of it. This is Ward Four. What the hell are you wearing? Is that trousers? Good God!'

'Government standard issue,' I lied. 'We need to talk. I'll come back. What's the quickest exit? Do you know?'

'The end of the corridor. There's a fire door to the gardens.'

'Do I need a key?'

Rory shook his head. 'It's only bolted. But you've got a few minutes yet. The nurse has gone off for cocoa. She always does that when the doctors have been. Makes it for the patients who are still awake too. There's a tiny kitchen off the ward where they make our breakfasts and hot drinks. It usually takes her about fifteen minutes to get everything done. She waits for the doctors to give her the all clear to leave the main ward. So far everyone in here is on the mend. Keep your feet up! Those screens are high off the ground. If anyone sees a flicker of movement they'll come over.'

'Are you unable to walk?' I tried to phrase it tactfully. In the low light I thought I could see the outline of both legs under the bed-clothes, but there was also a frame under there, lifting up the sheets. I had no idea what that meant.

'Only for the moment. I had a fresh load applied yesterday. They should wash out the wound tonight and then we'll see if it's worked.' I must have looked blank because he added. 'If the gangrene's gone.'

'I don't know much about medicine,' I said, 'apart from some basic field training, but I thought gangrene had to removed by surgery?'

'Oh for goodness' sake, girl,' said Fitzroy's voice in my head. 'Stay on track. Flirting with ex-suitors is not what the Service expects of you – especially when it had nothing to do with your mission. He's told you this isn't Ward D. He doesn't know where it is. He's as use-less as ever. Move on!'

'Maggots,' said Rory. 'I got them to put maggots in the wound. It feels rather odd, but it's not painful and they eat all the dead tis-sue. Besides I'm not going to object to a few wee beasties if they save my leg.'

I had to tense all the muscles in my body to stop my impulse to get away from the wee beasties at once. 'You mean they're under the covers now?' I said.

'For the sake of . . . Alice, get on with the bloody job,' growled Fitzroy in my head.

Rory's teeth flashed in the darkness as he grinned. 'Exactly.' The smile faded. 'But you do know about the rate of mortality here, don't you? It's far too high. I've even heard the nurses talking about it. Something is very wrong. I think there's a killer amongst us.'

I didn't respond. Soldiers are by the nature of their job killers. It's hard to get a man to kill another man even in war. Fitzroy had told me he'd already seen some of the local soldiers the BEF had been sent to train and support deliberately missing their aim, because they couldn't bear to kill another human being. For most people it is a taboo you never want them to overcome. However, veteran soldiers have, and there is always a fear that men who have been trained to kill might come to enjoy that power. Like Cole. One of the best assassins in the Service, who Fitzroy had trained but kept on the tightest leash possible.

The silence spread between us. 'How does he or she kill?' I asked eventually.

'You think it could be a woman? I can't believe that. Anyway I don't know. So many of us don't make it.'

'So there is no proof of any murder?' I asked.

'Insipid paranoia,' said Fitzroy sneeringly.

'There's the statistics,' said Rory. 'They are much too high. Even Dr Mitchum thinks so, and he's the chief surgeon. I overheard him say so.'

'You said the surgeon at the – what did you call it – clearing station, was a butcher. Do you think perhaps he got his hands on quite a few of you coming out of France and that's what's causing this?'

'I did,' said Rory. 'But Bob Darlington died suddenly last night. He hadn't been operated on. He was only here for observation. Got banged up escorting us back. Bit of concussion. Nothing more.'

Internally I made a decision. 'I've volunteered here as a trainee nurse. You'll see me around the wards. We can tackle this together.'

Rory's eyes twinkled in the dark. 'Like old times.'

Fitzroy groaned loudly in my head.

'You wanted me dead last time you saw me,' I said as lightly as I could. Revenge would serve no purpose here.

'I am very sorry for that,' said Rory. 'I was in a bad place. Fitzroy had made me almost mad with jealousy. He is obsessed by you. He did everything in his power to keep us apart and from what I could see you were blindly obedient to him. I even thought you were lovers. Did you marry him in the end?'

'*Fitzroy*? No, I married Bertram.'

64

'And he doesn't mind you hanging out with Fitzroy and his crowd.'

'I think he would rather I didn't,' I said, 'but he won't prevent me from doing my duty.'

'Is that what Fitzroy is calling it now?' Rory's voice took on an ugly tone I remembered all too well. Fitzroy had warned me when I had thought being betrothed to Rory was the right choice that Rory's flaw was an ugly, deep vein of jealousy.

'The relationship between Fitzroy and myself is purely professional. If you have a problem with me it's better I work alone.'

Rory breathed deeply. 'I owe you many apologies,' he said. 'I don't tend to see clearly when *that man* is involved. You should hear what they say about him in the –'

'Unquantifiable rumour isn't helpful,' I said, cutting him off. 'I've stayed too long. I will see you tomorrow or the next day. Be careful.'

The nurse had yet to return, so creeping out from behind the screens, which I remembered to realign neatly, was easy enough. One man stirred in his bed as I passed, but as he was one of those with a bandage over his eyes I didn't unduly concern myself. The door being largely glass meant I couldn't stand around. I pulled the coat tight around me and strode out, heading towards the exit Rory had mentioned. I hoped being bed-bound hadn't given him a false perspective.

The corridor was empty and silent as I strode towards the door. It was only now it occurred to me that if I unbolted the door there was no one to close it behind me. It would be obvious someone had come this way. I couldn't see another option, but it was sloppy work. However, when I reached the door I found it was already unbolted.

I walked out as casually as I could, keeping my head slightly lowered as if deep in thought. My best guess was that someone had gone outside for a breath of air or more probably a smoke. The door opened easily and in a moment I was outside.

The gravelled area lay in front of me. A cloudy dark starless sky hovered oppressively above me. But the sudden fresh air, after all that disinfectant, was surprisingly heady. I had done a complete U-turn within the building. I closed the door behind me and staying in the shadows I did a quick visual sweep of the area. I saw no obvious figures and certainly no glow of a cigarette end or ruddy embers from a pipe being smoked.

Several ambulances stood waiting on the forecourt. It would be possible for someone to hide in them or among them. I edged my way along the building. As I did so I discovered two things. I was still some distance from the front door. At night I always find it harder to work out dimensions and routes, but clearly there was an area of the hospital through those wood and glass partitions in the lobby that didn't connect with the wards I had seen. Could that area have an entirely different entrance? The only thing I noticed – and this was by the pure chance of the moon breaking out from behind a cloud – was that I was not the only one active in this area.

The sudden beam of moonlight bounced off something metallic mid-way down the drive that led to the ambulances and the forecourt. I rested back against the wall in the deepest shadows I could find and waited for my eyes to adjust. Gradually, I made out the hazy shape of a vehicle. Either I was more tired than I thought or it kept changing. Then I realised the vehicle wasn't some kind of weird morphing car – of course it couldn't be – the silhouette changed because people were moving around it. I felt confident it was more than one person. Did this have something to do with leaving the door unbolted? Was I witnessing information being passed to a traitor?

Once beyond the ambulances the driveway offered no protection. I would be totally exposed if I approached them. I could try and work my way along till I reached some vegetation, but without crawling on my belly for the last part I couldn't see how I could approach them unseen. I also had no weapon and no one to call on for help.

I took off my glaringly white coat, and stuffed it under a bush. Fitzroy would have crawled through the grass, I had little doubt. If he'd been caught he'd have defeated the men in hand to hand combat or threatened them with his gun. I was in quite a different league: a lower one. It was agonising, but I made the choice not to go after whoever this was. I worried that the information being passed would cost lives – lives I should have saved. But the reality was, getting myself killed and dumped in a ditch somewhere wasn't going to do anyone any good.

Instead I used the time these men were occupied to sneak along the building and dash past the brilliant white statues by the front door. Only when I was on the other side did it I start thinking about how I was going to get back into the building. I really had made the most awful hash of things. The important thing was to remain uncaught.

Nature, if nothing else, was on my side. The wall leading up to the dorm windows proved to be thick with ivy. In my dark clothes with my short stature I shouldn't be visible to the men by the car. I took hold of a handful and tugged. It held. I began to climb. As I climbed I discovered that ivy is a rich paradise for a variety of fauna, mainly of the eight-legged type. I have no particular fear of spiders, but like most females I am not keen on them nesting in my hair, or attempting to crawl down the inside of my collar towards the bare flesh of my back. Moreover they were accompanied by a wide selection of small creatures, some of whose passage made me violently itchy. However, I had been in far worse situations and instead of freezing and calling loudly about my predicament I climbed stoically and silently on. As long as I made it back inside unnoticed, my report on this night excursion could be mercifully brief, lacking in embarrassing details which really weren't to the point.

'All going jolly well, isn't it?' sneered the hateful man's voice in my head.

I had at least left the window ajar. I tumbled quietly and professionally in, landing in a sitting squat, and commenced immediately ridding my hair of spiders.

'And where exactly have you been?'

I jolted upright to see Merry sitting on the end of my bed, her arms crossed and an expression of fury on her face.

Chapter Nine

I am again accused of being in love with Fitzroy

'Really, really well, don't you think?' Said that hateful voice in my head.

'Who have you been sneaking off to meet?' hissed Merry.

'Let me get into bed,' I said. 'I can't let anyone else see me like this.'

'Just tell me this whole nurse thing wasn't cooked up between you and Major Fitzroy so you could sneak off to asides with him!?'

'Asides? You mean assignations?'

'That's what I said.' I could almost hear Merry's lips thinning and her arm bones tightening.

'Don't be ridiculous,' I said pulling my jumper over my head. 'I'm married to Bertram.'

'All the more reason for you to want to get away from White Orchards.'

I wriggled out of my trousers, undid my rather modern bra (surprisingly supplied via the agency for work in the field) and pulled my gown over my head. I stuffed my black clothes in a bag and dived under the cover. Only then I realised how cold I had got wandering around outside.

'What were you wearing?' said Merry. 'If that wasn't for a man . . .'

'It's a new design,' I said. 'It makes it easier to put on and off without a maid and it restricts your movements far less. I could get you one if you like. I order them from London.'

As the lightening sky peeked under the edges of our curtains I saw a flicker of interest cross her face. Then her lips tightened again in such a way I thought they might snap like elastic does when you stretch it beyond reason. 'Oh no, you're not bribing my silence.'

'I think you mean buying your silence with a bribe,' I said. 'And I'm not trying to. Feel free to tell Bertram about my wanderings when I get home. I'm happy to explain it to him.'

I wasn't, but Bertram had signed the Official Secrets Act so I could at least tell him my actions were relevant to a current mission.

'You'll have come up with some story by then,' said Merry. 'You're far too clever for your own good. And to think I used to think of you as a friend. You're even godmother to my little Mikey. For shame, Euphemia, for shame!'

'Oh, for heaven's sake, when did you turn into such an untrusting gossip hound? I'd never cheat on Bertram. I adore him.'

'And Fitzroy adores you. Oh, Euphemia, I know he's charming but you should have resisted.'

Despite the cold night air, I sat up fully in bed. 'I do not find Fitzroy in the least charming. He's irritating and conceited. I've never known anyone who could make me so angry so quickly.' Even as I said this I felt a touch of guilt. Everything I was saying was true, but I could have added that I trusted him more than anyone in the world, I knew he had a good heart despite his annoying nature, and he could even be good company when he chose. I'd rather enjoyed our drive back across France. And I knew he'd give his life for mine in the field – as I would for him. We were comrades and I valued him deeply. However, I had not the tiniest inclination to become another one of his conquests. I saw no way of explaining the nature of our relationship to Merry, who had clearly made up her mind.

'If I am to believe you – if – what were you doing outside?'

Damn and blast it! (Maybe some part of Fitzroy was rubbing off on me.) I gave a deep sigh. 'Rory McLeod is downstairs on one of the wards. He believes the rate of people dying in this hospital is too high. He thinks something funny is going on.'

'Oh,' said Merry. 'Oh, Oh, OH! You're *working* with him.'

I shook my head. 'If you mean Fitzroy, as far as I know he's still up in the Fens – although I suppose he could be back overseas again. It's all kicking off and he's needed.'

'Rory. Rory's here. How bad is he?'

'They wanted to amputate his leg.'

Merry's right hand rushed to her mouth, 'No!' She gasped. 'Not Rory. He was such a handsome man. Tall and blond and – you were engaged to him.'

'No, yes, yes, and yes. I broke it off. But he found a way for them not to amputate it. He's recovering slowly, but he thinks he's seen too many people die.'

'How could that happen in a hospital?'

'I don't know,' I said. 'But I already know there's things not right here.'

'What?' said Merry. Her arms had come uncrossed and she was leaning forward intently.

'Look, I know we're whispering, but we can't be sure someone won't overhear. Let's find time to talk tomorrow. I could do with getting some sleep before breakfast.'

Merry nodded. 'I'm in, am I?'

'Of course,' I said. 'Why did you think you were asked to come with me? The Major knew he could trust you – after what you did for me that time I was in jail.'

Merry nodded. I imagined her eyes would have sparkled but the light wasn't right for it. I sank back down into my bed and closed my eyes.

A moment later, or that's how it felt, the bell rang. I staggered down to breakfast with Merry, still straightening my uniform. I thought coffee would be too much to hope for, but to my delight there seemed to be a bottomless urn of the stuff. I nibbled on toast and drank as much coffee as time allowed. My eyes felt tired and itchy. Someone came to tell us we would be having a lecture this morning before spending our first afternoon on the wards. My brain struggled to take in what she was saying.

A hand took my arm. 'C'mon,' said Merry. 'Let's find the ladies' powder room.'

I allowed her to lead me away. I blinked and tried to fit the daylight images around me onto the memories of my night-time exploration. The ladies' lavatory turned out to be sensibly situated half way between the refectory and our dorm. Merry went in and pushed open each of the doors to the cubicles. Then she leant against the open door. 'We're alone. C'mon, quick, spill!'

I'd had a bit of time to think over my story, but it was rough and I knew it. Hence I pretended to be even more tired than I was, and slightly incoherent.

'The Major heard about the discrepancy in deaths that Rory mentioned . . .'

'So it's true!' said Merry.

'We don't know,' I said. 'I'm here to find out. It's also the first kind of hospital like this since – oh, the Boer War or the Crimea. It's being assumed that the casualties should be much lower with modern medicine. However, no one had a clear picture of how the Germans are fighting, so it might be something they are using on the battleground that makes wounds more deadly.'

'Like?' said Merry.

The plumbing gurgled. 'Dirty bullets,' I said desperately. 'There's a rumour they dip them in toilet water before firing them. Coats them with all manner of nasty stuff. They think the wounded will catch cholera!'

'Toilet water? The soldiers have toilets on the battlefields? Are they tiled nicely? What do you take me for?'

'They have latrines,' I said. 'Holes dug in the ground. I was trying to spare you the worst of it. They're more like dung heaps.'

Merry's face paled and she dashed into one of the cubicles. I heard the sound of her vomiting. 'See?' I called to her. I took her place against the door.

Merry came back out wiping her hand across her face. 'You're looking green around the gills.'

'How did I let you talk me into this?' said Merry.

Before I could make any kind of answer we were both startled out of our skins by a knock on door. 'Ladies, out! Time for lectures.'

'Here we go,' said Merry, looking far from the embodiment of her name

The lecture felt far longer than it was. Our Matron, whose name turned out to be Susan Wickers, but Matron-to-you, turned out to have one of those monotone voices. Possibly attuned to attracting attention across a vast plain, she bellowed information at us in a manner that must have been as exhausting to do as it was to listen to. But we all dutifully weathered the storm, making notes in the little notebooks we had been given. It was impressed upon us that our books may be used for nothing else, and that we work on our drawing skills, as sketches of anatomy and dressings would feature heavily in our training.

'Policy is we have clearing stations near the front,' bellowed Wickers, 'which should feed into a nearby hospital. There are already staffed clearing stations to back up the field medics and the signs are we will only need more. However the local hospitals are yet to be established. The best of you may well find yourself stationed at a clearing centre.

'When a wounded solider arrives at a clearing station they are classified into one of three categories. The *slightly injured* who will shortly be back in the fray, *need hospital* after initial attention, and lastly the ones who are *beyond help*.

'The latter we make as comfortable as possible, but we have to primarily turn our attention to those we can save. Every dying solider deserves a dignified death, but in the heat of battle this often proves impossible. We cannot sit by the dying like ministering angels. It is as well now that you face the reality of death. There will be many men who cannot be saved. This is the nature of war. If we have the medicines to spare we relieve them of their pain, and we visit them as much as we can in between tending to other business. A kindly word to a dying man should never be under-rated. A gentle touch of the shoulder, a wiping of the brow – all such kindnesses mean so much to the dying. Every soldier knows that a nurse or doctor will do their utmost for them and clearing station staff are exceptionally valued as they bear some of the accidental risks inherent in being near a battlefield. No enemy will attack a hospital in the civilised world, but it is not unknown for artillery to fire amiss or stray bullets to catch out a member of staff.

'A clearing station nurse requires nerves of steel. She will see the most upsetting and distressing of injuries often on young and once-handsome men. She must be prepared to face their injuries with kindness and action. No nurse must ever look on a wounded man with horror, no matter what she feels inside. We are there to assist the doctors in their fight against death. There is no space or time for histrionics.'

A hand rose. 'Ma'am, is this war not so unlike any other, so near to home, that it is difficult to predict? You speak as if it has all already been thought out. How can you know what to expect?'

'A reasonable question, Channing. We have the great history of Florence Nightingale, who changed our profession for ever, but also the Great British Empire has seen its fair share of wars across the globe. All that we have learned during those times has been thought over by those who knew this war was coming. Great Britain is never unprepared. All senior army nursing staff have been fully briefed on how to deal with this emergency, and all possible avenues have been thought through and prepared for.'

'Gosh,' said Merry quietly at my side, making a note on this in her book.

I heard it quite differently. Matron, who presumably had an army rank she wasn't using with us – another question – was dispensing stories to comfort the masses. She hadn't soft-soaped the awfulness of what happened on the battlefield, but she'd made it sound noble and been clear only the best would be allowed to get close to the battle. There was an inherent message that the harder you worked, the more you put yourself in the path of danger, the better person you were. As for the whole, 'we've worked everything out', I knew that to be nonsense. Even the rawest army recruit has heard the saying, 'No plan survives contact with the enemy.' I knew I was good at thinking on my feet, but I also knew I wasn't the kind of person who could deal with coming under fire and neither being allowed to retaliate nor move around freely. I was not of the mindset of those who could passively comfort patients while their own lives were under threat. That didn't mean I didn't admire medical men and women who did so. There, I was already buying into the mythology that it was a good thing to be a battlefield nurse or doctor. It was certainly a great thing for one's fellow man, but in terms of personal survival it was far from being a good option.

'Right, Stapleford, you can go first,' boomed Matron's voice. I pulled myself away back from my musing to see Wickers holding out a bandage to me. 'Replace a shoulder dressing. You can use Merrit as a model. We won't be bringing in water today, but you can mime what you could wash. Come forward, the pair of you.'

For the first time I wished I'd looked at Fitzroy's wound more closely. As I approached Merry with the bandage hanging limply from my hand, I realised he would have struggled with dealing with it on his own, but I'd never thought to offer to help. I'd been too angry with him.

Merry looked up at me. 'Wash your hands first,' she said quietly.

Accordingly I mimed placing a bowl of water before me and washing my hands. I then replaced it with another bowl of water. I took off the imaginary sling. 'I take it you wish me to imagine taking off her – I mean his army tunic?'

'For now, yes. Although you will often find clothing has been cut away to give you access to the wound.'

I carefully peeled the imaginary clothes off the imaginary wound, washed it, and then attempted to redress. This was the point at which everything went wrong. In my hands the bandage gained the properties of an eel, slithering out of its neat coil. I managed to catch it before it touched the ground, and wound it around Merry who was looking more and more like an Egyptian mummy. By the time I was attempting to attach a sling whose material seemed large enough for a tent, and under which the small-framed Merry was disappearing, the class could no longer contain its giggles.

'Enough,' said Wickers to all of us.

'Ladies, can you tell me what Stapleford did wrong?'

'Everything,' called Ruth from the back of the class.

'Her first mistake?'

'She attempted to bandage the wound without first placing a proper dressing on it,' said Margaret. 'You would never put a bandage straight on to a wound.'

'But I only had a bandage,' I said indignantly.

'A nurse's first action on changing a dressing is to ensure she has everything she needs,' said Matron. 'One cannot leave a patient half-finished to find whatever one might have forgotten. He may present a danger to himself and possibly others.'

'She didn't pull no screens round the bed neither,' said Rose, who had adopted the role of Ruth's devoted side-kick.

'Less important,' said Matron. 'Screens and curtains are a nicety we are privileged to use here, distant as we are from the action, but they may not always be available. Now, girls, off to luncheon. Stapleford, remain behind I need to speak with you.'

The others filed out. Merry gave me a last pitying look.

Susan Wickers sat down at desk at the front of the room. 'It wasn't my intent to make fun of you, Stapleford. Given your background I expected something better.' It seemed Wickers did have a level lower than boom. The final sentence was delivered in what sounded close to a conspiratorial whisper.

'I'm sorry,' I said. I had no intention of giving away my status without further information.

'What do you know?'

'A number of ways to stop bleeding,' I said.

She continued to look at me.

'Cauterisation, or use of a tourniquet.'

'Would you ever use a neck tourniquet?'

'Not to save someone,' I said too quickly.

'I see,' said Wickers in a way that suggested she saw too much. 'As you have signed the Official Secrets Act it appears we can use you on Ward D. However, I am not sure you will be of much use. I suggest you study hard and learn quickly if you expect to be put through. I'll not have anyone on that ward who doesn't pull their full weight. Do you understand me?'

'Completely, ma'am,' I said. Fitzroy would have called her a Napoleon. She wanted full control of what she saw as hers. Unless I opened up about my mission and gave her all the details, she was going to continue testing me to the limits.

However, I had been well trained. 'I will endeavour to do my best,' was all she got out of me. I was pretty certain I heard her grinding her teeth as I hurried off to find what was left of luncheon. That I had made an enemy of her was certain. Whether she was an enemy of the Crown remained unclear.

Chapter Ten

A learning curve

The next five weeks passed in a way both remarkably calm and remarkably demanding. Shortly we were to have a test to see if we were to be allowed on to the wards to do the most rudimentary of tasks on our own. By the end of those weeks, it was clear to me that I had to find my own way on to Ward D and even on to the general wards to speak to Rory.

Every day in the dorm started off with a competition in bed-making, and woe betide anyone whose corners were less than exact. Mostly we self-inspected, but if a girl performed poorly continually away from Matron's sight, it had been impressed upon us that we should report her – for the sake of the patients. I understood the idea in principle, but instead of bonding our little group it split us into cliques who warred for supremacy. Merry and I were a single camp. I wasn't universally liked, but nor was I hated. Merry, as usual, managed to rub along pretty well with everyone, but she loyally stayed with me despite inducements to join one of the more popular sets. Margaret had become very much of a loner. She kept herself to herself and acted, I thought quite unconsciously, as if she was better than everyone else. Ruth and Rose were something of a terrible twosome, loud-mouthed, lower class, but where Ruth clearly had some intelligence, Rose was more spite and slyness. Fat Elsie and poor Wee-wee Mary bounced around between groups like untethered kites. (A very heavy, gravity-defying kite in Elsie's case. She overcame the size of individual portions (which were fair but not large) by offering to eat up whatever anyone else left. As we were all on orders not to waste food, this offer was taken up more often than you might imagine. Anyone who had been part of the escorted visit to the wards and visited the burns unit or the facial disfigurement unit tended to come back with less of an appetite than usual. There were twenty of us in total in this intake, but the others after initial observation I had written off as being compliant and dedicated.

What I am saying is that we had all become rather institutionalised. We strived to conform, to do what was asked of us and be seen to be improving. It was driving me crazy. It didn't help that in all of this time I had heard nothing from Bertram. I knew Fitzroy would not encourage me in sending out a message, but he knew I was going to fret about my husband being sent off on some ridiculous mission of his. It would have been the work of moments from Fitzroy to forge a line or two from husband, allowing me to know all was well with Bertram. I knew he wouldn't show Bertram how to do it, but as an accomplished forger it would have taken no time at all for Fitzroy to have settled my nerves. This made me think that he too might be back in the field. In which case who the hell was handling Bertram? It had been agreed sometime ago he could only be an asset due to his health, so handing him over to someone else would be a serious step and only taken because mission parameters had gone awry.

I needed to get out of here. I needed to find out what was happening with my husband.

Which meant I couldn't possibly wait another – who knew how many weeks – until that wretched Matron allowed me on to her special ward.

No one would believe a female doctor. I didn't even know if there was such a thing in the army. I worked with a department that, for all the complaints I could have listed about it, was realising more and more how useful women could be. In this it was ahead of its time. The vast majority of the dominant sex were more likely to pat women on the head and tell them to get back to the kitchen, remarking how their neat little feet let them get adorably close to the sink.

Anyway, if I couldn't be a doctor I would promote myself to

qualified nurse. My plan was sketchy at best, but I knew I would have to enlist Merry's further help. So after an escorted visit to the burns unit, when we were meant to be writing up our notes, I dragged Merry out for a walk.

'They can hardly object to us getting some fresh air as long as we finish our notes later. We've been cooped up far too long.'

Merry hesitated. Like me, she was born a country girl and she hankered for the outside as much as I did.

'Besides, I need to talk to you.'

'About . . . stuff?' said Merry.

I nodded.

'Well, it's about time,' said Merry, grabbing her cloak from its peg.

We walked a reasonable distance into the grounds, and I stopped at a fortunate bench that was on a small rise, so I could see all around us. I sat down, drawing my nurse's cloak close about me. The wind whipped at our faces somewhere between the cold coming off the sea and the cooling sun of a late summer afternoon. Birds called from somewhere down the lane towards the wood that lay beyond the grounds.

'It's difficult to believe there is fighting going on anywhere,' said Merry. 'It's so beautiful here. Peaceful.' She turned to smile at me. 'They say it will be over by Christmas.'

I could imagine Fitzroy in my mind's eye shaking his head sadly. 'Let's hope so,' I said. 'I don't have any privileged information on what's happening at present.'

'Will you later?' said Merry eagerly.

'It depends. Depends on what the Major tells me.'

'You work for Fitzroy, don't you?'

'On an irregular basis,' I said cagily. Merry knew I had been used as an asset before. I didn't want to acknowledge to her that I was now a field agent. 'Certainly he asked me to look into this hospital,' I admitted.

'You've not got that far, have you? Or have you been doing things in the night again?'

'No, I nearly got caught that first time. I hoped to get onto the wards properly by now. Even being allowed to wash the floor would have been useful, but Matron seems determined to keep us sequestered.

'Yeah, they have cleaners here. But if you want to mop floors I bet they let you do it at the clearing stations.'

'No thank you. Listen. This is what happened last time I tried to explore.'

'Smugglers!' cried Merry when I had finished, making me very glad no one else was around.

'Smugglers?'

'You know, the fellow who ditched the coat – obviously not a doctor, they're so proud of their white coats. Have you seen how they strut about? Anyway, we're by the sea. And he sold stuff to the people in that car – don't you see? They obviously took it out to sea. Smugglers! The south coast is rife with them.'

'I think he was stealing medicines, but I doubt they were going abroad. I expect he had someone to sell them to – drug fiends, or doctors who can't get the ones they want since the war started.'

'Well, that's a kind of smuggling,' said Merry. She was now frowning. 'My version was much more romantic.'

'Yes, it is. But I've managed to gather a registered nurse's uniform. So when it's time for the shifts to change I thought I could go on to the ward . . .'

'You're crazy. If they catch you . . .'

'That's why I need you.'

'You want me to be your look-out?'

'Yes, but if it does look like I'm going to get into trouble I need you to provide a distraction – which won't get either of us caught.'

'Like what? A fire alarm?'

'Good God, no,' I said, startled. We'd recently had a lecture on the fire drill. We'd been allocated stations, but a full drill was out of the question as it involved moving patients who simply should not be moved. 'I'm not trying to kill anyone.'

'So what would I do?'

'What do you think you could do?' I said. I had a couple of ideas, but they weren't up to much. I didn't want her to know that.

'I suppose I could threaten to jump out the window. You know, saying it was all too much. That would get a lot of attention – unless the other nurses decided to try and keep it quiet to save my career. I'd have to find somewhere that lots of people would notice me at night.' She frowned in thought.

'A little drastic,' I said. 'Besides, you might need to stand in the very spot I wanted to get past.'

'I could find someone and say I was woken up by a scream.'

'And have everybody scour the hospital until they found me?' I responded. Merry opened her mouth, but I held up a hand. 'However, the principle is a good idea. You could say you'd woken in the night to go to the loo, but noticed someone in the grounds. Then they would be searching outside. That might work.'

'I was going to say that,' said Merry, but the muscle in her right cheek twitched and I realised she was lying. I was so pleased with myself that I had finally found Merry's tell I gave her a bright smile. (Finding tells in people you've known a long time is always harder.)

'What's more,' said Merry, 'I'm actually rather good at bird calls. We could use these to communicate. Listen.'

The first noise she made sounded like a cow in labour. 'Mmmmooocooooo!'

'Cuckoo!' said Merry brightly.

The second noise sounded like a scalded cat: 'EEEeeeekwaaah!'

'Swan!'

The third noise sounded like a hen: 'Cluck cluck!' But when I guessed this. Merry gave me a condescending look and said, 'Blackbird. I don't think you know your birdsong, do you, Euphemia – and you the lady of a country estate.'

'It isn't something I'd studied,' I admitted.

'Merrit taught me. He said I'm terribly good at it.'

'He must love you very much,' I said with complete sincerity.

Merry then gave such a perfect imitation of a wood pigeon that one flew over and perched in the tree beside us.

'That was impressive,' I said. 'It strikes me that some of the more exotic sounds might be most useful in locating you.'

'I can call them to alert you of people coming,' said Merry.

'Yes. Yes you could. Using the diversion of a man in the grounds would be a good emergency step if it looked like I was about to be caught. The best thing would be if I arranged some kind of signal if I needed help.'

'Or I could follow you around and see how things went.'

'Then we'd both get caught. I think on the first run. I should head into Ward D at change-over, and you can signal when the shift is coming back on duty.'

'I thought you wanted to speak to Rory?'

'I do, but we don't know what's in Ward D. It might answer everything.'

'You mean they might be running experiments in there on patients? Killing them?' said Merry, her eyes very wide.

This hadn't even occurred to me. 'It's a possibility we need to check,' I said, keeping my face as straight as possible. I thought it very unlikely the British Army would experiment on its own. It occurred to me for the first time, that if Rory proved right about more people dying than they should, it could be down to a doctor's incompetence. But then, I hadn't had more than the briefest conversation with Rory. I knew he had been a sensible and very observant man, but he had also obviously been in the fighting. I'd seen the result of Fitzroy going overseas, and he was a man I would have thought had more sang-froid and resilience than most. He'd intimated he had been involved in battles before. Yet, when he returned he had been far from his usual self. It could be that Rory too was changed. If I thought Fitzroy might have become paranoid and overly suspicious, could it not be that Rory, subjected to the horrors of war, now saw death everywhere? His previous life as a butler, and even briefly an asset, would not have prepared him for what he saw.

The situation was untenable. All the information I had acquired was either lacking significant detail or was unverifiable. I'd really been landed in a hornets' nest this time.

82

I blinked back to reality and realised Merry was still watching me closely.

'Are you running through plans in your head?' she said.

'Of course. Let's get on and walk a bit more, there's somewhere I want to see.'

Merry jumped up. She was eager for adventure.

'We need to seem as if we are merely going for a walk and talking about ordinary things,' I warned. 'Let's go over what we were learning on the burns unit today. It will make typing up our notes later much easier.'

She gave me the kind of look my little brother would have done if he'd answered a summons to the kitchen expecting to be fed pie, but had found homework awaiting him on the kitchen table instead. Interestingly enough, Merry and I noticed different things about the earlier gruesome version of show and tell (very popular in our village school), so we were able to add to each other's knowledge while we strode (as only a country woman can) over the hospital's park.

All the while I chatted with Merry, I was fingering the key in my pocket. It was the key I had taken from the white coat I had found in the potted plant. Over the past weeks I'd tried it surreptitiously in any door where I thought I could be unobserved. I had established that although the dorms did have locks on them, this key did not fit and I had never seen a key in or near the lock. Neither did it fit the refectory door, for which I had had unjust hopes. I often went to bed feeling hungry and the opportunity for a late night cocoa and a sandwich at midnight would have been much appreciated. I didn't have Fitzroy's knack of substituting food for sleep, but I found I could ameliorate my tiredness with a well-timed snack.

I tore my mind away from food. What I now wanted to try was the back door into Ward D. If Ward D's patients were admitted and treated separately from the rest of the hospital then there had to be access for both ambulances and doctors on the far side of the building. Since visiting the recovery rooms on my midnight stroll, I had deduced that the operating theatres must be close by, which meant that so must Ward D. However secure it was, the patients would need easy access to the operating rooms. It was possible they had separate theatres for Ward D patients, but that seemed to go against the whole concept of the hospital. Having patients who needed operations and not being able to access the full facilities seemed to make no sense. After all, during the operations the patients would not be able to spill any secrets.

No one had told us we couldn't go around the back of the building. We were simply kept too busy to easily find a time to go for a long stroll. Our visit to the ward today had been cut short by the sudden arrival of a new influx of patients. We were fairly chased out of the way. This had left Merry and I able to go for a long walk with little fear of notice. When we had left the main hospital it had seemed a case of all hands on deck. Of course, if we rounded the back of the building and found several ambulances outside Ward D then I would have to rethink my plan.

Chapter Eleven

My luck looks up

The wind blew our hair to bits as we rounded the building, but we were in luck. The yard here lay empty. I backed in against a wall out of the wind and tried my best to tuck in my hair.

'Right you stay here,' I said to Merry. 'Make one of your animal noises, loudly, if you see someone coming.'

'They are bird noises, and how do I explain why I am doing it?'

'I'd find a spot out of sight but not too far away. If anyone does find you, say you have stomach ache or toothache. Right, go and find somewhere to hide.'

I took the key out of my pocket and tried the door. It fitted. I turned it in the lock and entered. I did wonder about the safety of locking the ward, but I imagined they must have a key hanging up inside the door. There had to be at least one member of staff on duty, but hopefully it would be another nurse. I would need to try and evade her, or hope she wasn't someone I had previously run into.

I opened the door quickly and walked in as if I had every right to the there. I didn't relock it in case I had to make a quick exit.

My first impression was that Ward D was both more spacious than the other wards, and darker. Then I heard the moaning. There was a dimness that hung over the place, but I managed to make out a bed where a patient lay, rocking slightly from side to side. The moans came from him.

The thick blue-striped curtains trailed on the floor with not one scrap of the afternoon sunshine breaking through. Instead low lamps stood beside twelve beds. These stood in two rows of six that faced each other. Between the beds were half-screens designed to give the patients some privacy. At the top of the ward a nurse sat, reading notes, at a large brown desk on which the brightest lamp stood. While her attention was occupied I took the opportunity to get out of sight behind one of those screens. If I kept my voice low the moaning should cover it. I felt bad for that patient in distress, but I assumed the nurse had not answered his calls because there was nothing she could do.

In this bed a man sat upright, propped up by pillows, intent on a newspaper crossword. He looked up with some curiosity. He had no obvious injury, but his blond hair had grown below his collar, so he must have been there some time. Many women would have thought him handsome, but there was a hint of a sneer in the way he held his mouth. His thin brown moustache only made this more pronounced. He regarded me with bright eyes, 'What ho, nurse! I don't think we've seen you before. You're a little beauty!' His accent came from the upper echelons of society, and his extraordinary manner of greeting led me to believe he came from a life of considerable privilege.

'Good afternoon, sir,' I said, taking out my notebook from my pocket. 'I am part of the patient liaison service. Is there anything you need or anyone I can contact to send you materials?'

'Materials? Can't think of anything I need. Got the crossword. The Old Bone-saw gives me his newspaper every luncheon. Can't ask for more than that. Food seems bloody good after army rations.'

'A bottle of whisky or brandy?'

'I say, are they letting us have a drop now?'

'Only the longer-term patients who are officers, sir. However the hospital cannot provide –'

The man waved my excuses away. 'Topper Toppingham will send me down a drop of the good stuff. Got his wound on practically the first day. Always was a lucky bastard. He's at Bathleigh House in Shropshire. Drop him a line from me, there's a good girl.'

'And you are, sir?'

'Captain Algernon Dwyer of the Somerset Dwyers.'

I obediently wrote all the details down. This helped me disguise my astonishment that Fitzroy had picked such a boor for his elite troop. Presumably when working Dwyer kept his thoughts to himself. I had taken an instant dislike to the man. This deepened when he said, 'Give an old man a kiss, girl? Lost half my foot in the service of King and Country. I'll never play rugger again and I was in the first team when I was up at Rugby, don't you know.'

'I'm grateful for your service, sir. But I don't think my husband would approve of my kissing soldiers.'

He made a swipe for my waist, which I managed to dodge. 'Oh, come on. What he doesn't know won't hurt him. Besides, if you're in here you signed the Official Secrets Act. This can be our official secret.

'I'll pass, thank you.'

'Jolly unsporting of you. It's not like I can chase you without Matron catching us. And she's worse than the Hun.'

'I think you must be confusing me with an entirely different kind of lady,' I said.

'Isn't it what all you nurses get into this for? Seeing a bit of gentlemanly flesh?'

'If I find a gentleman I'll let you know,' I said, and nipped behind the next screen.

In this bed I found Corporal Potter, an engineer, who had been exploring the possibilities of digging tunnels when, 'The whole ruddy thing came down on top of me, miss. Still, I reckon I got some information about the type of earth there and what we might be able to do. Can't say I enjoyed myself, miss, but I miss the other lads. Looking forward to getting back out there when the doc gives me the all clear.' Cpl Potter, who turned out to have expertise in explosives, had been brought up in an orphanage and couldn't think of anyone who could send him anything. I made a note on my sheet to get Mrs T to anonymously send him some chocolate or cocoa powder. He was more than happy to chat. 'Him next door being not one to talk to the lower ranks and it being nice to stretch my laughing gear around a good conversation.' I knew I was spending too long with him, but he seemed a genuinely nice and lonely man.

Eventually I moved on. If I had to visit all twelve beds to find Fitzroy's four, Merry would need to hide for a very long time. Plus, I only had so long before the next shift appeared.

The next man was asleep. His head was heavily bandaged, so I didn't feel I could disturb him. The name on his chart said 'Lecky' along with 'serious concussion'. I let him sleep and moved on. The next man proved to be a Sgt Hipple, who was desperate for a decent plate of haddock and chips. I dutifully noted this down. These men were so eager for what were essentially tiny treats – things they had thought about during their time under fire – that I realised I would have to get Mrs T to somehow deliver them all. 'Odd thing that, miss. I kept thinking if I get shot now then I'll never have another paper of fish and chips.' He sighed. 'I could almost taste the vinegar, I wanted it so bad.'

'I'm sure we can sort something out,' I said, and his stoic military face broke into a glorious grin.

The fifth and sixth patients turned out not to have been on Fitzroy's list of names. I ended up putting them down for six packets of French cigarettes and a side of beef 'for the missus when I get home.'

This was definitely going to test the ingenuity of my housekeeper. But with patient number six I had reached the point where I had to cross the ward if I wished to continue. I imagined Merry outside getting more and more anxious. Time was running out, but I needed to make the most of this opportunity.

I couldn't be obviously sneaky or the man who had been telling me about his love of beef would know something havey-cavey was up. So taking a deep breath I walked straight across the ward, looking slightly to one side, so the nurse didn't have a clear view of my face. Half way across I heard the bang of a steel filing cabinet. and realised she must be away from her desk. I quickened my pace and arrived at the beside of Hobson. 'Just Hobson, ma'am. We don't use ranks in the outfit I belong to. It's whoever is best at whatever we're doing who leads – we all know each other's capabilities. Not much use for rank then. What did you say you were doing?'

I explained again about my patient liaison role. 'Never heard of such a thing,' said Hobson, who was a man in his mid-thirties with spiky black hair. 'Seems a bit odd to me.' This wasn't said in a hostile tone, but he did sound wary. 'When did they think this one up?'

I decided to tell some truth. I wouldn't be surprised if Fitzroy had taught his people some of the lie detecting skills he had taught me. 'I'm actually still in training. My lecturer wanted us to come up with ideas to keep up morale. I suggested this. She suggested I try it out and see how difficult it would be to do for the whole hospital. I've signed the Act, so she suggested I tried it on this ward. If I'd done it on one of the main wards, it might have become common knowledge and then we'd have to deal with everyone.' I sighed. 'She's right, too. The men have been asking for the weirdest things. It's becoming difficult to see how this could work.'

'It's a nice idea, I'll grant you. When you're away from home you always miss something badly, see? What that thing is varies from man to man. I miss the smell of burning leaves, the colours of autumn, and early sunsets. Do you have good sunsets where you come from, ma'am?'

'Actually yes, quite stunning ones, but I can't think how I could box one up for you.'

'That's the point. A lot of us want what symbolises the essence of our lives here back home. Most men call for their mothers when they're dying.'

I started at this. Hobson nodded. 'Yeah, they want the safety and security of when their mothers looked after them. Probably remember their mothers telling them they'd never let anyone harm their little darling boy. As if that's a promise they could keep. I killed my mother when I was born, so I'm not so sentimental about them.'

Even if I hadn't know the name I would have recognised this as someone attached to the Service. He was doing his best to shock me and see if I gave myself away as something other than what I was pretending to be. A little heavy-handed perhaps, but he was right to question an unknown nurse with an unusual story coming on to the ward. If I could have thought of a normal reason that didn't attract attention, I would have said that. But I hadn't come up with anything better. I had to play it out. 'So if you're not into mothers, what would you like? And is there someone who can supply it?'

'I'd like a knife. A five-inch blade with a rugged edge and a sharp point. Something good for cutting away the dross in your way.'

I didn't flinch. I had expected something unpleasant. 'I imagine there are times when a knife would be useful to a spotter,' I said.

His right arm darted forward. His hand formed an iron-like grip around my left hand. 'So who told you I was a spotter?'

I looked him straight in the eye. 'Bird spotter. I thought that was what you meant. Needing to clear the undergrowth to make a hide to watch birds.'

He smiled. It was the kind of smile even a mother wouldn't have loved. He was missing a tooth on the left upper side of his mouth. His eyes were cold and flat. His top lip twitched in something between a sneer and a snarl.

'You thought I was talking about bird spotting?'

'You're hurting my wrist,' I said. 'Could you please release me.'

'If I'm a problem, call for help.' He paused. 'You can't, can you? I don't think you're meant to be in here at all.'

Things were beginning to feel a bit sticky. 'I know Fitzroy,' I said. 'He'd not want you to blow my cover.'

'Fitzroy who?'

'Your commander during your last mission. Captain – now Major Fitzroy.'

The pressure on my wrist eased slightly. 'Why would you be working for the Major?'

'You must know I can't tell you anything,' I said. It felt a bit like bolting the stable door after the horse had bolted. If he wanted to, Hobson could blow my cover completely.

'Bit of an impasse, isn't it?' he said, still not releasing me. I had the sense he liked seeing me struggle. I knew some of the men Fitzroy had trained were, by any sane person's reckoning, nasty pieces of work. I'd met one: Cole. A man who took pleasure in killing. I'd always thought it was better he was in the Service than running

90

around loose. I also knew the measures Fitzroy took to control him were far from gentle. I could only hope he exercised the same influence over Hobson. I thought hard about what I could say to remind him of Fitzroy's methods without asking or revealing anything particularly secret.

'I wouldn't have said so, no. Fitzroy's trainees tend to recognise each other.'

He sneered at that. 'I doubt he's trained you for much outside the bedroom.'

'Do you know how to feel a pulse?'

'What?'

'Move your fingers here,' I guided them with my free hand. 'You must know that a pulse changes during a lie?' This wasn't entirely true – at least not all of the time – but I was fairly sure Hobson wouldn't admit to not knowing anything in front me.

'Yeah.'

'Ask me how many people I have killed during my missions.'

'You're not going to be able to compete with me!'

'I don't expect to,' I said. 'But you wouldn't expect me to have killed anyone to look at me, would you? Or even to be capable of it.'

'Easy enough for you to snuff a man out when he's relaxed.'

I allowed a flash of anger to show in my eyes. 'I have never been sent on that kind of mission.'

'Hmm, strong steady pulse,' said Hobson. 'Maybe you're the Major's little whore. I hear he likes 'em dark-haired.' He paused, clearly waiting for my reaction. I slowed my breathing and did my best not to give him one. It must have worked because he said, 'So how many men have you killed.'

'Two that I know of. There may be more, but those would have been deaths as indirect consequences of my actions rather than direct actions.'

He let me go. 'I'll give you the benefit of the doubt. If it turns out you've lied to me, I will find you and kill you. You won't hear me coming.'

'I wouldn't expect to after Major Fitzroy's training.'

91

I got up while I could. My legs felt a bit shaky, but I managed to tense my muscles and stop them from trembling. 'I'll do my best not to disturb you again,' I said.

'You'll do whatever you need to do. Say hello to the Major for me next time you're snuggling up to him.'

I didn't bother answering. More than anything I wanted to bolt from the ward. But I went behind the next screen. In the bed lay a boy. A pillow propped him up a little, but for some reason he couldn't sit up properly. He regarded me with bright eyes. 'Surely you're not old enough . . .'

'To serve my country, miss? Spent a lot of my life on the streets. Not a lotta grub. Means I grew up small – or so the Major said.'

I must have shown my shock. Because he gave me a wink. 'Nah, it's all right. I'm one of the Major's too. Not that he was a Major when I met him. He was a Captain. Like you almost called him.' He tapped the side of his head. 'I've got very good hearing, Miss. Besides, made me think you were more likely to be telling the truth. Reckon you must have known him before this – this little party.'

I sat carefully down on the end of the bed. 'You must be Wilkins.'

'That's it, ma'am. I won't ask the name you're using with old bugger-lugs next door. Not sure how well he hears, but he's an evil b—,' he hesitated, 'an evil what–der–yer–call–it, if you get my meaning.'

'Thank you,' I said.

I got a cheeky grin in response. 'Wanna know how the Major became the Major?'

'Field promotion, I imagined.'

He gave a low crack of laughter. 'Yeah, kind of. The unit we were in, well, rank wasn't meant to matter. We had a commanding officer and the rest of us were, well, the rest of us. Only Major Dwyer somehow learned that the Major was only a Captain and he started being difficult about it. Saying he should be leading the final –' he caught himself in time, took a deep breath and finished with a vague, 'final bit.'

'I shouldn't imagine Major Fitzroy liked that,' I said.

'Understatement of the century, ma'am. Hadn't really thought of him as the kind of man who excels in hand to hand, after what we'd been doing. Seemed an intelligent, careful type, who moved with the skill of a fox's ghost, but not someone you'd expect to leather you. Dwyer hadn't marked him like that either. The fury in him when he gave Dwyer what for. Bloody terrifying, if you don't mind me saying. Then when Dwyer was on the ground the Major was all cool as a cucumber again, as if he'd just been to tea with the vicar, not beating a man half to death. I remember him combing his hair back into place and saying, 'Put the kettle on, Wilkins. I could do with a cuppa.' Then he adds as he's walking away from Dwyer lying on the ground groaning, 'I'm giving myself a field promotion to Acting Major. You can refer to me as the Major now. Nice to know they let him keep the rank.'

I couldn't hold back a smile. 'That sounds very like him.'

Wilkins tilted his head to one side, assessing me. 'Reckon you are one of his. Most ladies would be fainting away at a story like that. And you are, whatever 'im next door says, undoubtedly a lady.'

I frowned. 'You may be right. This isn't my first outing.'

'So 'ow can I help?'

I shifted closer to the boy and lowered my voice. 'Do you remember seeing anyone go up to the hayloft in the barn?'

The boy paled. 'I've been trying to put that night out of my mind.' He nodded down towards his prone body. 'I got some really bad burns. They won't even let me look when they change the dressings.'

'I'm sorry to hear that.'

'The Major got me out. Carried me over his shoulder like I was a lump of coal. Me clothes were still on fire. There weren't no time for 'im to do nothin' about it. He ran like the devil. It were raining heavy like, and the flames went out, but me clothing went on smouldering. I don't think either of us realised. It were only when we were clear that he rolled me on the ground. Finally put the fire out, but well – I was all burnt up. Crying like a little kid, I was. The Major were right decent. He got me home even though it slowed us down. By rights he should have left me.'

93

'I don't think he would have seen it like that.'

'No, bit of a maverick I reckon.'

'The hayloft?'

'If it's important to the Major I'll try and remember.'

'Thank you. I'll come back in a day or so.'

I stood up to leave. 'Miss,' said the boy, calling me back, 'none of them are a bad lot. Bit rough around the edges maybe. We was chosen for being different, but we stand by each other. Them others are the closest I've ever had to family. The Major got me out that night, but both Dwyer and Hobson pulled my – well, got me out of difficulties more than once. I did the same for Lecky too.'

'Brothers in arms,' I said smiling.

'Something like that, miss. Unless you've had to put your life in another's hands you won't know what I'm talking about.'

'I know. I'll be back when I can.'

The ward door opened. I moved back instinctively behind the screen. I'd taken too long and the next shift was coming on.

Chapter Twelve

Night–time manoeuvres

I was lucky. Despite the handover the first thing the new staff did was head towards the nurse's desk to check with her if there had been any developments. I took the chance and walked quickly towards the door without looking back. It was open. I left, slowing my walk as much as I could bear. No one would remark on a nurse leaving the ward, but one sprinting as if the hounds of hell were after her would draw attention.

However, Merry had no such qualms. I had no idea where she had hidden, but now she approached me at what, if she'd been a horse, would have been a thundering gallop. (It's perhaps a little unfair to comment on the weight she had put on after the birth of her son. Although it did do an excellent job of reminding me I needed to start getting up early and going for a run. With Fitzroy unable to exercise I'd let my fitness slide on a trip back from Monaco.)

'Where the dickens have you been,' hissed Merry between panting breathes. 'I thought you'd been nobbled.'

'I had a lot of people to talk to,' I said. 'I didn't hear you call that the shift were coming back.'

'You didn't 'ear me call?' said Merry, her voice getting louder. 'I was ruddy woodcocking myself blue in the face. Can't you hear the way I'm chuffing like a bleedin' steam engine?'

'I thought that was your lack of fitness,' I said. 'After all, you're not used to running.'

'Not used to running! Not used to running! You try living my bleedin' life at walking pace. Not only am I running around after the baby, but I'm doing my work and Merrit's *and* keeping that ruddy allotment going. All my bleedin' sister does is sit around like Miss High and Mighty, occasionally playing with Michael and telling me I should be spending more time with me son.' She leaned forward with her hands on her waist, struggling for breath.

'Merry,' I began, but she straightened up.

'I reckon you and my sister would get on just fine,' she said, and with that stormed off towards the hospital. I walked in the other direction for a while, partly to give her time to calm down, and partly so I wouldn't associate with a small raging termagant. This wasn't the Merry I knew.

I had hoped our time together training and then my efforts to use her gently as an asset would prove an adventure for her. Now, I was beginning to realise that the strain of having a newborn in the house, a sister to whom she was not close, and a husband away at war, had taken more of a toll on my friend than I realised. She was volatile and unhappy. Completely unsuitable for me to use on a mission. I would need to help her in a big way when we got back to White Orchards. I'd get the gardening boy to help her with her vegetable patch. I'd ensure she spent more time over at the house with me. I'd even let her bring the baby. I wondered how Jack would react to that. He'd either become a little playmate or he'd try and eat the child. He was as unpredictable as his master.

Unfortunately, this latter thought was on my mind when I gained the hospital entrance, causing a small smile to play on my lips. Merry was waiting for me. 'I'm glad to see you find it all so amusing,' she said. At least her voice was low, but her eyes shone with anger. 'I was stupid to think you and I could remain friends.' To my horror she dashed away a tear. 'To think I was going to apologise to you, and you were laughing at me all the time, behind my back.'

'Merry, I have never . . .' my voice trailed off. She had turned her back on me and was walked up the stairs. Her back so straight even my mother would have approved. I climbed the stairs slowly after her, deliberately not catching her up. It was time for dinner. I expected we would both feel better after a good meal.

When I entered the refectory I saw Merry sitting with Ruth and Rose's crowd. She saw me and turned away so haughtily another time I would have smiled. Haughty didn't suit Merry. I chose a seat near the window where three nurses I didn't know were gossiping together. I let them be and helped myself to a substantial amount of food. I had a lot to think about.

Back in the dorm I changed openly into my black clothes. It sparked a lot of comments.

'I'm going for a run,' I explained. 'I can't run in a skirt.'

'You're as good as naked!' said Margaret. 'Don't try and tell me you're still wearing a corset!'

'Of course not, but I am wearing a brassiere.'

At this Margaret slumped down onto her bed as if she had fainted. By now everyone in the room knew enough to know she was faking it. We all ignored her. She sat back up and glared at me. I did up my shoes.

'What if there's a man in the grounds?' said Merry.

'Then he had better look out,' I said. Rose tittered at that, but quieted almost immediately under Ruth's baleful glance.

'I'll come with you if you like,' said Elsie.

'That's very kind of you,' I said. 'But I always run alone.'

Merry eyed me, but said nothing.

'You should take her,' said Ruth. 'If anyone tries to molest you, she can sit on them. That'd be effective.'

Elsie fled the room biting on her fist.

'You're a mean one, Ruth Bakewell,' said Wee-wee Mary, 'Why you thought you could be a nurse I've no idea.' She got up to go after Elsie.

'Call of nature, is it?' said Ruth. 'Still no control over that bladder?' Mary gave her a filthy look, but left without another word. Merry and I accidentally locked gazes. The expression of dismay on her face matched what I felt. The women had had their cliques, but the atmosphere had turned poisonous. Merry raised her eyebrows and shrugged. She too didn't understand this sudden turn of affairs. I leaned over and said quietly to her, 'Talk at breakfast tomorrow?'

She nodded. It wasn't exactly a truce, but I could tell the viciousness of our dorm mates had shaken her. I glanced round as if checking if I'd left anything out of place. What I wanted to check was that the window was still wedged ajar if I couldn't get back in through the front door.

I left the dorm and headed downstairs. I made it out of the door without running into anyone. I tampered lightly with the lock of the main door. I couldn't afford to do anything too clever and draw attention to myself.

We were meant to sign out if we intended leaving the grounds, but I felt certain no one would expect me to go for a run longer than lapping the building. I knew if I paced myself I could run for ten miles. I had no intention of going that far. However, I did have a plan that might for once produce some solid results. After that I intended to see if the porter's unattended desk was vacant again tonight, and whether the telephone remained connected. It was incredible to me that a telephone might be unattended, but then again I had not seen anyone try to use it.

Outside I found the night air mellow, slightly too warm for running, but here near the sea I thought it wouldn't be long before the air cooled. I stopped by one of the enormous statues. I could see no one out here. Lamps either side of the front door glowed, and there were four lampposts in total along the drive, I assumed in case an ambulance turned up at night. Although the leafy lanes around had no lighting at all. Instead, the countryside was sunk into the pitch blackness all country people know well and became used to navigating. Even before my training I'd had to become good at memorising the environment. It had been either that or never go for an evening walk in the Fens again. Marshes and bogs surrounded my home, and a mistaken turn could end in far more than simply getting your feet wet. People drowned in the bogs.

I'd been taught to stretch before I ran. A practice I found pointless. But I hadn't had the chance to run for a while so I dutifully did so. Whilst readying my body, I called up the layout of the hospital in my mind's eye. After my walk with Merry I was fairly certain I knew how most of the departments and wards fitted into the hospital. As yet there was no security in the grounds, something that would have to change if the war continued, but for now I didn't worry over running into a guard or eager young soldier with a rifle. What I wasn't wholly sure about was all the exits and entrances to the building. That made tonight's operation a bit of a hit or a miss, but at least no one would die if I didn't get it right this time.

Light spilled from multiple windows of the hospital. I clung to the shadow of the walls until I reached the edge of the building. Then I moved off into the night. Breathing deeply, I smelled flowers and mown grass. So much nicer than the constant smell of disinfectant that filled hospital life. My limbs protested at first, but after its initial complaining my body fell into an easy loping run. For a woman brought up to wear corsets and sit properly it was a true pleasure to run. With it came a sense of freedom and personal power. I was fitter now than I had ever been. I knew only too well my form-fitting clothes were a scandal, and that even at White Orchards I would not have worn them during the day in full sight of my tenants and servants. Although more than once Fitzroy had taken me out wearing a coat to some countryside location, only for us to leave our coats in his car and run a circuit of five miles or more. But then when he was in professional mode he would neither have noticed or cared what I wore as long as I was free to move and, most importantly, kept up with him.

An owl on the hunt hooted and further away two foxes called to one another. Whether they were fighting or mating I couldn't tell. All around me I heard the rustles and twitches of nocturnal wildlife. I knew that it would unsettle many people, but I rather liked the thought that while humans were busy killing each other, mother nature's other children were ignoring their idiocy and going about their nightly business as usual. The rubber soles, so quiet in the hospital corridors, did not provide a good grip on the grass. I avoided the noise of the gravel and had to correct my gait frequently to stop myself from falling. After a while I found my centre – although my thigh muscles were already starting to complain – and carried on. I had set out on a wide circuit of the hospital. I timed my run so that I should complete the circuit and be at the end of the lane some fifteen minutes before I had seen the car there on that first night.

Now, I was moving without any conscious thought of body control. The rhythmic movement warmed me and my pulse had settled into a steady beat. I considered from my newly learned medicinal knowledge (which I knew was far from complete) what was actually happening in my body. It occurred to me, not for the first time in my nursing studies, that the human body is a rather wonderful thing. This of course then led to thoughts of injured soldiers and the bitter waste of life war brought.

Fitzroy and I thought alike that war was a failure. He had been working far longer than I to avert it, but when powerful people determined on a collision course, all we in the Service could do was provide information in the hope of producing a swift victory and minimising suffering.

This led me on to thinking about Rory. I had yet to speak to him again. He doubtless felt I had ignored him and thought him ridiculous, but I knew he had a sound mind. If he had noted that the fatality rate was too high then there would be a reason. Although, I admitted, it might be that the fatality rate was due to the unusual nature of the injuries inflicted by war, and the general suffering and ill-health that fell upon men in the battlefield. Fitzroy had refused to let me be involved anywhere near the frontlines. I'd protested, as I felt I should be able to do my bit as well as any man, but secretly I was relieved at his insistence. I did not doubt my choice to serve King and Country, even if Fitzroy had, from a certain perspective, tricked me into swearing the oath. Bertram believed Fitzroy had set out to entrap me, but I thought it was more likely he had taken advantage of circumstances. It was what he had trained me to do.

I was reflecting on how annoying he could be when I saw a thin wedge of light widen, slowly at first, then quickly expand into a rectangle before being just as quickly extinguished. I knew I was near the back of the hospital now, and it appeared that someone had made what they thought was a stealthy exit. I had no desire to intercept them, but if it was who I thought it was, I needed to get ahead. I quickened my pace, widening out to avoid them. The figure stood out against the light from the hospital briefly. It was a man and he was walking quickly.

I redoubled my efforts. I couldn't think of any way to slow him down, so I would have to go even faster. I still had a good third of the circuit to run. I mentally ran through how I might shorten it, but I would have to be sure I didn't cut directly into his path or come within his hearing.

I was no longer enjoying my freedom. My lungs hurt. My breath rasped. My thighs had ceased being sore, but were now quivering like jelly. If I kept going at this rate I was going to hit a wall of exhaustion at which point my hamstrings might hobble me. I might collapse gasping on the ground or I might manage to break through and keep going. I didn't like the odds.

Just when I thought I would have to fall back and attempt this another night, the man paused by a small outbuilding and then disappeared inside it.

This structure had been on my mental plan as an obstacle. I hadn't thought deeply about its use. I'd assumed it was something to do with the gardener. I rather wanted to follow him in. This could be another avenue of investigation, but did I want one? I had too many open threads as it was. I slowed down to a jog. My whole body trembled and I quickly realised that stopping now would mean my muscles were liable to seize.

I alternatively jogged and ran to my original target. Keeping well clear of what I deemed most likely to be my target's route, I finally reached the tree I'd set my heart on.

The lane at the end of the drive was clear and dim. The darkness leavened by the lampposts. After a quick check around me I climbed up to the second branch in a few quick fluid movements. (As a child I would hide up a tree from my mother, reading books I had borrowed from my father's library. It was my proud boast there wasn't a tree in the county I couldn't climb. I have never let that skill lapse. Fitzroy always said I went up a tree like a bear after honey.)

I made my way up until I came to a good V between the second main branch and the trunk. I'd chosen a sturdy elm and I quickly found a comfortable perch against the trunk that not only kept me out of sight from the ground, but allowed me to stretch out my legs and cool my muscles slowly, so they didn't seize. Aglow from the exercise, it was rather relaxing. I felt much as one does when one emerges from a hot bath. A little heady and tingly in a most pleasant manner. All I had to do was remember I was up a tree and not relax too much.

Long before my mark appeared a car drew up near the bottom of the lane. I heard rather than saw it, as whoever was driving kept the lights off. The engine went quiet and the car merged nicely into the shadows of the lane. I heard the scratch of a lucifer and then although the car remained invisible a red dot glowed below me, like the evil eye. (Smoking a cigarette when one is trying to hide is a very bad idea.)

I leant my head back against the tree and waited. On a summer's day it would be a lovely place to sit and read.

It was some time later I noticed a flicker out of the corner of my eye. The light from the lampposts pooled on the lawns in perfect ovals, like fallen moons. It was the edge of one of these light wells that had been disturbed. I sat up straighter. I realised I had relaxed enough that I had, if not slept, at least become much less aware of my surroundings.

I glanced down to see the car still there. The red glow was gone. The man from the hospital finally broke out of cover and crossed to the car. He was carrying a large bag that hadn't been with him before. I strained my ears to hear.

He spoke in a low whisper. I thought I heard something like 'more difficult'. Though low, his voice had a whiny insistence. I guessed he was asking for more money for whatever he was selling. The voice that answered his was muffled, but terse. I didn't need to hear the words to know that the whiny one wasn't getting his way. The man outside the car wheedled again. This time the only answer was a grunt. There was the noise of leather rubbing against metal and I guessed the bag was being handed over. Some more muffled exchanges and I heard the engine roar into life. The car eased off slowly into the night. Whoever was driving was certain of himself and not prone to panic. There had been a smoothness to the exchange that despite my man's whining had been professional.

The man stood watching the car leave – as I had hoped he would. I edged my way along the branch. I'd chosen a strong branch that wasn't too high. The light from the lamppost allowed me to see where he was. It also partially illuminated me – and this had prevented me getting a decent look at the car. But now came the part I had planned for. The car and its occupant were intriguing, but my focus was the lone man.

I readied myself. He looked up. I dropped on him like a stone.

There had been a danger when he looked up that he might have cried out, but this was my chance and I wanted to be certain I landed on something squishy rather than the gravel drive. I had a quick image of his face, mouth agape in horror as I fell.

Even with that second's warning he crumpled under me. I adjusted myself so I landed full on his chest. Then I punched him hard in the face.

Chapter Thirteen

Ivor cuts a deal

For a moment I thought I'd killed him, then I heard a faint sound. I lowered my head slightly and realised he was whimpering like a beaten puppy.

'Don't hurt me. Please don't hurt me. They made me do it. I didn't want to. Please don't hit me again. I think my nose is broken.' This was not a person who became silent when terrified, quite the opposite. He had a scarf wrapped around the lower edge of his face. I pulled it free to check I was dealing with a man, and not a woman or a child. The five o'clock shadow scraping against my fingertips convinced me this was, all other indications to the contrary, a fully grown man, if no combatant.

I sat back slightly. I kept enough pressure on his chest with my knees that his breathing was laboured. For all I knew this weakness was a ruse.

'Would you care to explain what you were doing?'

'Not really,' he whimpered.

I glared down at him, hoping there was enough light to create a halo around me and make me a threatening shadow. I waited.

'That wasn't a question, was it?'

I shook my head.

'I was going for an evening stroll and the man in the car stopped to ask me for directions?'

'Is that a question?' I said, keeping my voice low.

'You believe me?'

I waited again. I was all too aware someone looking out the

window might glimpse us from the hospital. But if I rushed this I risked losing control or worse letting him get away.

'Do you?'

'No.'

'Oh, Gawd help me! What you going to do with me?'

'I haven't decided yet,' I said, thinking this was the kind of answer that was most likely to elicit the truth.

'My face hurts.'

'I could hit you again.'

'No, no thanks. I wouldn't want to put you out.' Despite the lack of backbone his sense of humour amused me mildly. I stifled any reaction.

'It's no trouble,' I said, raising my fist. He cowered, covering his face with his hands. I felt a little sick.

'Please don't. You don't want me. You want them. I'm no one.'

'Talk,' I said, my fist readied. In reality I thought the chance of my being able to hit such a weak, defenceless man slight, but he didn't need to know that.

'I owe Jimmy Pratt money.' He said it as if it should mean something to me. When I didn't answer he continued, 'I got in too deep at one of his games. I was trying to earn money to get me poor old mum some medication.'

'Spare me the sob story. You have access to as much medicine as anyone might want.'

'I do *now*. They got me the job. I can only steal to order. They get angry when I don't.'

'So you've already tried skimming, have you? What did they do?'

'Let's just say my fingers aren't all as agile as they used to be.'

'So your dear old mum still doesn't have her medicine – if she even exists . . .'

'She does! I swear on my father's grave, she does.'

'And your debt?'

'They said they'd tell me when I was paid up.'

'Hmm.'

'Yeah, you got it. I ain't ever going to be free. Oh, Gawd help me.'

'This isn't Jimmy Pratt's operation any more, is it?'

'No. He sold the debt on.'

'So who do you work for you now?'

'I don't know, I swear. There's this big bugger of a bloke who drives the car. His name is Bill.'

'How did you know what to do?'

'They leave instructions for me. There's a loose stone in the wall a mile from me house.'

'How do you know to check it?'

'The stone's brown one way round, more of a beige if it's put in the other way. I walk past it every day on my way to work. I can tell the difference, but not many people would notice. If I see it's changed I have to go back after dark and get the message.'

'Is it handwritten?'

'No, typed – and I can't see anything odd about the keys.'

That made me frown. 'I take it you'd like to be out from under this particular master's thumb?'

'Depends who was taking me on.'

'Someone who could keep you out of prison,' I said.

'What do I need to do?'

'Carry on as usual. When I need to speak to you I'll leave three stones in a triangle beside that shed you visited tonight. As soon as you see the signal come to this tree at eight that evening. Understand?'

'Yeah.'

'If you try and do a runner I will hand you over to the police. That is if your current master doesn't find you first.'

'I know when I'm caught. You might as well known I'm Ivor Cuttle. What do I call you?'

'Ma'am,' I said, and rising quickly, I turned and disappeared into the shadows. Within a moment I was back in my trees. I saw Ivor stumble to his feet. He doddered around a bit as if he was drunk, but I reckoned he was in shock. When he crossed the path of the light I could see a dark stain on his front and his face was covered in blood. I wondered if I had really broken his nose. Luckily he worked in a hospital.

There wasn't much more I could do tonight. I made my way back to the front of the building. Now the adrenaline was fading I could feel the soreness beginning to seep throughout my body. I was truly going to pay for my lack of exercise tomorrow. Never again would I skip my fitness regime, I swore, as I limped to the front door. The piece of cloth I'd stuck in the door had done it's job and I was able to slip inside.

I scouted around the lobby and checked the corridor was clear. Then I lifted the telephone from the desk. The cord was of reasonable length. I checked the porter's cupboard door. It was unlocked. I took the phone and crept inside. There was nothing in here, but a stack of shelves, a stool and a small table. I didn't stop to check what was stored here. Instead I picked up the receiver and told the exchange to connect me to a number that she would rarely have to try.

'Sunshine Removal Services. How can we be of assistance?'

'I need a special vehicle,' I said, which was code for asking the receptionist to secure the line.

'We have one available for the following three minutes.'

'Is Fitzroy available? It's Alice.'

'I am afraid that employee is currently on holiday' Which meant he was in the field. That surprised me. Almost as much as her continuing to speak in code despite the secure line. I supposed war changed everything.

'I would like to set up an outing.' Which meant I wanted to run an operation.

'One moment, ma'am, let me check your file.' There was some clicking on the line. I sat frozen waiting. Why was Fitzroy out? Wasn't he meant to be handling Bertram from England – what had changed? All the time my ears were straining to hear if anyone was approaching. It wouldn't be easy explaining what I was doing in the cupboard. I'd strung together a story about being homesick, but even if that was believed there would be a punishment. If that was expulsion, I was in deep trouble.

'Ma'am?'

'Yes?'

'I'm afraid your recent invoice is still unpaid. We could send one of our people to collect? Are you still at the same address?'

'I am. That would be fine.' This meant I wasn't cleared for running my own operations without Fitzroy overseeing them. I felt this was reasonable. I'd rather counted on his back-up.

'Can you tell me if Fitzroy's vacation is due to end shortly?'

'I'm sorry. It isn't a package holiday.' This meant it was a sudden response mission.

'So will someone else collect?'

'Indeed. Our time is up.' So someone else would come to talk through my idea. I didn't yet know many of the people from HQ. I'd met some of the other trainers, but for the most part Fitzroy had kept me on a tight leash.

The telephone line went dead. I peeked out around the edge of the door, keeping my head low to the floor. I looked under the desk. I couldn't see any feet, so I came out and put the telephone back on the table. Then I half crawled around the table, only standing when I was clear of it. The lobby stayed empty.

I walked up the stairs to the dorm. I wondered if I had the energy for a bath and decided I did. There were certain times when we were meant to bathe. Not least to ensure that hot water supplies were available when needed. My muscles were punishing me with every step. If I didn't sink into some hot water tonight there was no way I was going to be able to walk tomorrow.

I made my way towards the communal bathroom. The corridor was quiet. I would have liked to go to the dorm to get my own towel and toiletries, but I needed to keep the chances of waking the others to a minimum. I hoped someone had left a towel and some soap behind. I'd noticed that the night staff were often so tired that I came across these in the early mornings. I kept my fingers crossed.

I was in luck. I found a comparatively dry towel and a soap cake still in its packet. I ran the bath with the taps at half turn. It was agonisingly slow, but I knew that the full weight of water tumbling into the metal bath was extremely noisy at the best of times. Now, in the middle of the night, it would carry in a deafening manner. I let the bath fill enough that it would cover me. I got into the steaming water. My blood rushed to the surface of my skin, turning it a rosy red. At the same time I heard a rushing sound in my ears as dizziness overcame me. As I was lying down, nothing happened. Except I was fairly sure I wasn't getting up and out any time soon. I hadn't allowed for the time I had spent outside sitting on Ivor. I was far colder than I had realised. Consequently, submerging myself in hot water hit me with the force of a steam train. After the initial disorientating rush I felt my eyelids flutter. How much water does it take to drown someone? I couldn't remember. Tiredness overcame me.

Fortunately the bathroom fittings laid on for nursing staff are not of a luxurious style. I did pass out, but the smallness of the baths and badly fitting plug meant that I was wedged in with my head above the water level. As I woke to the pale light of dawn coming through the window my first thought was I had fallen asleep outside in a ditch. I felt frozen. My neck ached. The bones in my neck crunched painfully as I struggled to sit up. The parts of me still in contact with what remained of the water were more wrinkled than a dowager's neckline. I eased myself up and slowly, more like an octogenarian than a supposedly field-ready spy in her twenties, I eased myself out of the bath. The towel was still there, so I started rubbing feeling back into my mistreated body. I felt cold and sick and tired and thoroughly fed up. As feeling returned to my limbs every part of me ached like I'd been beaten with a hammer. I couldn't help wondering if this was a usual day in the life of a spy. Fitzroy had once told me that it was mostly extremely unglamorous and dangerous work, it was simply that he made it look good. I owed him an apology.

At this point I remembered I had promised to meet Merry for breakfast to try and repair the damage in our friendship. I liked this idea about as much as I would have liked to have awakened with my bathtub filled with eels. I wrapped the towel tightly around me. I hadn't been in the Service that long, but already my body was changing. I was thinner, more wiry and I had no fear the towel would slip. My concern was rather that its owner would recognise it and demand it back.

I balled up the rest of my clothes. They were muddy and sweaty. I picked up my shoes and walked to the dorm as if this was normal behaviour for me. My bare feet sounded loudly on the shiny floor and I left wet footprints behind me. There was nothing I could do about this, so I lifted my chin and walked with confidence, though the thought of running into the matron like that turned my insides to quivering jelly. However, I managed to get to the dorm without running into anyone. When I went in, no one, other than Merry, paid any attention to me.

The women were again divided into smaller groups or sitting on the edges of their bed alone. The atmosphere in the room was thick with emotion. I made my way to my bed without speaking to anyone and begin to dress quickly. Even putting on fresh clothes warmed me. The draught from the wedged window blew painfully cold against my naked skin, but I didn't close it. I wanted it to be the usual thing that it was left open. It remained my emergency return route.

Before the bell even rang some of the trainees had left to go to breakfast. 'Hurry up,' said Merry, 'Or they'll nab all the good stuff.'

As far as I knew, up until yesterday this had been a group, who if not all on the very best of terms with the others, tended to ensure we all got our fair share of the food, so we could do our work well. The escorted visits to the normal wards were becoming longer, and it seemed likely to me, whatever test they might have planned for us, that working on the wards shadowing other staff must be coming shortly.

I raised an eyebrow at Merry, but bent down to do up my shoes. I shouldn't have been surprised that they were as muddy as I had been. After a moment's indecision I consigned the unknown owner's towel to shoe-cleaning rag and did the best I could. Fortunately the bathroom had been warm and moist, so the mud hadn't dried on and I was able to do a reasonable job. I threw the towel under my bed.

Merry gasped. 'It's not mine,' I said. This induced another gasp.

I got up and headed towards whatever remained of breakfast. Merry followed.

We managed to find a decent plate each and withdrew to sit alone by the window.

'So what's going on?' said Merry.

Chapter Fourteen

Officially on Ward D

I thought hard about where to start. Currently I was in the process of setting up an asset to infiltrate into the black market. I still had to investigate Rory's assertion that something funny was going on with the standard patients here – to be more exact, that someone was terminating them unofficially. Then I had to find the traitor among Fitzroy's people on Ward D – if I could even get back in there. And finally, I had just learned that my handler had gone into the field on an emergency mission, and I had no way of discovering what was happening with my husband.

'It's got a bit complicated,' I said.

Merry tilted her head on one side and bit into a piece of toast. It's quite a skill to eat toast hostilely, but she was doing a good job. 'There are several things going on . . .' I paused and consumed some eggs and bacon. As soon as I had the first mouthful I realised how hungry I was. Regardless of Merry's hostile crunching, I shovelled a lot of food into my face. My mother would have been appalled at my manners, but I had expended a great deal of energy and breakfast for trainee nurses was not a leisurely affair.

'What are they?' said Merry.

I pointed with my knife to my full mouth.

'You're acting as if you haven't eaten for a week. It's disgusting. What is wrong with you?'

'I've been busy.'

At this point an expression came over Merry's face that struck me as both unusual for her and most familiar. It took me an egg and two rashers to work out why I knew it. It was the expression I wore when Fitzroy was being particularly obscure and I really, really wanted to throw a teapot at his head. I checked to see there wasn't one close to Merry's hand. I had had incentives not to throw things at my handler, she hadn't.

'I can't tell you much,' I said. 'I'm sorry. But I can tell you I am trying to ferret out some very bad people who are doing terrible things. I'm not allowed to give you details.' I shrugged. 'It's not that I don't trust you personally, but I could be shot for saying more than this.' It was a better explanation than I had ever been given as an asset. It was also one that would have calmed me.

'I know,' I continued, 'I've been asking you to take a lot of things on trust. I also now realise that I grossly underestimated the effect on you that Merrit's joining up, leaving Michael with your sister for these weeks, and having given birth less than six months ago, would have. It must have felt as if your life was out of your control. I mean, Michael is wonderful, but I can only imagine how demanding new babies are. Then as proud as you are of Merrit signing up, you must also be angry with him for leaving you to cope alone – at least I would be. And now you're separated from Michael. I don't know how that feels, but when I came to Stapleford Hall to work as a maid I missed Joe terribly, and he was only my little brother.' Another thought occurred to me. 'Oh Lord, when you look at those soldiers your fears for Merrit must soar.' I leaned across the table and placed a hand on one of hers. 'I am so sorry, Merry for dragging you into my business. I had no right.'

Merry pulled her hand away as if my touch burned and ran from the room. I sighed. I would have to go after her, but perhaps the kinder thing to do was to give her some moments to collect herself. I looked at the untouched toast on her plate. It would be a shame to let it go to waste.

Merry had taken refuge in the bathroom. A room I felt disinclined to enter ever again. There was no lack of decent powder rooms to house someone having a good sob, but no, she had to go into to the room of baths. I found her crouched in one of the dry baths, sobbing her eyes out.

113

She looked small and pitiful, but she had curled down in such a way that there was no way I could reach out and give her a hug. That's not to say I've ever been much of a person to hug those close to me. My mother had brought me up to keep my distance from relatives and associates. Although I now hugged Bertram, we never exhibited our affection in public. In fact, the only person who had ever had physically manhandled me in the presence of others was Fitzroy. Although I don't think one can consider being tugged across gangplanks during stormy weather or being hauled up the side of snowy cliffs a sign of affection. It had been most useful grappling, but definitely not affectionate.

I sat down on the floor, so my head was level with Merry. 'I am most awfully sorry.' The words tasted ashy in my mouth, but what else could I say? 'I won't involve you in anything else. We do genuinely hope to open a small hospital at White Orchards, and an understanding of what that may involve will help enormously in liaising with the army and setting things up. I'd also have thought that some basic nursing knowledge might be useful when raising children. I never fell out of a tree, but Joe did on several occasions. He even broke his arm once. He was terribly proud of the cast.'

Merry gave a small watery laugh. 'Sounds just like a boy.'

'Am I forgiven?' .

Merry levelled her gaze on mine. Her eyes were bloodshot and red-rimmed. 'I must look a sight,' she said.

'Yes,' I said.

'Now, don't go soft soaping things so you don't hurt my feelings. Tell me like it is.'

'You need to splash your face with a lot of cold water.'

Merry nodded. 'I feel better for a good cry. I should have done it earlier. I've been carrying all that stuff bottled up inside me. All that stuff you said. I didn't know you underst . . . understood . . .' She blinked back tears and hic-coughed, 'hat I was feeling. I should have known better. We've been through a lot, you and I. If you don't understand me then who will?'

'So am I forgiven?'

114

'I'm thinking about it. Pass me that flannel.'

I did so.

'Whose is it?' I asked.

Merry ran it under the cold tap before applying to her eyes. 'Probably the same poor twit that left their towel in here. Whoever it is is going to find it hard to wash.' We both gave a slight giggle at the thought of someone else's mild misfortune.

Merry redid her bun. 'Right,' she said. 'I'll forgive you on the condition you involve me in what you're doing . . .'

'I can't tell you –'

Merry held up a hand. 'I know you can't tell me nothing, but it's a good distraction. I've got all my learning, as much as we've had, down pat. Why those other women are taking so long, I don't know. They must have brains like mince. I need something else to think about. Besides, tangling with a little danger adds a bit of spice to life.'

'If you're sure. I'll tell you what I can.'

'It'll still count as doing my bit, won't it? Doing my bit for the war effort?'

'Very much so,' I said. 'And it will be easier with your help.'

'So, did you find out which of the women is nicking the drugs?'

'What?'

'That's what got them all so riled up. Matron wanted whoever stole the stuff to own up or we'll all be in for it. Only no one will confess. They're all blaming each other.' She paused. 'It wasn't you, was it?'

'No.'

'All right. I thought it might be part of your mission or something.'

'No, definitely not.' I was pleased my voice was level and calm. Inside my mind was racing. I'd got the impression that Cuttle was good at what he did and covered his tracks. It certainly appeared he'd been lifting stuff for a while. Why was Matron only noticing now?

'But you know something about it?' persisted Merry.

115

I decided to give her a half truth. 'I know there's been an issue with medicine being stolen, but it's been happening for some time. I have no idea why the hospital has only noticed today – yesterday?'

'Matron came in to see us when you were out for a run and delivered her ultimatum.'

'I think I will need to go and see her.'

'Lucky you,' said Merry.

I checked my time piece. 'We'd better hurry. We're on the general surgical ward today. We should try to get more information from Rory about what he knows. One of us will have to distract our supervisor.'

'You want me to do it?'

I shook my head. 'I think we have to be more flexible than that. Whoever gets the chance to sneak behind his screens and talk with him should take it and rely on the other to cover. It would be even better if we both did, then we could compare notes. It would be good to get him to tell his story twice. The second time people often remember more.'

'Right, let's get going,' said Merry. 'How are my eyes?'

'You'll pass.'

I'd been right to think that our training would now centre around the wards. What I hadn't counted on was that this was the time Matron chose to separate me from the herd and send me into Ward D. I could only hope none of the patients would mention my previous visit. If I got the chance I would say that their requests had been sent for. I made a mental note to write a letter home tonight. So far I hadn't found the time to write, but then Bertram wasn't there and even if Fitzroy had been we hadn't agreed a written cipher for this mission. Which, thinking about it, was remiss on both our parts.

We arrived shortly after everyone else from our dorm had lined up along the edge of the general surgical unit, which comprised six wards. Fortunately Matron arrived after us. A group of doctors, one out in front like a mother goose, was followed by several goslings in white coats clutching clipboards. Matron bustled behind them, giving the impression she was shooing them out of the wards so she and her staff could get on with the serious business of nursing. And perhaps she was.

Having seen them out of the double doors at the end of the corridor, without breaking stride she turned back towards and came to a stop in front of us. It all felt rather like watching some kind of dance performance, albeit done by various forms of livestock. At this point it occurred to me that I might be coming down with a fever. Either that or the time I had spent in this institution had been detrimental to my mental well being.

'Ladies, good morning. How many of you are there this morning? Fifteen? I understand two of your number have decided this profession is not for them. Another unwisely drank some old milk and two others are in bed with the sniffles. Although if they allow a cold to floor them they too should think twice about the usefulness of them taking a place on this course. So pair up and we'll have two of you on each ward and two working in the kitchen today. Stapleford, you're with me. The rest of you go and report to the nurse in charge of each ward. Bakewell and Channing, you can start in the kitchen. It always takes the two of you longer to settle. Some kitchen chores will soon get you into the swing of things.'

She walked off smartly. Then she threw over her shoulder, 'Stapleford, follow me.' I cast Merry a glance that I hoped conveyed both my helplessness and my desire for her to continue with our plan to talk to Rory. The expression she returned signified little beyond her bemusement. I sighed. Having been used to working in a partnership where we could easily read each other, the difficulties of an amateur arrangement hit me hard. Merry's bright, I told myself, she'll do the best she can.

Matron, despite her age and maturity of figure, had set off at a cracking pace. As we had been taught never to run – it sent the wrong signals to the patients – all I could do was walk briskly after her, but with little hope of catching her until she stopped. I felt rather like a puppy on a very long leash, which is undoubtedly what she meant me to feel.

She headed down through the wards and towards the back corridor that led to the operating theatres. I swallowed. The idea of assisting the surgeons was not something I was keen on. I wouldn't say I was squeamish exactly, but there is something about people rummaging around in someone else's guts that makes me feel oddly light-headed.

When she reached the corridor, she turned the other way towards the exit and I felt a flood of relief. It did occur to me that this was the door I had taken on one of my nocturnal sorties, but as she barely slowed her pace to open the door, I didn't get the impression she was trying to make a point.

She led me around the back of the hospital and up to the entrance of Ward D. She pushed open the door – I noted it was unlocked – and walked on to the ward. She didn't stop until we reached the nurse's desk. A tall blonde woman with a face not dissimilar to a horse's stood up.

'Matron,' she said in an alto voice.

'Nurse Evans, this is Stapleford, one of our new trainees. She's a quick learner and is cleared for work in this section of the hospital. As you are rather straining at the seams I thought I'd let you have her for the afternoon. She can certainly do any chores, plus simple dressings and checking patients' statuses. You can keep her till supper. If you're happy with her work I can send her over again.'

Without waiting for an answer, she nodded to Evans and me. 'Sister. Stapleford.' Then she was gone. My first thought, I confess, was an unworthy one. If I was here until supper, what was going to happen to my luncheon? I had the sense not to comment on this, but it must have showed on my face.

'We eat luncheon in the kitchen off the ward after the patients have been fed,' Evans said. 'You'll find most of the staff here are rarely in the main part of the hospital. We're severely understaffed – as I am sure you can imagine. There's no lack of nurses in the Corps,

118

but ones who have our level of clearance normally have had other responsibilities.'

She paused to see if I wanted to add anything. I didn't.

'Well, then, you can start by familiarising yourself with the kitchen. Fill the urn and bring it round the patients. There are biscuits, but they are only allowed one unless they have had a procedure in which case we usually allow two. When you have given them each a cup, you can take requests from the staff for tea. We always feed and water our patients first. After all, they are the ones who have been to war.'

'Yes, ma'am,' I said. Nurse Evans had an air of authority about her. I guessed she couldn't be more than ten years older than me, but she exuded capability and strength.

'Sister. You call me sister on the Ward. If you work here long enough you will get to call me Sarah off duty, but only if you meet Ward D standards. We have the best survival rate for a ward of our kind in the country and I intend to keep it that way.'

I caught a flicker – could it be of concern? – in her eyes when she spoke of the survival rate. Could she have heard something about the rest of the hospital?

'If things really go bad I will be going abroad to run a clearing station. I am already looking for the best to accompany me. You may only be a trainee now, but show promise and I will consider you.' She said this as if it was a great prize.

'Yes, sister,' I said. 'Thank you. May I go now?'

She nodded and returned to her paperwork. I headed for the kitchen. I was aware of another two nurses circulating on the ward. Considering they only had twelve patients I was a little muddled as to why considered themselves understaffed. Part of this was answered when I moved past Evans' desk. Back here between her desk and the kitchen were another twelve beds I hadn't noticed. Between these beds were full side screens, but the ends were left open to the passageway between them, so I could see the first patient on the right easily enough. He was straining to sit upright, his mouth open in a silent scream. Bandages smothering his crown and forehead. His arms were also swathed in them, but most obvious of all were the leather straps that were holding him in place around his torso, waist, wrists, forehead, and ankles. As I came into view he reacted violently, pulling hard on his restraints, rolling his eyes and working his mouth frantically – although no sound came out. The muscles in his neck were bulging. Any moment he might tear himself free. I hurried past.

In the next open cubicle a white-coated man had his stethoscope out and was listening to the chest of a man, who stared past both him and me into the distance and drooled. I could hear the doctor speaking quietly. At his side stood a small red-headed nurse, holding a number of files. 'Excuse me,' I said. They both turned quickly towards me. 'The patient in the next bed is straining hard against his straps. It looks as if he might be about to burst a vein in his neck.'

The doctor, who I now saw was young, not much older than I, said, 'Nurse White, take Cuttle and sort out Major Cummings.'

'Yes, sir,' said the tiny nurse and scurried off.

The doctor held out his hand to me. 'Dr Carlisle.'

'Euphemia Stapleford. I'm one of the trainee nurses.'

'I imagine you're more than that if you're allowed on this ward, but it's a bit don't ask, don't tell at the moment, isn't it?' He smiled. The corners at the edge of his blue eyes wrinkled and I caught a distinct twinkle. 'Don't let what you saw with the Major frighten you. His head straps keep coming undone. I don't like securing anyone, but he keeps trying to open the windows and climb out. We think he wants to get back to his men. Mutism induced by shock. So we can't tell. It's for his protection rather than ours. We don't keep very violent patients here.'

'I see,' I said. 'I've been sent to make tea.' Which sounded rather a silly thing to say. 'Wouldn't it help if some of the Major's men visited him? Or are they still on active duty?'

'All dead,' said Carlisle, picking up the files from the bed where the little nurse had left them. 'As I said, mutism brought on by shock. Mine's a milk and two when you're finished with the patients.' He turned back to the man in the bed, who was moaning softly. 'Nurse White will be back, Harry. Don't you worry.'

I made the tea in something of a daze. Fitzroy had talked about the toll war took on soldiers, but I'd taken it simply as another fact to include in my calculations. Meeting these men made me realise the reality of the situation. It was no longer a question of how long, or what circumstances, were liable to induce a form of battle fatigue or how long a man might be in the field before some kind of injury was inevitable. The issue had moved from the desktop world of paper and pen, and into the area of body and soul.

As I poured the hot water into the urn I saw my hands were shaking badly. I wondered if I would ever be able to help plan logistics again now I had seen the bloody face of war. Some of the men I had worked alongside had called me extraordinarily brave for a woman, but I knew I could never survive facing what the men in this ward had. The relief this brought me made me feel like a coward. I loaded up my trolley and wheeled it down to the bottom of the ward. Before I had seen the spotters as a problem to be solved, now I saw them as something much more.

One of the day cleaners in their distinctive pink-striped overalls came in to fill her bucket. She patted my arm. 'I know, dearie. It's a bit of shock to see men like that, but you'll get used to it.'

I consoled myself that although I had let my emotions show at least they were in tune with my cover. I thanked her politely and rolled the trolley out.

I started with Potter, as Dwyer appeared to be asleep. He showed no sign of recognition, but he perked up enormously when he saw the tea. 'Oh, good old char. You don't know how much I look forward to a decent cuppa. I hope you made it proper, nurse. Those urns are a right – (he started to say a rude word and changed it) difficulty, aren't they? Give me a good teapot any day.'

I smiled at him. 'Milk and two,' I guessed.

'Three if you don't mind. I'm building up my strength.'

'Of course, three it is. I take it you'd like a biscuit too?'

'You are a darling,' he said sincerely. His eyes intently followed the path of cup and saucer. 'Do you mind leaving one on the side for the major? He gets a right grump on if he misses his tea.'

'But it will go cold. We're told not to wake patients,' I explained.

'Then he'll drink it cold. As long as it's there with his biscuit it'll be all right. Trust me, love.'

I did as I was told. I'd hardly set the tea down on bedside locker before Major Dwyer opened an eye. 'Ho, ho,' he said. 'Am I dead? Is this an angel I see before me?' He looked over. 'An angel with tea. So the vicar was right. The afterlife is a paradise.' He sat up, smiling, and running a hand through his hair. 'A new nurse. Come over and introduce yourself to a fellow. There's a good girl.'

Pleased he hadn't recognised me, I had already taken a step back, so I evaded his outstretched arm.

'Come on, nurse. Got to play fair with a one-legged man.'

I gasped in shock. 'He's still got his leg, nurse,' said Potter. 'It's rather banged up, but he'll walk again, not like some of them in here.'

'Potter, you freakish little gnome, stop spoiling the field.'

I took their interchange as a chance to move on. This time when I came to Lecky he was awake. He had thick black hair that currently stuck out at all angles and large chocolate brown eyes. A wiry man, his frame appeared tall and skinny. When he smiled, his eyes glittered and I got the impression this was a man who could, as Corporal Potter might have put it, play people, especially women, like a piano. I imagined he and Fitzroy had got on particularly well. He accepted his tea gratefully.

'Don't mind Dwyer, miss. He's an odd sort. Always has to prove himself somehow. He's laid up in bed, so obviously he has to be grabbing a woman. In the field he were always challenging the other blokes. Wanting them to see he could do everything better. Reckon he was frightened by a mirror when he was in his cradle.' He gave me a charming smile.

I pulled the trolley over slightly. 'That can't have been a good situation.'

'Nah, it were dangerous. He were too busy thinking of himself.

Weren't paying enough attention to what were around us. Almost got us done up one time. Major brought him into line though.'

'Really?'

'Oh yes, no flies on Major Fitzroy. He beat him to a pulp – or near enough. Started to pull his socks up afterwards.'

'Is that the way it normally works? When someone is insubordinate?'

Lecky gave a small laugh. 'We're not regular army, miss – and the Major, I'm not sure where he sprang from, but he were even more irregular than us. Damned good at his job though. Hadn't put him down as much of a fighter until he went for Dwyer. After that there weren't any of us would dare speak a word against him. Even behind his back. Moved as quiet as anything, he did. You never knew where he would pop up next. Mind you, if you did your job well, he'd recognise you for it.'

'It sounds like you liked him.'

'He's worth a thousand of that lot like Dwyer. All posh words and flash trousers. I'd follow the Major into hell and back. I wouldn't follow Dwyer to the end of the street.'

I made as if to hide a smile.

'Can I get a second biscuit, miss?' said Lecky, pushing his luck.

I pretended to think about it. 'Tell me something interesting and I might consider it,' I said, trying to be arch. (I never feel I can pull it off, but I was hoping the uniform might help.)

'You're the same woman as came in here yesterday. Pretending to be patient liaison. I pretended to be asleep.'

I dropped the smile and handed him another biscuit. 'Very good,' I said.

'So, what you after? You've a pretty face, but I give you fair warning, if you're ferreting out secrets for the enemy I'll gut you like a fish myself.'

So much for working under cover. I leant down as if brushing something from his bed. 'There was something odd about your mission. I'm here to uncover that. And as for gutting me – you wouldn't find me as easy as a fish.'

I straightened. Lecky grinned more broadly at me. 'You're my kind of girl. I'll have a think on what you're looking for. Although right now other than Dwyer being such an arse, I can't think of anything . . . I'll think on it, as the bard would say.'

I managed to offload the rest of the teas fairly quickly. When I got to Hobson he only said, 'I see you're getting to know the team.' Just enough to let me know he recognised me and was watching what I was up to.

Wilkins, who I'd spent the most amiable conversation with, knew me. He was the only one I wanted to know who and what I was. 'That were quick, miss,' he said. 'I haven't remembered anything about the hayloft yet. I am trying.' He lowered his voice. 'I think I worked out what you're doing though. The Major thinks we were set up, doesn't he? Does he think someone signalled from the hayloft?' He watched my face as I did my best not to give anything away. 'Oh my Jove. Crikey Mikey! Does he think one of us set the signal? Does he think we've a traitor among us.'

I sat down on the bed immediately. 'You must never repeat that, Wilkins,' I said firmly. 'It could put you in great danger.'

'What's a bit of danger between friends, miss?' He gave me a quick cheeky smile. For a moment he looked very much younger than his age.

A cleaner came by mopping the floor. We stopped talking until she was past. I wondered how she must have felt about signing the Official Secrets Act. When she was out of earshot we picked up the conversation again.

'You're hardly in a fighting fit condition. I don't want you to get hurt – again,' I said.

He gave me an odd look. 'Yeah, whoever set that signal did for me all right, didn't they? I'm going to wrack my brains. If there's a traitor among us still alive then I want to know. What will the Major do about it?'

'I think you can imagine,' I said. I slipped two biscuits into his saucer and wheeled the trolley away and towards the top of the ward.

'Just leave the tea by the beds, nurse,' said the red headed nurse

124

I'd seen with Dr Carlisle. 'Someone will come by shortly to help them with it. If you could lay out tea in the little room off the kitchen, we'll come and grab it when we can. Have one yourself. Tea break lasts ten minutes. When it's over, go and collect the cups and wash them and the urn out in the kitchen. Then report to sister. She'll tell you what to do next.'

Chapter Fifteen

A young man comes calling

The rest of my day on Ward D passed in chores, bandaging, serving food, and helping clean up both the instruments and the patients. None of these were demanding duties, but I was kept almost constantly on my feet. By the time Sister Evans let me go, my feet ached with every step and I felt bone weary. The knowledge that the others on shift would do at least another four hours made me feel humble. I was fit, but goodness only knows where the doctors and nurses were finding their stamina. They were amazing.

I popped into the powder room to splash my face and tidy my hair before supper. A very wan-faced individual with sunken eyes confronted me in the mirror. I looked as bad as I felt. I staggered into the refectory, and responding to a call from Merry, took a place beside her.

'You look worse than you did after your first day as a maid,' said Merry.

'Thanks. I'm not used to being on my feet all day. You don't seem too bad.'

Merry reached for another piece of bread and dunked it in her soup. The ghosts of my ancestors shuddered, but I didn't say anything. Watching me, Merry picked up her bread with the fingers, sucked the soup out of it, and dunked it once more. 'That's impressive,' she said, 'your eyebrows wiggled a bit, but you didn't shudder. You must be getting used to being with the common folk again.'

'I'm inured. Major Fitzroy's table manners make yours look like those of royalty.'

126

Merry paused. Her bread dripped into her bowl. 'Really, he had perfect manners when he dined at my house.'

'You had Fitzroy over for dinner?' I said surprised, but Merry wasn't listening. Instead she had moved on to helping herself to a leg of chicken from the table server as she moved onto the next course. It had to be said they fed their doctors and nurses well here, but then they needed it.

'So anyway, I saw Rory. He's doing much better now. He can stand on his leg again. Of course, it's never going to be right. They think he will always walk with a cane, but it's a lot better than losing a leg. Also means they can't send him back. He thinks he might try reapplying to the police. He said, all that stuff you, Bertram, and he were involved in left him with a desire to change things for the better. He said after the war no one will be using butlers. Can you believe that? You should let Giles know. Why didn't he volunteer?'

Reeling a bit from this volley of information, I responded weakly, 'He has flat feet.'

'And he became a butler?'

I shrugged. 'So has Rory changed his mind about what he thought?'

'You mean too many deaths?'

'Not so loud! Yes, that's what I meant.'

'No. He still thinks there's something odd going on. He wants to talk to both of us, but it's not easy. We managed to exchange a sentence or so every time I visited his bedside – tea and whatnot, but the sister on that ward is very keen on ensuring we don't waste a minute. Always something to do, she says. I think she makes half of it up. She had me scrubbing the windows with vinegar and newspaper. Don't they have cleaners for that?'

'I suppose she could have been trying to distract you,' I said cautiously, 'but it's more likely she was worried about having a whole load of trainees around, who she doesn't know yet.'

'Trying to keep us out of mischief?'

'Or making mistakes.'

'Humph,' said Merry, frowning. 'Anyway, there's a thing they do called walking therapy or some such thing. They take patients outside for fresh air. Rory is going out every morning and evening. He's determined to get better. We can volunteer to help. All we have to do is be human walking canes. I thought one of us or both could volunteer. Then we could get to have a proper conversation.'

'I'm expecting to be back on Ward D again tomorrow. Could you volunteer me for one of the evening walks? I don't think they'll let me off the ward before supper. They're quite short-handed. One of the other nurses told me they were using some of the nurses who work in the operating rooms on the ward when there was any slack in the surgical cases.'

'What's so special about the ward?'

'It's the kind of thing you might overhear.'

'Like swear words? I can deal with that.'

I shook my head.

'Oooh!' said Merry, 'like the special things they've been doing?'

'If patients are delirious or under partial sedation they can't be responsible for what they say.'

'So this *is* like the other stuff you do? Well, I know Fitzroy! Can't I work on Ward D with you? Especially, if they're as short-handed as you say?'

'It's not up to me.'

'But you could explain about my knowing Major Fitzroy. About us coming here on his suggestion.' Her speech slowed as she said this last sentence. 'Is there anything I should know?'

'About Ward D? Nothing more I can say.'

'No, about the Major making such an effort to get me to accompany you?'

I shrugged. 'He didn't speak to me about it and I'm useless at reading him,' I lied.

'I expect he meant I was to help you with your investigations. You should tell Matron, and explain I'm in on it. What are you doing in Ward D anyway?'

'Assessing their security measures to see if they should be used elsewhere. I have to write a report,' I said desperately, trying to think of something boring that wouldn't interest her.

'Oh,' said Mary, and turned her attention to getting the last slice of spotted dick.

I didn't go out that night. I needed rest and I felt I had set as much in motion as I could. The atmosphere in the dorm remained tense. I'd forgotten to ask Merry if there had been any progress or if Matron was still planning to punish us all. It would have to wait. Whatever happened, it was unlikely to have anything to do with my mission as none of the others were allowed on Ward D, but then I had learned you find the oddest things when you turn over stones. I would ask her tomorrow. With luck it might have all blown over by then. Or it would all end up in a pair of stockings. My sleepy brain reminded me that stockings made both excellent disguises, pulled over the head to distort features, and were useful in strangling people. (Fitzroy had once said they could be used to mend cars, but I really couldn't see how.) I should consider everything. I had time . . .

And it was with my brain descending into nonsense that I dropped off into a sound and dreamless sleep.

I awoke early even for the hours the hospital kept. I decided to take a bath and get an early breakfast. I wanted some quiet time to mull things over before the tasks of the day made that nigh impossible.

Soaking in a decadently hot bath, I suddenly wondered if the nurses' rift could be stoked by a lost towel. In small insular communities, and none of us had been allowed off campus since arrival, such things could acquire ridiculous importance. After I had had breakfast and the others were still in the refectory I should dispose of the one under my bed.

I timed it perfectly so I arrived back when the dorm was entirely empty. I was on my knees, fishing under my low bed, when the door opened.

'Stapleford,' said Matron's voice. 'What are you doing? I have better things to do than chase around after you all morning.'

My fingers had touched the towel, but now I did my best to shove it further under. I stood up brushing down my uniform. 'Tidying, Matron. I'm not late for duty, am I?'

'No, no. You're not. But your young man is here to see you and I've been told (she placed an unusual emphasis on 'told') to let him take you out. I'll expect you back after lunch. Report direct to Ward D when you return.'

'My young man?' I said blankly.

'Yes, Stapleford. He's downstairs waiting for you in the lobby. I should change into civilian clothes if I were you.'

She closed the door. My heart jumped into my mouth (even though I now knew that was an impossibility) and I felt quite breathless. Bertram? Could Bertram be here? I hurried to change and needlessly tore two pairs of stockings in my efforts to dress quickly. I half walked, half ran down the hall in a quick scuttling step.

In the lobby there was only an army captain. I stopped, disappointed. I was about to search the nearby corridors in case Bertram had wandered off. Could he know Rory was here? Then the Captain turned at the sound of my footsteps. His handsome face broke into a broad smile. He walked quickly forward and took my hands. Then to my utter surprise a man I had never seen before uttered, 'Darling,' in an impassioned cry and kissed me on both cheeks. 'It is so good to see you. I've missed you so much. I've got the motor outside.'

Out of the corner of my eye I saw Merry, Rose, and Ruth emerging from the corridor and all staring at the Captain and I. Merry's jaw had dropped. She'd obviously witnessed the kisses. But the Captain was still speaking.

'Your sweetheart of a matron is letting me have you all to myself this morning. I even get to take you to lunch. I thought we'd try that little place by the coast you loved so much. The one with the garden and the funny squint-eyed cat.'

'The ginger one,' I said, my brain working furiously. 'That would be lovely. Let's go. I don't want to miss a moment.' I slipped my hand through his arm and walked him briskly to the door before any of the girls could demand an introduction.

Outside, by an ambulance, was a sporty little car. The Captain opened the door for me and took my hand as I climbed in. I gave him a dazzling smile. Within moments we were roaring off down the drive and turning off into one of the little hedgerow lanes that surrounded the hospital. My new best friend appeared to either not care if anyone else was coming in the opposite direction, or believed his car had a divine right of way. I'd been driven by Fitzroy, who I'd always thought was the most reckless driver, and by my husband, who was simply the most appalling driver, and both of them seemed like paragons compared to this maniac. The fact I was also a skilled driver made me appreciate how very near we came to overturning as the Captain barrelled around a curving bend that rose sharply. I decided to wait until he stopped before I spoke. I didn't want to detract from whatever little attention he was paying the road.

Eventually, he pulled over onto a grassy verge that overlooked a wide view of open sea. 'We shouldn't be overheard here,' he said. Then he turned in his seat, stretching one arm along the back of his and said, 'Well, here I am. The answer to a maiden's prayer.'

He wore a Captain's uniform, but I'd been with the Service long enough to know people rarely wore their actual rank. Fitzroy's people adored playing dress-up. Fitzroy has continued to be vague about what, of any rank, I am assigned, so I had no idea if I could pull rank on this 'Captain', but I doubted it. I reminded myself silently that I was in a military institution and if I hit a senior officer during time of war I would not get away with it, like *some* other people did, and I might even be shot. Thus, I did my very best to be polite. 'May I ask, Captain, what exactly the performance at the hospital was intended to achieve?'

The smile widened. 'You played along quite toppingly. I thought we did rather well. No one would ever know we hadn't met before.'

'Indeed not,' I began. He spoke over me.

'Oh Lord, forgive me. I should introduce myself – I am Captain Reginald Lacey. Same department as yourself, different cubby hole as it were. With old FR off about his own business your message was routed through to me. Got a little idea of something you can do to help us, I hear?'

Deep breath, I told myself. He can't help being an inbred idiot. 'Well, Captain, I think we ought to straighten out your arrival first.'

He frowned. 'You don't think they bought it? I'm rather good at acting. Did a number of plays when up at Oxford.'

'No, I think they bought it all too well.'

'I'm not sure I follow you.'

'I am Mrs Euphemia Stapleford. Mrs.'

'Ah. Oops. Have I made a bit of a FUBAR?

'Did you get to see my file?'

'I ran an eye over what they had, but FR has kept his cards pretty close to his chest where you're concerned. Been an asset for a number of years, haven't you? You must know how it works by now. Left hand and right hand operate on a need to know basis.'

I didn't ask him how long he'd been with the Department, I merely reached into my pocket and brought out my token. (I usually keep this in a much more private place on my person, but I had a hunch I might need it when I was told someone was waiting for me.)

'Is that FR's? Did he give it to you?' His voice and eyebrows rose in united shock.

'It's mine. My code name is Alice. That should be in your files.'

'So you're married and an agent? Aren't you awfully young to be doing this?'

'I imagine I am a couple of years older than you,' I said tersely.

'I mean, possibly . . . couldn't, wouldn't say. But I'm a man.'

At this point I considered banging my head off his dashboard, but I feared the only damage would be to myself. 'Major Fitzroy inducted me as a full agent.' I considered saying that Fitzroy and I had just completed a joint mission to Monaco. But then I had no idea of his clearance level.

'Well, I'd heard FR often works outside the mainstream, but this does rather take the biscuit. Give me a moment to get my head around this. I don't suppose you and FR are . . .'

132

'With respect, Captain, I would be extremely careful about what you say next. Major Fitzroy is my training officer.'

'Ah, yes, right,' said the Captain, turning a rather pretty shade of pink. 'I'm ballsing this up a bit, aren't I? Oh Lord, language! I'm terribly sorry.'

'You can't have heard Major Fitzroy swear if you consider "ballsing" anything other than bad grammar.' I decided to take control of the situation. 'I have a minor member of a black marketeering gang under my influence. I'd like to use him to either work with other assets in the area or to infiltrate the black market in general. He's happy to do whatever I want if I keep some minor loan shark off his back.'

'Well, that would be easy enough to do. Do you trust the fellow?'

'Not at all. But he could also be useful to me on my mission here.'

'What, training to be a nurse?'

'I won't be completing the training. It's my cover.'

'Really, that's a bally shame. We're going to need good nurses.'

'I don't wish to sound immodest, but Major Fitzroy said he "wouldn't waste my talents during this war on bandages and bedpans".'

'Always to the point, old FR,' said Lacey, moving from pink to red at the mention of bedpans.

'How well do you know Major Fitzroy?'

'Well, not actually met the gentleman to speak to, as it were. Saw him once across a meeting, he looked flinty and cross. Apparently when he's not undercover he's dreadfully antisocial. Heard all about him. Bit of a departmental legend in a way. I'd tell you about his latest exploits with the BEF if I could . . .'

'I know how he became a Major.'

The Captain's eyes grew very large. 'You do? Have you had contact? Only we've sort of lost him.'

'Lost him?'

'As I said, he tends to play off book. There's a rumour he took his mistress on a mission to Monaco recently. Then meandered back through France enjoying her – er – company. What a dog, heh?'

I did my best to imagine my eyes turning to cold steel. Lacey winced slightly and shifted in his seat. He looked out across the sea. 'So you're wanting help, turning this fellow?'

'No, but I would like permission to run him myself. I'd also like to link it with anyone else running someone of a similar nature to coordinate.'

'Yes, well, I think the least I can do is agree, Alice. As for the linking part, I'll log the project and put a request in. It'll probably be one of the more normal missions we're running. There might be a bit of relief from the higher-ups that we're also able to do the ordinary.'

If I'd wanted to, I felt, I could have taken quite a lot of this amiss. I decided not to. 'Can I see your token, please, and I'd like to know your code name in case I need to refer to you in future.'

'Oh, what? I suppose if we're being by the book.' He fumbled in his pocket, but eventually found his token in the glove compartment of his car. I think my expression said it all, because he mumbled several apologies. 'And your code name?'

'Peregrine,' he said. 'Like the bird.'

I put it entirely down to Fitzroy's training that I didn't giggle. Although on the whole this man made me more likely to fear for our country than laugh. Perhaps he had hidden talents. Very hidden.

'So is honey trap more your kind of thing, usually?'

'Captain Lacey, can I suggest we start thinking about where you are taking me for lunch? I have a heavy schedule ahead of me this afternoon and I need a good feeding.' His colour had calmed, but his eyes were squinting in such a manner that along with his frown, I realised he was still confused about my role. 'I do not seduce men for the Department,' I said. 'On my last mission I killed two people. I regret neither incident. As for what kind of spy I am, I am what Major Fitzroy made me.'

'Sounds a bit scary-biscuits.' This came with a nervous smile.

I returned a small, tight unfriendly one. 'That's about right. Lunch?'

Over lunch, in a sweet little restaurant by the sea, we made public small-talk. I learned he had two younger sisters who were determined to marry their beaus before they were sent off to war. His father was close to apoplexy with the cost of it all. Peregrine intimated that a little help from the black market might be appreciated. I decided to miss the suggestion. On the whole I decided he appeared a fairly harmless sort of an upper-class twit. I couldn't imagine why the Department would employ him. I doubted Fitzroy would even have given him the time of day.

Chapter Sixteen

Wilkins

Lacey delivered me back to the hospital directly after lunch. This had been a little early, so when I arrived back what would have been my shift were still at their lunch. I went upstairs to the dorm to change into my uniform. I had got so used to it, it had felt odd to wear a normal dress again, and my hat had felt very different from the overstretched little cap I was currently expected to wear.

I had a little time, so I decided to get some air before my afternoon duty began. I went for a brisk walk. The weather was quite lovely, and it would surprise no one that anyone with time would try to catch some fresh air. Indeed I saw quite a few other solitary figures and even small clusters of staff enjoying the day. It struck me then that everyone I saw was young. With the exception of a very few senior staff, the entirety of the hospital was staffed by young men and young women. All of whom were in the prime of their lives, complete with the stamina that brings, but also the inherent love for life and fun that youth brings. I did hope that between their long stints on the ward there were other entertainments. I wondered if I should suggest to Matron that the staff could get up a series of skits for the patients. I imagined her reaction would be one of unqualified disdain, but if Fitzroy was right and all this was only the start of something much longer, these people were going to up against the second worst of it. Fighting on the battlefield, risking one's life, would be terrifying. For those trying to piece together the survivors, often against the odds, the loss of patients would be demoralising yet unavoidable. I made a mental note that when Fitzroy and I were on better terms I must talk to him about my ideas and how we could introduce them into the heads of the right people. It's always better to make someone think the whole thing is their idea.

I lingered for a moment by a small out-building, while I idly shifted three stones into a triangle with the point of my shoe. Then I made my way back to the main building. I hesitated in the hall, thinking I would like to explain things to Merry, who might be thinking the worst of me, but decided that I would have to give her the benefit of the doubt that she still believed in me. I couldn't risk annoying the Sister of Ward D. Matron might have got me in there – under orders – but it was up to the Sister if I stayed or not. Accordingly, I arrived early for my afternoon shift.

'Good afternoon, Stapleford,' Sister said when I reported. 'Several of the men were asking where you were. You seem to have made quite an impression.' I watched her carefully trying to figure out if this was a bad thing. Her face remained quite impassive.

'I am trying to do my best, Sister,' I said. 'I know I have a lot to learn.'

She nodded at that and sent me to the sluice to wash out the bedpans. I didn't take this as a punishment. Someone had to do it, and I was the most junior member of staff present. I was lucky the cleaner had just finished sluicing out 'a nastiness', as she put it, that she'd had to mop up, so the entire room was mine. It made things a lot easier as I was about to use several sinks at once – one for soaking, one for scrubbing, and one for rinsing. And some of these bedpans really did need soaking. I was finishing the last and worst of them, when I thought how my mother would look if she could see me now. A bubble of giggles rose inside me.

'I say, it's not often we have a nurse who enjoys this duty.'

Dr Carlisle stood in the doorway. I finished what I was doing and put the pan on the side to dry. 'I can't say I enjoy it, Doctor, but I realise it has to be done. I was actually somewhere far away and thinking of something else entirely. I found it helped.'

'I can see. They're positively sparkling. Sister normally has to make the trainees do it again.'

'I'd rather do it only once,' I said, with a smile. 'How is the ward? How is Major Cummings – and Harry, was it?'

'Excellent memory,' said the doctor, standing aside and ushering me out. 'Major Cummings is still trying to escape to rescue his men, but physically he is much improved. I will need to see about sending him somewhere they can help his mind. Although I am not hopeful of his recovery.'

'Will you send him to others for examination?'

Carlisle shook his head. 'If I had my way I'd send him to live quietly in the country and hope that nature might help with his distress. He's not mad. He quite understands on one level his men are dead, but on another he is completely unprepared to accept it. I don't feel we should force him to accept reality before he is ready. The only thing is I'm not sure he will ever be ready. If that is so, the question is what to do with him. I fear he is only one of the first to be affected like this by the war – and we cannot let him or others like him back into general society.'

'You certainly cannot do so while the war still rages,' I said. 'The effect on the morale of both the women left behind and the men called to join up would be terrible.'

'I predict there will be no place for men like this after the war either, Nurse Stapleford. No one will want to remember them.'

'That would be truly terrible. Major Cummings and his like have given everything to defend us.'

'You are assuming we will win.'

'Naturally.'

'You're very certain.'

'The British services are the best in the world,' I said.

'That sounds like a line you've been taught, Nurse. I only hope you're right and this thing ends quickly.'

We were now approaching Sister's desk. He broke off and disappeared back in the part of the ward that housed the disturbed. I watched him go, wondering about his loyalties. Was I being over-suspicious? If he had somehow slipped through vetting or perhaps replaced someone legitimate, could he be here to receive information from one of the spotters? Perhaps even to help the guilty escape?

'Nurse? I asked you to do the afternoon teas!'

I flinched. 'Sorry, Sister. I was wool-gathering.'

'It looked to me as if you were thinking of something – or someone – more corporeal. I should tell you the whisper on the grapevine is that you were taken out this morning by your high-ranking lover, while your husband is at home. It's not good to get that kind of a name for yourself.'

I felt myself blushing. 'Honestly, Sister, there is no truth in that. The man who picked me up was my devil of a little brother. He thought it the greatest joke. He never thinks about the ramifications of his actions.'

'If that is true, I feel most sorry for you. I also suggest that you correct the gossips before the story gets more embellished. There's little enough entertainment for staff around here, so they will take it where they can get it.'

I nodded and scurried off to make the tea. The rounds went much as the previous day's had done. Dwyer was awake, so I had to be even more agile, but other than that things were moving along quickly enough. Then I came to Hobson.

'So how's it going?' he asked me. He was propped up in bed, and there were heavy frown lines on his face that suggested he was in considerable pain. His eyes were cold and dead. If he hadn't spoken I might have wondered if he was still alive.

'I'm learning,' I said brightly, as I poured his tea. 'I barely have a handle on one thing then I'm learning another.'

'Yeah, that's a pun. I get it. Cup handle.' He put his hand on the saucer as if to take the tea, but I could tell he hadn't taken the weight of it. It meant I was forced to stand there with him.

'I've been watching you,' he said. 'When you came in that first time you had quite a different gait to now.'

I had adopted a false step for the liaison nurse. Such things reminded me to stay in character. I decided to play dumb.

'I suppose I was moving around the ward more slowly.'

'You know exactly what I mean,' said Hobson. 'You're much more clever than you let on. More deceitful, too. I heard you lie to the Sister. I could hear the lie in your voice.'

'Nonsense,' I said. 'You were much too far away to hear our conversation.'

'I've excellent hearing. That's part of the reason I'm here.'

'I think you've been laid up too long. Your mind is playing tricks on you,' I said in what I hoped was a brisk no-nonsense nurse voice.

'Whatever you say,' said Hobson. 'But you should know I'm watching you. You're not who you're pretending to be. Now, that might be all above board with the boys upstairs or it might mean you've slipped through the net. But I've got my eye on you. If you're doing anything to harm the men in here I'll personally introduce you to my other specialist skill: the garrotte.'

'Take your tea now or I will drop it,' I said.

'Got to you, have I? That's a sign.'

He took the teacup and I moved on without looking back. Was that a double bluff or was he merely reacting to an inconsistency he'd noticed, as I had to Carlisle's comments: with suspicion. A veritable mass of rumour and intrigue seethed underneath this hospital's calm aura of respectability.

Wilkins gave me a winning smile. 'Couple of biscuits, miss? You know how I'm your favourite.'

'You're a cheeky young man,' I said. But I put two of the best biscuits in his saucer. He was still more in a prone position than sitting up. 'Do you want to sit up more?' I asked.

'Nah, thank you, miss. Can't bear the full weight of the sheet on the rest of my chest. Still recovering from the burns. Don't you worry. I'll be right as rain in a few weeks.'

I pulled the trolley in close. 'Did you remember anything?'

'I reckon I did remember something, miss. There was someone who went up into the loft. They wanted a bit of a smoke. There was a load of hay in the barn, so it must have seen the safest thing to do. Must have been bad luck the light was spotted by the enemy. I don't

140

want to give you any names as I reckon the fellow that did it likely doesn't know it was his fault we got nabbed. I wouldn't want to put that on anyone's conscience. We all make mistakes, don't we?'

My heart quickened. Fitzroy had said he'd seen a light on leaving. He had been clear it was more likely a lamp. To my mind, there was the vague possibility it was light from the fire below and Fitzroy, in the chaos of getting his men away, had mistaken that for a lamp. He would have been searching for reasons they had been caught, even then.

'I would have thought the others would have noticed anyone going up for a smoke.'

'No, we were all asleep. I only woke up because he had to step over me.'

'I'd be much happier if you could tell me who it was. I'd make sure his side of the story was heard. If it was a mistake –'

'They might shoot him. Make an example of him.'

'Not in this case. It's more important that we know what happened. I could even keep it off his record.' I had no idea if I could do this, but my priority was to get the name.

'Sorry, miss. Nothing doing. The chap saved my life on more than one occasion. I reckon that's a clear sign he's a good 'un. He might not be the most social-skilled, but he's helped keep us all alive in his own way.'

I thought of saying, he kept you alive until he could corral you all in the barn, but Wilkins' face was already looking mulish.

'Is there anything I can do to convince you to give me the name? It's more important than you might realise.'

Wilkins, perhaps caught by the earnestness of my tone, didn't immediately decline. He had the grace to give my question some thought. 'I reckon,' he said at last, 'that I would tell the Major. I'd trust him to do the right thing.'

'Major Fitzroy?' I said. The man Lacey had just admitted to me that the Department had lost. I have to say this didn't worry me as much as anyone else being listed as MIA. (Fitzroy often deliberately got 'lost' while working away on missions. 'Saves anyone interfering', he told me.) Still, the issue remained that I had no idea how to get hold of him. 'If I got the Major here, you'd tell him?'

Wilkins nodded. If I could get him to trust me half as much as he trusted the Major I might be able to get the truth from him. He was no longer flatly refusing to say who he'd seen. This was progress.

Chapter Seventeen

Coming to terms with Cuttle

When the time came for me to leave for supper, I was extremely weary. I also had to go and meet Cuttle at eight p.m. I decided to head into dinner early and miss seeing Rory (again). Merry could relay the discussion to me. I would try and attend one of the outside sessions that didn't clash with my Ward D duties. I didn't like the idea of anyone in the hospital being helped on their way, either through negligence or maliciousness, but finding the traitor among the spotters could lead to Fitzroy and I unearthing a major traitor in the senior ranks of the army. That would undoubtedly save a lot of lives. Having someone trying to wreck our war from the inside was an untenable position.

Fortunately they had started laying out the food in the refectory, but only one nurse and a handful of what must be new trainees were there. I helped myself to food, and then found a solitary corner. It would give me the space to think while I devoured my chicken pot pie and treacle tart.

It seemed then that I had three suspects: Dwyer, a dyed in the wool womaniser, who if Lecky were believed suffered from some kind of insecurity complex. He also had no reason to like Fitzroy, having been beaten (literally) by him when Fitzroy decided to assert his authority in an unusually bloody fashion. Could this story have been embellished by the group? Dwyer was clearly the only upper-class man amongst them and that wouldn't have added anything to his already low popularity. But it wasn't like Fitzroy to turn on one of his own men. If it was true, then Dwyer must have driven him to the edge. But I couldn't put that incident to causing Dwyer's possible betrayal, because the signal that was sent must have been arranged before they left for France if it was Dwyer's doing. Or if Fitzroy was right and Dwyer was only a small link in a chain that went to the higher echelons, then he wouldn't have arranged the signal, he would only have been following orders, so his crossing swords with Fitzroy was immaterial. Except . . . if he was a traitor, wouldn't he have wanted to keep his head down and convince everyone he was a jolly good egg until the time came to act?

That made it more likely to be Lecky, who was something of a charmer. He'd used his big brown eyes on me, but his ability to flirt charmingly and inoffensively with me would doubtless translate to knowing how to get along with his comrades. He'd also showed an empathy that surprised me. He understood Dwyer's brashness, and while not suggesting I forgive Dwyer for it, showed himself as a compassionate man. I suspected that last bit was part of the act. I had an idea of what Fitzroy was training these men in, and empathy and understanding would not be a high priority. It might well be a barrier to some of the things they were called to do. When he felt he was doing what he must, Fitzroy could be colder than ice and completely dispassionate. He would want these men to either be able to adopt that state of mind when necessary (as he himself did), or preferably to be the kind of individuals who always thought in that manner.

Again, it made Dwyer the misfit of the group. Could it be that whoever was the traitor at HQ had added him into the mix to make Fitzroy's mission much harder? Could it be Dwyer was working for the traitor without knowing? He hadn't struck me as in the least perceptive, so I had to acknowledge this could be true. On the other hand, if there had been a signal lamp whoever lit it knew he was betraying the unit.

Hobson, who reminded me strongly of Cole, the assassin Fitzroy had trained, was much more the kind of man I would have expected Fitzroy to pick for this mission. Cole and I mutually despised one another, but I knew he fulfilled a function the Service needed. He also enjoyed inflicting pain and had once bruised my throat so badly in practice Fitzroy had knocked him out. However, Hobson seemed acutely defensive of the remaining spotters. He also had exceptional hearing and was highly observant. He was ideal as a spotter. But was he loyal to King and Country? My gut told me he wasn't an opportunist or an idealist. I suspected he would enjoy being a spotter – the danger, the close-quarters killing, and the sense of superiority taking an enemy by total surprise can bring. I couldn't see a good reason why he would endanger that. If we were not in the hospital I would have had his life looked into and watched his spending habits. Although I would have needed an entire crew to do this. He would have spotted one man (or woman) tailing him too easily.

And then we came to Wilkins. He said he had a name, but there was an outside chance he was playing me. Despite his youth and apparent vulnerability I had not ruled out he was the traitor. I also knew that Hobson would have heard all of our conversation. If necessary I was counting on Hobson to defend Wilkins if the real traitor attacked him.

I could put Wilkins out as bait. I could tell them Fitzroy was coming and see if that caused anyone to act. But to do that I would have to be sure of Hobson. I had no back-up here.

I started on my tart. What if I told Hobson my plan? He'd protect Wilkins from Lecky and Dwyer, and I could count on him to notice if Wilkins started behaving oddly. If Hobson was the traitor himself then it would be very difficult for him to act against Wilkins without being caught. It seemed most likely if he thought Wilkins was going to name him that he would try and abscond. Setting up Wilkins' murder to look like someone else, when he remained wounded and had no help, was less likely. But of course, he was a spotter. A man trained to act on his initiative and think on his feet in the field.

I finished up my tart. With Fitzroy missing, it seemed like my best plan. It would mean risking Wilkins, but I believed that risk to be low. Plus when I told Hobson of my plan I would have one final chance to assess whether he could be the traitor.

I cleared my plates and took them to the counter. I felt lighter than I had done for days. I had gathered information, and I thought of a way I could use it. There was an excellent chance I would be able to expose the traitor. Also, if Fitzroy had been wrong about all of this – made paranoid and edgy by a deeply disturbing mission – nothing would happen. No one would be hurt or accused. I could even frame it to Hobson in such a way that implied it was a test of the other spotters and their loyalty, rather than the suspicion of his commanding officer.

I managed to entirely miss the others coming in for supper. I didn't bother changing before I went outside. I collected a coat, more to hide my particular appearance than for warmth as the nights were still warm, and headed out to meet my very first asset, Ivor Cuttle.

Cuttle was early. He was leaning on the wall of the outbuilding that was out of sight of the main building and smoking. Dusk had not long started to gather, but the glow of his cigarette stood out sharply. He straightened up when I came round the corner. 'So you're here. And there was me hoping the whole thing was a bloody nightmare or someone's bad idea of a joke. It's not, is it?'

I shook my head. I watched him throw his cigarette down and stamp on it. An idea came to me. 'Can you get me some of those?'

'I expect so. What's it to you?'

'All part of our deal. Can you get them to me by tomorrow.'

Cuttle looked up at the sky. 'I don't think it's going to rain tonight, do you?'

'No, what's that . . .'

'I'll leave a packet on the sill by your dorm. You sleep next to the window, right?'

I nodded. I didn't like the idea that he'd taken the trouble to find out where I slept. I would need to ensure that the window could open ajar, and no more, while I slept. Failing that, I would have to booby trap it.

'Right, that us done?'

'We've barely begun. My department is prepared to remove your concerns – and by that I mean your creditor and by extension

146

your debt. Do I need to say that should you entertain the idea of gambling again during your work with us there will be serious repercussions.'

'Oh, come on! A man's private life is his own!'

'Your gambling allowed me to gain leverage over you. I wouldn't want to put you in the position where someone else could do the same.'

Cuttle frowned, obviously thinking. Then he said, 'Hey, I might not be lily-white, but I ain't no traitor. I wouldn't ever betray my country.'

'Then there is nothing to worry about, is there? For now, what can you tell me about what is going on in the hospital?'

'I thought you were interested in my buyers?'

'I am. We'll come to that another time. Right now I wanted to know if anything out of the norm is going on. I've seen you everywhere. Even on Ward D. Can you explain that?'

'I'm not on Ward D. I'm sometimes asked to help strong-arm one of the patients. Happens to most of the orderlies. Hate doing that myself. Those poor sods.' He spat on the ground. 'Anyway, I'm in and out in a moment. I don't get the chance to overhear nothing – and they only call us in when they've got no choice.'

'So you know what Ward D is?'

'Sure, it's where they put the ones who've been on the secret missions. They don't want just anyone hearing the poor sods' mindless mutterings. Not that you'd get anything out of the ones I've been asked to help handle.'

'So anything odd?'

'There?'

'Anywhere.'

'Well, there's that big row among your group of trainees. Getting bad, so I hear.'

'Tell me.'

'Well, you have to know . . . Oh hang, on you think it were me? Nope, not guilty. I'm not that stupid. I take a little bit here and there. I build up my stocks. I know better than to go in and grab a bottle of stuff. They like you to think it's all accounted for, but there's always a bit of leeway. They're all run off their feet. But they generally try to keep little discrepancies quiet. Your lot are well in for it, because it's all liable to come out that their accounting ain't that good.'

'Do you know what was taken?' I said.

'A lot of morphine. And that's another thing I'd never do. I wouldn't leave those poor sods without anything. I'm not an utter bastard.'

'No, you're the soul of generosity.'

'That's closer to the mark than you might think. I reckon a lot of my stuff goes to doctors who can't get meds for their patients now the army is buying it up lock, stock and barrel.'

'So you're merely providing a redistribution network to make things fairer?'

Cuttle shifted his feet. 'Kind of.'

'What about the woman I heard you with?'

Even in the lowering light I could see the blood drain from his face. 'I ain't no grass.'

'That is, in fact, exactly what you are.'

'I've changed my mind. I'm not doing this. I'm out.'

'The only way out is in a wooden overcoat.' I thought I'd gone too far, but Cuttle leaned back against the wall again. He must read some of the novels I did. He didn't laugh in the way Merry might have.

'Bloody hell. You've told your superiors who I am, haven't you?'

'Of course, otherwise you might have been tempted . . .'

'I'm no killer.'

'Anyone can kill, man or woman, if they're desperate enough,' I said.

'Maybe you can, but I can't. When it comes to violence I am lily-livered.'

'But you wanted to protect someone, this woman. Is she a lover?'

Cuttle gave a sudden crack of laughter. 'Her, no. Not my type. But she's not a bad sort. Her mother's ill, dying, but insisted on being at home. Doctor won't give her any strong painkillers unless she's in a hospital – and she won't go. I give her a little something now and then. There's no money passes between us.'

'But she helps you.'

'Only because we struck a deal. She appeared when I was on the job – and as I said I don't hold with violence, especially against a woman. Though she could take me one hand behind her back. We came to a deal. She's not worth your notice.'

'What does she do?'

'If I tell you . . .'

'Tell me.'

'Not saying. She's been here for years. Very popular with the staff. She's a hard worker and no one has a word to say against her. I'm being totally truthful with you here. It's all very well me being in your hands. I'm a big boy and I can look after myself.'

I raised an eyebrow.

'Dropping out of that tree on me was hardly fair. Anyway, I'm not handing over another poor soul who is only trying to do the best for her family. Arrest me if you must. I ain't telling. I might be a gambler and a thief, but I've got my own standards.

'All right,' I said with feigned reluctance. The reality was I couldn't care less this incidental character. I wanted bigger fish. 'You continue to be a good boy and I'll look the other way where your friend is concerned.' It did confirm one thing I'd suspected. Cuttle might be a physical coward and general low-life, but there was a streak of good through him. I was pleased. It was going to make him much more pliable than some wooden-headed thug who didn't care a jot for anyone but himself.

'That all?'

'Almost. I've heard reports the death rate in this hospital is oddly high. What do you know about that?'

'There's a lot of soldiers with battlefield injuries that were barely patched up before they were put on a boat to cross the ruddy Channel. It's hardly surprising a lot of them cop it. And that's not including the ones who throw themselves out of the open windows. Why

149

do you think they keep the nutters on the ground floor? All the bleeders get there is a bit of a scrape. First week we were receiving two of 'em threw themselves out of the fifth floor windows. That's when they moved the mental cases downstairs. Couldn't live with what they'd seen or what they'd done. Who knows? You're not getting me into that war for love nor money.'

'If you're working for us you'll be exempt from conscription.'

Cuttle pulled a handkerchief out of his pocket and wiped his forehead. 'I get shaky just thinking about them. They look at you with those dead eyes. Right through you that look goes, like it can see into your soul and past it to something . . .' He shivered. 'Still, silver linings and all that. Maybe it won't be so bad working for you.'

'For now, I want you to carry on as normal. But keep your eyes peeled. I want to know if anything out of the ordinary is happening.'

'Right you are. But you mean . . . still supplying?'

'Act as you normally would.'

'I'll delay next week's delivery on account of things being a bit dicey at the mo. I've got extra stock, but they don't know that. I reckon the most normal thing is for me to tell about the situation. If they're insistent. I can whine a bit and give them some of my extra stock. Sounds the most believable to me. 'Cos I tell you what, if one of you girls don't fess up to this theft this place is going to be crawling with police – and you can't keep that kind of thing quiet.' He paused. 'If the police . . .'

'You'll be safe,' I said. 'We'd let them question you for appearance's sake, but you'd be let go. We can ensure that.'

'Right you are. Bit of an adventure this. Maybe I'll enjoy myself yet.' He didn't sound overly cheerful, but I could see he was trying to talk himself into his new role. I bade him good night and made my way back to the hospital building. I only hoped Merry had fallen asleep by now. She was bound to have heard about Lacey and that wasn't a conversation I wanted to have tonight.

Chapter Eighteen

Despatches from the front line

Once again my trick of leaving the front door open had worked. I didn't know whether to be pleased with my ingenuity or appalled at the lack of security at the hospital. I still had an uneasy feeling about Dr Carlisle. I couldn't quite put my finger on it, but something was off.

I decided that while the lobby was empty it was time to use the phone. I went through the usual procedure, but was then told to hold the line. After several whirls and clicks a familiar voice came on the line.

'Good evening, ma'am.'

'Griffin! Is the Major with you?'

'No, ma'am, I am afraid he is still away. I've been brought in to be a – er – message taker, and to help in any small way. I can only apologise for Captain Lacey being sent out. An excellent gentleman in his way, but not exactly one of us.'

I took this to mean not someone who worked covertly. 'I did assume he must have other skills.'

Griffin coughed politely.

'So how can I help, ma'am?'

'The arrangements I agreed with Lacey are now set in motion. Accordingly I need to make good on my guarantees.'

'I have his *report* here.' The way he said 'report' made it sound as if it was done in crayon. 'It should suffice.'

'I need to call my housekeeper and arrange for some items to be forwarded.'

'I don't believe Major Fitzroy would approve of that, ma'am.'

'Too much of a trail. Oh dear. I rather foolishly posed as a liaison officer and promised to contact some of the men's families to arrange deliveries of desired items.'

'It sounds like a good plan in the moment, ma'am, to inspire trust.'

'But in the long term it was . . .'

'All things have consequences. If you could let me know the names of the men and their desires I will see what I can do. Anything they receive will be sent from the Liaison Office rather than their families.'

'It is a bit of a long list.'

'Please tell me it's not the entire hospital, Alice?' said Griffin, for a moment dropping his butler/batman act.

'No, only the surgical patients in ward D.'

'Very good. Fire away.'

I listed the items from memory. I could almost hear his eyebrows raising at some of the requests. When I finished he said, 'I don't think this will be a problem. Was there anything else?'

'As Fitzroy is still on holiday, I have a plan to find the person he wants to speak to here.'

'I see,' said Griffin, caution sounding in every note of his voice.

'It was what I was sent here to do.'

'Yes, ma'am, but I got the impression the Major was hoping you would be working in a passive manner. A subtle and discreet one,' he placed emphasis on the last phrase.

'You mean like he tends to do?'

Griffin gave a small laugh, which he quickly turned into a cough. 'The Major can operate with the utmost discretion when he finds it necessary,' he said.

'I hope you're not scolding me, Griffin.'

'I wouldn't dare, ma'am. I do know that the Major was greatly concerned that he would not be available for you. He remembered he had promised to be here to answer any calls from you. It caused him some distress to think you might feel he had broken his word.'

'I only wanted to let you know that if anything goes wrong, Fitzroy needs to speak to Wilkins.'

'Ma'am, are you about to put yourself in serious danger? The Major would not want you to do so without back-up.'

'Hmm,' I said. 'How is Jack?'

'Pining. But I have discovered he is partial to foie gras, and I find an occasional treat helps his mood.'

'So he is no longer at my home? I take it then that . . .'

'Ma'am, this line is as secure as possible, but you may be overheard. Please be careful what you say.'

'I'm in a cupboard, Griffin. But I take your point. Neither of them have returned.' I tried not to let the stress sound in my voice. Sweat was forming at my hairline, and my heart was thumping in my throat. My eyes brimmed. 'Who – who is running the earlier mission now?'

'I cannot answer that question, ma'am.'

'Is he still alive?'

'I have no reason to believe he is not. We are speaking of your husband I assume? And not the Major.'

'I rather think the Major can take care of himself. Are you concerned about him?'

'As you know, the Major has a habit of disappearing and reappearing. Please be assured he has done and is doing everything to assure your husband's safety.'

'Are you saying that so I won't worry?'

'No, ma'am. I am saying it because it is true. He feels most responsible for Mr Stapleford.'

I swallowed, pushing down unreasonable sobs that were threaten to bubble up. 'May I add, ma'am, that you are under enormous strain working alone with possible unknown hostiles. Please take care.'

'No one is shooting at me yet. I am surprisingly competent for a woman.'

'For anyone, ma'am. But when we fear a loved one may be in danger, and we are over-tired, foolish decisions are too easily made.

I know that to my cost. I am certain the Major will be back in the near future. Could your plan wait until he returns?'

'It's already rolling. I'll be careful, Griffin.' I paused. 'If anything does go wrong, please let Fitzroy know I don't blame him and that I apologise for my shocking behaviour at White Orchards.'

'Ma'am, I really do think you should wait.' Alarm sounded in Griffin's voice.

'Good night, Griffin,' I said and hung up.

I replaced the telephone. It had occurred to me it was very conveniently placed for my use. I suspected that Matron, perhaps even the Sister of Ward D, knew of my extra-curricular activities. Not in detail, but enough to ensure I could ring up HQ if I needed.

Grateful yet again for my rubber-soled shoes, I crept up the sloping corridor and quietly into the dorm. I felt both tired and wired with worry. What would happen if someone like Lacey took over handling Bertram? It could be a disaster. I undressed quietly. A few hot tears ran down my face in the dark. This wasn't like anything I had previously done. All the people I loved and trusted were scattered to the winds.

I got into bed and was immediately reminded that one such person was still present.

'What the hell do you think you're up to?' hissed Merry.

I didn't answer. I only turned over and tried to sleep. I shed many silent tears before the oblivion of empty dreams overtook me.

In the morning I awoke to find Merry's bed empty. Groggy-headed from a disturbed night, I dressed and headed for the refectory. I was almost there when Merry barrelled out of the door at top speed. She was holding a cloth bundle in one hand, but with the other she took me by the elbow and turned me with such force that I would have had to make quite a fuss to get free. 'We are going to eat our breakfast outside,' she said in a falsely cheerful voice. 'You've been looking peaky. The fresh air will do you good.'

'But I'm hungry.'

'I've got food. Don't whine.'

'Do we have time?' I protested.

'We won't go far.' Merry marched me out the front door, across the lawn, round the corner, and to a little sheltered bench that was getting the full heat of the morning sun. 'I noticed this on the walk last night. The walk you weren't on.'

'I didn't get off Ward D in time. What did you bring?'

Merry sat down next to me, but she placed the bag strategically behind her. 'Before I share anything with you, I want to know, who the hell is that army captain? The one you were canoodling with in the lobby yesterday.'

'Oh for heaven's sake! I'm hungry and I've got another long day ahead. Give me some food, pleeeeease!'

'Because the gossip is he's your boyfriend. I grant you he's handsome, but you've got a husband back home!'

I sighed. 'I've been telling people he's my brother, and it was his silly idea of a joke.'

'There's no way that was Joe! He's still in school.'

'And about a foot shorter. Or he was last time I saw him. No, it was the best I could come up with at the time.'

'So, who is he?'

'Who the hell do you think he is, Merry?' I said, distracting her with one hand and grabbing the food bag with the other. I opened the parcel between us. The blissful aromas of hot toast, sausages, fried potatoes, and buttered muffins reached up and caressed my nose.' I grabbed a muffin. Before I bit into it, I said, 'If you think I would cheat on Bertram then go and find yourself another best friend.'

The muffin oozed melted butter all over my tongue as I chewed its glorious springy texture, and tasted the tang of salt and yeast. 'Mmm,' I murmured involuntarily.

'It's only a muffin,' said Merry, taking one for herself.

'I'm working day and night. I need food.' I took a sausage.

'More secret stuff then. I suppose the Captain was like Major Fitzroy.'

I shook my head. 'He is nothing like Fitzroy. He's an idiot.' I picked up a chunk of potato between my fingers and bit into it. I wondered why I had never tried eating without cutlery before. It was so much quicker and easier.

'Who's an idiot? The Captain or the Major?'

I consider for a moment while I chewed. 'Fitzroy can be idiotic about some things, like any man. But professionally, he's very acute. Captain Lacey, on the other hand, was lent by another department. He didn't even have the sense to read my file properly.' I distracted Merry by looking over her shoulder, while I took another sausage and a muffin. I combined the two with my fingers. 'That's why he didn't know I was married.'

Merry's gaze focused on my hands. 'Your table manners have really gone downhill. And you've taken more than your fair share!' She grabbed a muffin.

'It's not my fault if you didn't bring enough!' I smiled. 'Sorry, I really am getting very little sleep and for whatever reason it makes me ravenous. So, will you go along with the story that Lacey is my brother?'

'Sure, although people will wonder why I didn't defend you before.'

'You can say we were at odds, but made up this morning. I'm sure you acted angry with me.'

'I was. Rory wants to talk to you. He was disappointed you weren't there last night.'

'I'm going to try my best to be there tonight. I have one thing I have to set up and then I'm free.' I saw how much it cost Merry not to ask what I was up to. 'What did Rory say? Has he noticed anything odd?'

'I told him about the missing morphine. Remember?' I nodded and she continued, 'He had noticed people weren't getting the same level of pain medication they were getting before. They're all a bit ill-tempered. You know, gritting their teeth and bearing it like proper Englishmen. Lots of quarrels breaking out. But he didn't say anything about anyone dying. But I did think, what if someone stole the morphine so they could kill patients? Overdose them?'

'It's a thought,' I said. 'But it's a bit obvious, isn't it? Before this

156

Rory had suspicions – and he has good instincts, like you, so I'm open-minded about what he said – but whatever might have been happening, it was subtle. Stealing this amount of morphine is blatant.'

The calm of the morning shattered in a cacophony of ringing bells. Merry and I looked at each other in dismay. 'What?' But anything else she might have said was lost as Matron ran out of the front door, followed by a host of nurses and doctors. She spied us. 'Here, girls, quickly!'

We hurried over. 'I'm meant to be on Ward D, matron,' I said.

She barely spared me a glance, 'Not today, Stapleford. We have wounded arriving.'

The bells in the hospital continued to ring as more and more personnel poured out of the door. Orderlies arrived with stretchers and gurneys. Doctors stood by grimly, while the nurses brought out a series of basic supplies and set them up. I couldn't help wondering why they would do that when the hospital was literally feet away. Then, as if answering the call of their mate, we heard bells coming from the lane as well. Within moments a host of ambulances was flooding up the drive.

After that it became well ordered chaos. Merry and I quickly understood our role was *everything else*. If an extra hand was needed to help carry a body or equipment we jumped in. If any medical supplies were needed we flew down the corridor to get them. Running, for once, being expected rather than forbidden.

As for why those supplies were needed, we got our answer when the first ambulance doors opened. Inside each vehicle were one or two pale-looking nurses, crouching between stretchers that had been placed on makeshift shelves to fit more bodies in. My immediate perception was of a dark, crowded interior. Then the smell reached you. It was the rank stench of every kind of bodily fluid, coupled with a distinct odour of decay. Groans and cries greeted the sudden influx of sunlight. The nurses jumped out, sometimes stumbling on their cramped legs, only for many hands to reach out and catch them. Before they allowed themselves to be led away, these girls, none of them could have been more than twenty, listed in details the casualties on board to the attending doctor.

As the men were brought out we saw bleeding that had broken out through bandages, splints half off, and men unconscious. 'It was a rough crossing,' said one nurse miserably, 'we did the best we could, but with all the rushing over rough roads and the stormy seas, most of what was done to help them has come undone. At least they're no worse off than when they were brought into the clearing station.'

Everyone was moving. Nothing was still. I ran hither and thither doing my best to help. My small knowledge of field first aid meant I could fix some of the splints and more desperate bandages, while the men waited for the next orderlies to be available. I saw Cuttle, sweat streaming down his face, as he hurried to lift another stretcher. His frame was small enough that it obviously took a great effort, but like the rest of us he worked without a break until the last man was inside. I saw Wee-wee Mary and Ruth kneel side by side to comfort a man who was clearly mortally injured. All differences between them forgotten as they focused on lessening the soldier's physical and emotional distress.

One young solider with most of his right leg missing asked me to find his right shoe as he was sure he would need it later. He gazed down unseeing at his bloody stump. Another, who looked no more than sixteen, asked me if I was his mother. It was only when I stopped resplinting his shattered arm that I realised his eyes were blank and blind. When I said kindly that I was a nurse, he began to cry. I patted his arm, unsure of what to do. I told him he was in hospital and everyone would look after him. I didn't promise he would be fine as I felt it was wrong to say something that might not be true – to offer false hope. Cuttle came over. He lit a cigarette and pushed it between the boy's lips. ' 'Ere, mate, have a drag on that. Be over to take you in in a minute, so make the most of it before Matron catches you.'

The boy managed to stop crying so hard. He inhaled. 'Thanks,' he said softly.

'Ain't nothing, mate. I'm Ivor, one of the gophers. You need to send a letter home or have a pretty nurse described to you, I'm your man. They all know me. You want something, you ask for Ivor and you got it.'

'Thanks.' The voice was a little stronger now.

'Ain't nothing, mate. You're a bloody hero, ain't you? Mind you, be a lot less bloody when they get you inside, huh?' This poor sally got a weak laugh. 'Look out. Here come your bearers. Lads, you take care of this one. He's a friend of mine.' The boy was carried off.

'That was kind of you,' I said to Ivor.

He shrugged. 'He weren't no more than a kiddie. Reminded me of me own brother.' He moved off to talk to someone else. I carried on retying bandages and even a makeshift tourniquet that had loosened, but thankfully not come off altogether. On the whole, the men had a cheerfulness that it was hard to understand. Even the ones in pain. 'You're being terribly brave,' I told one chap.

'Nah, Nurse. I'm happy. I'm out of it now. They can't send me back into hell.'

'It's a kind of euphoria they all tend to feel when they are back on home soil,' said Matron at my arm. 'I saw it in the Boer War. Give them a week or so and they will start to remember what it was like and what they've lost. For a few of them it starts almost immediately in their dreams.'

'It's terrible,' I said. 'How do you cope with seeing so many broken souls?'

'I'd rather be doing something to help them than knitting socks or drinking tea at home,' said Matron. 'Once you've seen the ravages war can produce, you never forget. You'll find all the girls are changed after today. The ones that stay will become some of the strongest women of our nation. The ones that can't bear it, and this is not work for all – they'll find another role. Once you've seen what war can do, no one can rest until it's over and the last man's home.

'Now, Stapleford, do you think you could take that nurse over there in and give her a cup of tea. She was the first out of the ambulances, and I don't believe she will leave until the last man is carried in.'

'Of course, Matron.'

'I happen to know it was her first trip into a fighting zone. She's holding up too well. Any moment now that stiff upper lip is going to shatter.'

'I understand. Might I take Merrit with me? She has more of a warm maternal nature than I.'

Matron nodded. 'You can take her into lunch with you both. After that the poor girl will want to sleep. See if you can get something inside her before she does.'

I found Merry and with the last man carried in, we scooped up the nurse, who proved to be terribly well spoken and as brittle as Matron had suggested. By the time we'd reached pudding she was crying so hysterically we took her out of the refectory. Matron, who someone must have sent for, arrived as we were leaving, and whisked her away. 'Change before you go to Ward D, Stapleford,' she said.

I looked down and realised I had the blood of several men on me. I hadn't even noticed. Merry hurried off to her ward. She gave me a meaningful look, which I decided to miss. I checked myself in the mirror of the ladies' room and ended up redoing my hair and washing my face. Back at the dorm I changed and checked the sill for cigarettes. To my surprise they were there. Cuttle must have climbed up during the night. I shivered. He might have a couple of good streaks in him, but I didn't like the thought of any man trying to peer between the curtains of a female dorm.

I put them in my pocket. I straightened my apron with the help of the mirror and checked myself over. I took a deep breath. It was time to begin my plan.

Chapter Nineteen

Hobson's Choice

Ward D was a haven of calm compared to what I had seen this morning. There had been no new admissions here, so I imagined the surgical wards must be overflowing. The initial days of my training seemed an eternity ago. The foolish rifts between the new nurses, the cliques, had irritated me, but I hoped that now we were into the seriousness of the work, petty feuds had been forgotten by the others.

It frustrated me enormously that I still wasn't getting to talk to Rory. I could only hope that between him and Merry they would start working out what was going on. If indeed anything was. The idea that someone had stolen so much morphine worried me enormously. It would be so easy to overdose someone on a busy ward and claim an overworked nurse or doctor had caused the accident. But then the very theft of the morphine itself would call any overdose into question. It simply didn't make sense.

I filled the tea urn almost without being aware of what I was doing. 'I see you're doing much better now, love,' said one of the cleaners as she passed by. 'The Lord's put us all here for reason. You have to trust he knows best.'

I smiled absentmindedly at her. My father had been a Vicar, so I had once been used to members of my family, or members of my father's congregation, talking about the Lord and what he wanted. Working in the Service, one didn't generally come across people talking about God, unless they were swearing. Still it was good to know that outside in normal life people trusted and took solace in him.

I did the tea round as quickly as I could. I exchanged idle

chit-chat and banter with the men, but I was going through the motions. When I got to Hobson, I stopped. 'Do you smoke?' I asked.

'I doubt there's a man in the King's army who doesn't.'

'I've got a packet for you if you persuade Sister you need to get outside for a bit and want me to be the nurse to accompany you.'

The cold eyes narrowed. 'What's this all about?'

'I've got a proposal I need to put to you.'

'Aw, darling, I didn't know you cared.'

'Not that sort of thing. Your chart says you can walk if you take it slow. Fresh air would be good for you.'

'And you've got smokes?' I lifted the top of the pack, so it showed just above my pocket. 'I don't know what you're up to, but I could do with a fag.'

I was finishing up the tea things, when Dr Carlisle came into the kitchen. 'Nurse Stapleford, it seems you have an admirer.'

I looked up without smiling. Inside I cursed Lacey once more. 'Hobson wants you to go for a walk with him.'

I hadn't expected the message to come from him, so my surprise was genuine. 'I see,' I said. 'How very odd.'

'It's not uncommon for a patient to become attached to, or even obsessed with, a pretty nurse.'

'Obsessed?'

'You're right to be cautious,' said Carlisle. 'Sister asked my opinion, so I said I'd come talk to you. It's undeniable that it does the men good to go outside when they're ready. Hobson asking is a good sign he's properly on the mend. However, men in this ward tend to be different from your average soldier. Harder. More dangerous. If you're uncomfortable in any way I wanted to let you know you don't need to do this. Another nurse or even I can take him. It's your choice. It depends on how you believe he sees you and whether you think you can handle the situation.'

'It's not a problem,' I said, drying my hands. 'Besides it gets me out in the fresh air too. It's a lovely day out there.'

He frowned. 'If you're sure. Stay close to the building. Within earshot. I could have an orderly go with you.'

162

'I'll stay within earshot,' I said. Then I smiled slightly. 'I'm not being impulsive. I will be careful. I have some idea of what Hobson is like. I know not to cross him – or bait him.'

'Very well, but no more than a quarter of an hour. He mustn't overdo it and I need to know you're safe.'

'Thank you, Doctor.'

I found Hobson sitting on his bed in a dressing gown, a stick lying on the bed at his side. 'They won't let me get dressed,' he said. 'And they want me to use this bloody thing.' He lifted the stick and let it drop on the bed.'

'Why don't we do as they say and get out of here? The sooner we do the sooner you get a cigarette. Besides, you can always break the stick when you're outside if you don't need it.'

'Yeah, I suppose so,' said Hobson.

'Personally, I think it's rather odd of them to give you a weapon.'

For the first time I saw Hobson break into a grin. 'Think I'm going to brain you with it, Nurse?'

'Hopefully not. I am, after all, the one with the access to not only this packet, but others.'

'All right then.' He stood up. 'I'm not coming to please you. I want to know what the hell you think you're up to. If you're a ruddy nurse I'm a milkmaid.'

'And the cap would look so good on you,' I said sweetly.

We walked out of the ward and into the sunlight. I learnt now that the door was only locked between shifts when fewer staff were at liberty to help stop any patient fleeing. Sister was extremely careful who she allowed to be on the ward during the change over.

Both Hobson and I looked up at the same moment to enjoy the sun beating down on our faces. 'What's up with you?' he said. 'You get to go outside anytime. I've not been out of that ward in months.'

He was leaning heavily on the cane and breathing heavily. I took his arm to help and urged him on. 'You've guessed I'm not usually the type that likes to be shut up in an institution all day. I value my freedom.'

'Can't say I'm one for too many rules, myself. Where are we going and where are my cigarettes?'

'There's a bench a little way off. It's sheltered from the wind, but still in the sun. They'll also be able to see, but not hear, us from the hospital. Dr Carlisle was very worried about me going off with you alone.'

Hobson carried on silently for a bit, trying to get himself into a rhythm of walking with the cane. After a short while he had adjusted. 'You're not scared of me, are you?'

'I would be very scared of you if I crossed you,' I said. 'But I have no intention of doing so.'

'Good to know.'

We reached the bench and Hobson sat down at once, clearly tired. 'If you're going to ask me to do anything physical,' he said with a slight leer, 'I have to tell you I'm not at my peak fitness.'

I ignored the innuendo and lit a cigarette which I passed to him. I'd seen his hands were slightly shaky on the ward and I didn't want to embarrass him or make him feel he had to show me how hard he was. It was only as I opened the packet that I realised I hadn't brought any matches. Fortunately, Cuttle had had more foresight than me and enclosed a lighter.

The cigarette felt odd between my lips. As I lit it I deliberately didn't inhale as I knew it would make me cough. Even so, as I passed him the cigarette I could taste the sour tang of tar in my mouth. I wanted to make the point that the smokes were under my control. Hobson took it from me. His hand brushed mine and I suppressed a shudder.

'So what do you want?'

'I do know Major Fitzroy well,' I said. 'Not in the way you originally imagined, but we've worked together a number of times.'

'I don't recall seeing you among the spotters.'

I shook my head. 'Our skills sets are different. I wouldn't be any use at what you do.'

'Don't like the killing? Or is it the danger?'

'Neither,' I said lightly. 'I make as much noise as an elephant when I am trying to be stealthy and my sense of direction appears to have been removed at birth.'

164

Hobson laughed out loud. 'Yeah, that would make you a liability. Plus a war zone is no place for a woman.'

I resisted commenting. Seeing the soldiers come in today had given me a whole new appreciation of what the men faced out there. The plain truth was that any man or woman knowing what they would face and actually wanting to go struck me as unbelievable.

I side-stepped the debate. 'Major Fitzroy told me about the final mission. How you were ambushed?'

'You've seen him?'

I nodded. 'He asked me to do this.'

'How is he?' The question seemed perfectly sincere.

'Thinner. His arm was still in a sling. He looked older. His face had more lines on it. He was pretty chuffed to see his dog again.'

'Jack, isn't it?'

I nodded. Amazed once again that the hardest of British men (and women) have a soft spot for animals, especially dogs.

'Yeah, he told us some tales about it. Very funny. He can tell a good story.'

'Yes, he can, but what he told me about your last mission wasn't a story. When you were leaving the barn – under fire and some of you literally on fire – he thinks he saw a lit lamp in the hay loft window.'

'You mean we were set up?'

I nodded.

Hobson struggled to get to his feet. 'He doesn't think . . .'

I laid a calming hand on his arm. 'He doesn't think anything. He set me to find out if he was right and you had been betrayed. His deepest fear is that it is one of you, but he has no idea who it might be. He asked me to find out.'

Hobson frowned heavily, 'And you don't think I . . .'

'No, I don't think you betrayed them. But I want your help finding out who did.' Then I outlined my plan for using Wilkins as bait.

Hobson listened intently to the whole thing before speaking. 'It's a dangerous plan. I don't like the idea of young Wilkins getting hurt.'

'That's why I need your help. To protect him. There's no knowing when the traitor might strike. I can't be on the ward all the time.'

This brought out another dark grin. 'You think you could take one of us, do you?'

I shrugged. 'Most of you have discounted me as a threat. I'm only another nurse to them. You're the only one to pay me enough attention to notice the change in gait.'

'Oh, the others notice you. It's just not their eyes they notice you with.'

I ignored this as well. 'So will you do it?'

'What if it's Wilkins or me?'

'Then the outcomes would be different but unique. I would know.'

'You think I'd kill the lad?'

'No, I think you'd do a runner, but I am certain enough it isn't you to let you in on my plan.'

'What does the Major think?'

'He's back in the field. That's part of the urgency of this. If there is one traitor in our midst there are likely to be others. Whoever we uncover is liable to know at least some of them.'

Hobson turned to glower at the sun. 'Right,' he said not looking at me. 'We can't have that. You send me the cable that says the Major is coming to see us and I'll spread the rumour.'

'And I will have some louder conversations with Wilkins about him wanting to speak to the Major.'

'I'll follow up on that later.'

'Then we have an accord.'

'It seems we do, Nurse Stapleford.'

'Call me Alice. That's my professional moniker.'

'Huh, like Alice through the Looking Glass? The Major always did have a funny sense of humour.'

Chapter Twenty

Round and round the garden

That evening, come hell or high water, I was determined to speak to Rory properly. Accordingly I presented myself to Sister in plenty of time to join the early afternoon walk. I explained an old friend of mine and my husband's was having to relearn how to walk. This was his second walk and he was already on the verge of giving up. I asked if I might be shifted to that duty for the next few hours.

'Normally, I wouldn't allow such a request, but Matron lent you to me with the strange but specific instruction that if you asked to do something, and I did not consider the request a liability in any way, you should be allowed to do it.'

'I did not know, Sister.'

She pursed her lips. 'Perhaps not, but now I am receiving two requests in the same day for you to go off ward, albeit one was with a patient. You know how short-staffed we are. I have learned not to ask certain questions on this ward, so I will only ask you this. Do you consider this action necessary at this time?'

'Yes,' I replied without hesitation.

'Then I will have to let you go, Stapleford. But if you wish to retain your position on my ward, I would prefer, and may come to insist, you prioritise the demands of this ward over all else.' She fixed me with what some would consider a steely glare. I thanked her politely and tried to act as if I was mildly intimidated. She sighed loudly as I left. She hadn't bought it in the slightest. But really, how can someone whose sole purpose is to heal the sick ever intimidate anyone?

I still had a few odds and ends to sort out. Although having Griffin to arrange things for me was infinitely more useful than speaking to someone like Lacey. I didn't know Fitzroy's batman well – I couldn't think of a more apt turn, but Fitzroy trusted him completely. A very, very unusual state of affairs – and it made me almost fatally curious about him.

I was so lost in my thoughts that I failed to notice Merry before she grabbed me by the waist from behind. My instincts kicked in until I heard her voice, calling my name. I released her. Merry sat up on the floor where I had held her in an downward arm lock. 'Bleedin' hell,' she said, 'we're meant to be learning how to cure people not kill 'em. At least I am.' She took my hand to stand. Then brushed herself down. The blood had drained from her face.

'Are you hurt?' I asked. 'I didn't realise – I didn't think – I reacted. I'm so sorry. I would never wish to harm you.'

'I remember how you were nifty with a candlestick in the old days, but you seem to have moved on a bit.' Her voice shook slightly. I realised I had given her a real fright.

'I wasn't trying to inflict harm. Only immobilise,' I said.

'Oh, that's all right then,' said Merry. 'Euphemia, what the hell have you turned into? I don't know you any more.'

'Let's go and find a cup of tea,' I said, linking my arm through hers, so she could feel how real I was. 'It will help. I'm still exactly the same person I always was. I may have acquired a few peculiar skills, but in all else I am unaltered.'

'Peculiar skills,' repeated Merry. 'That's one way of putting it.'

I had the strangest feeling that rather like a kettle she was building up steam. I walked us as quickly as I could to the refectory, and drawing on my old skills from when I had worked for Richenda, I plied her with cake and tea. (I had to bribe the cook heavily to dig into her larder, but I knew the Service would recompense me.) Living on her husband's wage as a chauffeur had not placed her on the poverty line, but from the way she regarded the cakes I knew that sugar had been something of a luxury. This time, at least, it sated her and she calmed down. By the time we had finished our tea and cakes, Merry was able to see the whole thing as a bit of a joke. She even believed me when I told I only knew one other manoeuvre; one that Fitzroy had shown me early on: how to escape from attempted strangulation. I promised to show her later. 'It's easy,' I said. 'Anyone could do it. You have to know how in the same way you have to know how to make a bed with hospital corners. It's a simple skill once you know how.'

Merry checked her watch. 'We need to get down to the ward. I got away early because I'm on the third supper shift tonight like you. They let us get a cup of tea and a biscuit if we're working later.' She grinned. 'I have to say this was far better than usual. The cook must like you.'

I smiled, thinking the cook certainly liked the inside of my purse. 'So what do we do?'

'We head back downstairs and meet them by an exit that's just off Rory's ward. There's quite a few of us on tonight. Matron wanted to get as many men out as possible, what with the new arrivals having to adjust and all the recent operations. She said it would be easier if we could get the old hands out the door, so the doctors could concentrate on the new arrivals. Makes a kind of sense.'

'It's good for us, anyway,' I said.

When we got to the rendezvous point, which as I thought from Merry's brief description was the door I had followed Cuttle out on that first night, it was to see a positive flock of nurses waiting for the patients to be brought out. The evening was even warmer than the previous night, so no one was wearing a coat. As they rustled around in their white starched aprons and caps I couldn't help thinking of the geese back on my childhood home, a vicarage with a small farmyard. Merry and I came to a stop at the back of the gaggle.

'How are we allotted to the men?'

'Don't worry,' said Merry. 'Rory will ask for us. I hope you don't mind, but we told Matron we'd all known each other before.' She looked up at me. 'We didn't say what we had been doing. That's all right, isn't it?'

'Of course,' I said. 'I think it's better not to give details of our

169

current home either, if there is a killer about, but I can't see any harm letting Matron know we are old friends. It's what I told the sister on my ward. Why I wanted to come.'

The door opened before Merry could reply and a hoard of wounded men poured out, accompanied by orderlies and a few nurses. I don't know if Merry thought this, but I couldn't help compare it to this morning's experience. These men were also scarred, maimed, and battle-worn, but instead of a brittle show of bravery or even despair, as the sunlight shone down on their faces there was a feeling of cheer. A fair amount of good-natured banter began with the patients implying they were being set up on a date with the nurse they were allocated.

'I'm taking these two,' said Rory, appearing by our side. He lent heavily on a cane, but he was upright. 'I'll fight anyone who challenges me – and I'm frae Scotland I'll have yer ken!'

He threw an arm around Merry's shoulders and mine, leaving him to wave his stick in the air behind us. 'I can repel attackers!' he cried.

It was some minutes before we could extricate him from the fray. Eventually nurses separated their charges from the main herd and we all headed off in different directions. 'We can't go out of sight of the building,' said Merry.

Rory had taken his arms from around our shoulders and was using his cane once more. 'Can we go to the bit of wall you found, Merry. It was the right height for sitting and I'm feeling a wee bitty sore today.' It was strange to hear Rory dropping in and out of Scots. When he had been working as a butler he had been most properly spoken. Under extreme stresses or emotions only did he resort to Scots. I realised he must be in a lot of pain.

'I'm sorry, Euphemia – for the arm around your shoulder. I need to convince them we were old friends.'

'You're trying to create an image of you as a Scottish Casanova among the men. I've heard you.'

Rory had the grace to blush. 'What does it matter if I spin a few wee tales to keep the men's spirits up?' He spoke to me. 'You didn't ask but I went in as a sergeant.'

'Your potential was obviously spotted,' I said politely.

We walked on a bit further. The lawn sloped up hill very slightly, but Rory's pace slowly dramatically. 'Not much further,' said Merry. 'The path's this way.'

She led us down a small paved path that formed a vennel through the middle of the hospital. I had a vague memory of noticing this, but I hadn't thought much about it except that I didn't want to be caught in the dark down there. I had assumed it was some kind of utility passage, which it seemed to be. We could only walk two abreast now, and Merry had taken the lead. We passed several large aluminium tubs on wheels. 'I do hope that's not where they make the soup,' I said. Walking alongside me, I could tell Rory was on edge. 'Do enclosed places bother you?'

'No,' said Rory. 'But you do. I wasnae very nice to you last time we spoke.'

Inwardly I reflected this was the understatement of the year. He had in fact been trying to get me prosecuted for murder.

'I hope you know I would have seen sense. I would have realised it couldn't possibly have been you – that you would never . . .'

'Would that be before or after I was hanged?' I asked, cutting to the chase.

'Och, Euphemia, you hurt me badly. I was head over heels in love with you. I would have sold my soul if you'd asked me. I would have done anything for you. I was like a man obsessed. Then *that man* came and had a wee chat with me. Told me I wasn't the right man for you. Told me to leave you be. Then you're engaged to Bertram, the closest I ever came to having a toff as a friend. The job he gave me at White Orchards felt like all my dreams come true, factor and driver to a decent man who called me a friend. Then you appear, engaged to him, and I'm out on my ear.'

'Bertram never fired you!' I said. Although my mind was still reeling from his comments of *that man* coming to talk to him. Had he?

'No, he didn't. But he kept you out of my way, and as you were nigh on always with him, and were going to be mistress of his estate, there wasn't a place for me anymore.'

'We could have worked it out.'

'Do yer not ken, lass, I was still in love with yer?'

I flinched. 'No,' I said softly.

'Seemed to me the best thing I could do was get away. You know who found me a job in the police. Or rather a special division of the police. Then I run into you again and in trouble and he's there hanging around you again. The marriage hasn't happened and you're running off into the night with him. I had to wonder if he'd been playing us for a long time. He wanted you and he got you.'

'If the man you keep alluding to is Fitzroy. I can assure you he never "got me" as you eloquently put it. Our relationship is and has always been nothing but professional.'

'He plays a long game, that one,' said Rory frowning darkly.

We emerged from the vennel into the bright light. I touched him very lightly on the lower arm. He flinched a bit, but I didn't remove my hand. He had to turn and look down at me. 'I'd like us to be friends. We meant a great deal to each other once. I still care for you as a friend. I don't know if you're willing or even able to be my friend as I hurt you so much, but know on my side I'm willing to try.' He frowned. I added quickly, so as not to be misunderstood, 'I know I made the right choice for my husband. You would have despaired of me as a wife. I'm far too wilful and independent. Bertram rather likes that. We have the most tremendous arguments, but we always make up the same day. I adore him for many reasons, but not least among them is for him not trying to change me. I think you would be happier with a far more gentle wife. My temperament would drive you to distraction.'

There was a long and uncomfortable silence. 'You may be right,' he said at last. 'I don't know if I can ever be your friend, but I'm willing to call a truce while we work this matter out. But it won't be like the old days, ever, Euphemia. We've all moved on a long way from then. Any innocence we had is lost. We see the world the bitter way it truly is. None of us are young and foolhardy any more.'

I bit the inside of my cheek, so I didn't say, 'You may have turned into an old fogey, but I'm not even twenty-five.' (That being the maximum age my mother had once told me that a maiden remained marriageable. After that, she had said, one becomes a maiden aunt and reliant on the generosity of others.')

'And you're even more mixed up with *that man* than ever, aren't you? From what Merry's told me, you go jaunting about with him. I wonder Bertram doesn't give him a damn good thrashing.'

'They actually get on rather well,' I said lightly. Though in reality the thought that Rory ascribed to the idea that I was one man's property reminded me of all the reasons we would not have been suited. 'But I am amenable to a truce.'

'It will make Merry happy,' he said, as if this was the most important thing. 'She thinks of us as family and hates to see an argument between any of us.'

I didn't answer. I couldn't see that this conversation could be continued in a useful way. Rory remained annoyed with Fitzroy. I couldn't imagine my handler warning him away from me. It simply wasn't the kind of thing Fitzroy would do. He disliked very much getting involved in other people's personal lives. I was continually surprised he made such effort with Bertram.

Merry had already reached the wall. I walked slowly enough to ensure I didn't leave Rory behind, but not close enough that we had to continue the conversation. I could hear him breathing heavily behind me, and I realised his leg must be hurting him a lot. He would hate me seeing that, so I didn't look back, but I strained every nerve to listen in case he fell.

The wall ran around the edge of a vegetable garden that was clearly a recent project. A few leafy plants poked up through the brown, crumbling soil, but many of them were little more than seedlings. Little dots of bright green against the rich earth. The garden was at the back of the laundry area. The building here was much plainer than the ornate front. It was more utilitarian, designed to be used not admired, with plain brick and simple windows. Opposite the forest stood, a riot of greens. Everything from a deep, dark emerald to lighter tones of teal. Even this early in the evening it was so quiet we could hear the sounds of nature stirring and preparing for the night hunt to come. A grey stone wall, similar to the ones you see at most British harbours bordered the country lane that lay between us and the forest. The air smelt sweet and fresh in that way flowers do in the moments before they close their petals for the night. The absence of the smell of disinfectant was akin to stopping banging ones head against a wall. It was lovely and oddly peaceful. It made it almost impossible to imagine that somewhere men were fighting each other to the death. Men who would never even know each others' names. If I hadn't seen the wounded for myself I might have thought it was nothing but a terrible story.

Rory sat down on the edge of the wall, sighing with relief. I hoisted myself up to sit beside Merry. Her feet dangled several inches from the ground, and she swung them to and fro happily. 'It's lovely here, isn't it?' she said. 'It always amazes me how much noise a few ill men on a ward can cause, what with all the staff coming and going, and the constant whispering of doctors, even the clacking of Matron's shoes grates on my nerves.'

Rory took a pack of cigarettes out of his dressing gown pocket, balanced his stick against the walk, and lit one. 'The sound of the birds at dawn before the fighting starts is both wonderful and terrifying.'

'Why terrifying?' asked Merry.

'He means that every time he hears it he thinks it may be the last time. That's it, isn't it Rory?'

He nodded and blew out some smoke. 'Partly, but there's also something about nature carrying on, paying no attention to what we're doing. Like maybe those birds will get caught in the crossfire today, maybe they'll fly away, but there'll always be birds. Always be trees. Nature will reclaim those bloody fields when all of us are gone.'

'Cheerful,' said Merry. 'But you're not going back out, are you?'

Rory shook his head. 'I need to exercise this leg to get back my strength, but it will never be properly whole again.'

In the old days I would have made a joke about that being because part of it had been eaten by maggots, but I didn't. I was too wary of insulting him.

'So,' said Merry, 'shall we tell Euphemia our plan?'

Chapter Twenty-one

If we could see us as others do

'Right,' said Merry, 'we still aren't completely sure something is wrong, but what with that morphine being stolen, we're extra worried. Yesterday evening we had a long chat about who had died and why.'

'She's learnt a lot about injuries, our Merry,' said Rory proudly. 'I'm quite in awe of how she could explain what had happened to the different chaps.'

'Thing is, we started to notice a pattern. I volunteered to check through and organise the paperwork today while the others were dealing with the new intake. Things do get confused and out of order when there's a sudden flurry of activity. Most of the other nurses hate the paperwork. They say they can never read the doctors' handwriting. So they were delighted when I offered to help.'

'Did it check out?' said Rory. 'Were we right?'

'I think so,' said Merry. 'It's hard to be sure, because the notes aren't as detailed as you might hope. Plus there's only six months' worth held in the hospital. After that it all goes off to an archive somewhere.'

'You're keeping me in suspense,' I said with a tight smile.

'Thing is, there's one too many people who seem to suddenly just up and die. Now, we know that can happen. So many factors and there certainly hasn't been time for any detailed checks. I mean, why would they? But the thing is, out of the ten most recent sudden deaths, eight of them were men who looked to be on the mend – and all had been severely injured, so they had no chance of a normal life. We're not talking a missing limb here. We're talking bed-bound, loss of more than one sense, half of their face blown away – things that would make living in society almost impossible.'

'But that's the point, isn't it? They were the men who had undergone the most traumatic shocks to the body, weren't they? Isn't it most likely they would be the ones where something undetected caused some kind of systemic failure?'

'Maybe,' said Merry. 'But it doesn't feel right. Rory, tell her about the man in the bed next to you. Corporal Edwards.'

'Must have been about twenty-five, I would think,' said Rory. 'He'd had a really bad time. One leg below the knee, one foot, and one hand gone. All amputated because they were so mangled. But he was as cheery as anything. Said he as long as he still had his . . .' Rory paused. 'You know. Down there. And one good working hand, and he'd be fine. I couldn't believe how he dealt with what had happened to him. I thought it was bravado, but yer ken the bawdy jokes never stopped. Only serious thing he ever said to me was, when he was lying on the field thinking he was dying he'd prayed and said "I don't care what happens to me just let me live". So as he put it, "turning into an article of pity with all senses remaining," seemed like a grand bargain to him compared to dying.'

'But he died,' I said. 'It sounds like he'd been through some awful physical traumas. You can't be surprised if he got an infection or even if his body simply gave up. Tragic, but not unusual.'

'But Matron is always saying how the patient's mood affects their recovery. It's the ones who have hope who usually live,' said Merry.

'I've heard that too,' I said, 'but hope doesn't beget miracles.'

'If you lasses would let me git a word in edgeways?'

'He's coming over all Scottish,' said Merry, 'we'd better look out.'

Rory threw her a filthy look. 'As I was trying to say, Edwards were a cheery soul, but also for what happened to him, a lucky devil. All his amputations healing up nicely. Not a trace of infection – Dr Mitchum started bringing other surgeons over so they could discuss his work and emulate it.'

'How did Edwards feel about that?' I asked.

'He loved it,' said Rory. 'He'd sit basking in the attention as if he'd been the surgeon himself. He even joked about charging display fees.'

'But he died?' I said.

'Yes, two nights ago,' said Rory. One minute he's telling the ward one of his long lewd stories and then when I wake up in the morning he's gone. I knew it the moment I opened my eyes.' He gazed away into the distance. 'When you've seen death come enough times, you get a kind of sense. You know when it's only the flesh left.' He paused to wipe the back of his hand across his eyes. 'Of course I called for the nurse. I even got as far as swinging myself out of bed. I stumbled across to him and felt for a pulse at his neck. He was ice cold.'

'He'd been gone for a while then?' I said gently. 'How did he look?'

'That's the thing,' said Rory. 'Completely peaceful. Not a mark on him I could see.'

'I'm sorry to ask, but can you think if you noticed anything at all out of the norm?' I said.

Merry was watching our faces in turn much as cat watches two mice play, with fixed intensity and bright eyes.

Rory shook his head. 'He looked empty, but otherwise . . .' he shrugged. 'But it doesn't make sense. Even Dr Mitchum challenged the nurses over what might have happened.'

'Did he think there had been foul play?' said Merry, looking ever so slightly ghoulish.

'No, I don't think so,' said Rory. 'He was upset as much about his model patient dying as about Edwards dying, if you see what I mean. But it was wrong. I know it was wrong. He didn't simply die.'

'Why do you say that?'

Rory shrugged helplessly. 'I don't know. Instinct?'

Merry tugged his sleeve. Rory shook his head. 'You have to tell her,' said Merry.

'It's daft.'

I raised an enquiring eyebrow. Rory sighed. 'I had an odd dream that night. Merry thinks it was an omen.'

'How very Roman of you,' I said to Merry, who looked at me in confusion and suspicion.

'I told you she'd think it was silly,' said Rory. 'She's not one to believe in superstitions.'

'Black cats crossing your path or walking under ladders – I don't believe in those,' I said. 'But I don't think we know everything. Sometimes strange things do happen.' I didn't share with them that I had once received my father's blessing via a medium to marry Bertram. I certainly hadn't gone looking for such a thing, but when I heard the voice coming from Madame Arcana I knew in my bones, and without a single doubt, it was him. I wanted to hear about Rory's dream, but I didn't want to make him feel in anyway responsible for Edwards' death. In case he thought he should have warned him or some such thing. On the wards I often heard the men painfully lament being unable to save their fellows.

'If you must know,' said Rory, 'I had a nightmare about being buried alive. It was hideously vivid.' He turned to me. 'Nothing like that happened to me over there. I never saw it happen to anyone else.'

'Could it be an older memory?' I asked.

'Like getting buried under sand on the beach by my brothers, you mean?'

I thought this was oddly specific, but nodded.

'No, nothing like that has ever happened to me.'

'When you found him how was he lying?' I asked.

'On his back.'

'Is that how he normally slept?'

'I think so,' said Rory. 'He looked relaxed. None of his remaining limbs were at an odd angle. At least I don't think so. I think I might have been in shock. I can't think why. I've seen more than enough dead men.'

'But not here,' I said. I leaned over to look him directly in the eye. I placed a hand on his arm. 'Not here,' I said, watching his reaction. 'where you thought you were safe.'

He started back so hard that I recoiled by instinct, snatching my hand away and almost falling off my seat. 'I'm sorry,' I said.

Rory stared at me. He shivered.

'It's getting cold,' said Merry, 'We should go back.'

'Your eyes,' said Rory to me. 'They're the same colour.'

'His eyes were open,' I said.

'Open but unseeing. Looking into me like he wanted to say something, but there was no spark left in him. No energy to do anything. Hollow windows. All broken. All broken up.'

'Definitely time to go inside,' said Merry. She picked up his cane and handed it to him. 'Come on, Rory. Let's go and find you some hot tea.'

I opened my mouth to ask something, but Merry gave me a furious look, so I shut it again. We took a side each to help Rory down the path. He gave his stick to Merry, so he could lean harder on me. At least this told me it hadn't been my touch that had revolted him. I wanted him to forgive me – for everything. But as his weight settled on me I realised this was not the Rory I had known. That Rory would never have let himself be held up by two women. His pride would have had him crawl, even over broken glass, rather than that. This Rory walked with a dragging leg, but I could see it was freshly bandaged. The maggots were gone and his flesh was healing. His mind would take longer.

Merry and I managed to make it back before the refectory closed. The benches and tables stood largely empty. Three individuals, with sagging shoulders, ate at different tables with an air of weariness that was almost tangible. It could also be this was the result of losing a patient. I'd seen how much these women invested in the men they were nursing. Even I felt a blow to the solar plexus when I saw a trolley with a covered human outline pass by, and other than Ward D, I hadn't got to know any of the patients. I tried to imagine how I would feel if one of the spotters died. I realised that even the demise of the unpleasant Dwyer would give me pause. It was the transition from living being to corpse that was so shocking. That a body could both look so like the person who had died and yet also not resemble them at all. I forced my mind not to go down the avenue of wondering where Bertram or Fitzroy were. It would do neither them nor I any good.

Instead I went to the serving hatch to enquire if there was any hot food available. The cook on duty was one of the older ladies with her stockings as wrinkled as her face, who I only usually saw in the background. I told her that we had been helping with the walking of the injured tonight and that our charge had had a bit of a turn. It had made us late for supper. The cook took pity on us and reheated a couple of pies, some potatoes, and gave us two slices of treacle pudding. She apologised that there wasn't any custard. I told her that we were very grateful for everything. Rather embarrassingly she called us young angels and then pattered off to finish clearing up and preparing for tomorrow.

Despite feeling rather down I managed to eat. Now I had seen a busy day at the hospital I fully understood the concept of eating when you could. Merry only picked at her plate. I wanted to say something comforting, but I could only guess what was going on in her head. Instead I ate my beef and kidney pie as quietly as I could and waited for her to speak. When I was re-salting my potatoes she exploded without warning.

'You turn everything to your advantage, don't you? It's all about you. Your plans. Your ideas. Whatever you think is important we have to investigate. It doesn't matter what we think. And you use people. Even old friends like Rory. You pushed him too far.'

'The memory overwhelmed him,' I said. As it had been her idea to get Rory to talk about Edwards and his nightmare, I didn't think she had a right to blame me. But neither did I want to end this evening at odds with her. 'It made me very sad too. Rory still has a way to go to heal.'

'You even begrudge him that? Leaning on you to get back to his bed? After all he's been through.' She gave a little half sob.

'Of course not,' I said. 'I meant it will be a while before he recovers from the shock of all that has happened to him. You heard him say he'd seen a lot of death over there. Then to wake and see the empty shell of a cheery, lively young man, when everyone said how well Edwards was doing, must have been a tremendous blow. Like being back in the war all over again.'

'Oh, you have an answer for everything, don't you? You're hard, Euphemia, that's what you are. You've got a heart of stone.'

Tears streamed down her face, but her face didn't portray sadness. She was frowning deeply, but also showing her teeth like a small but extremely angry tiger. It wasn't Merry's fault that her short stature made her so endearingly sweet or her dark ringlets and wide eyes made her seem almost doll-like. I wanted to pick her up and hug her, but I rather thought she might dig her teeth into my neck if I did so. Besides, she now knew where the jugular artery ran.

'I felt very sorry for Rory . . .'

I got no further. Once again I had said the wrong thing. Merry stood and hurled her words like spears. She was standing now, but not shouting. Servants learn not to shout. Instead she spoke in a harsh, hissing whisper that dripped vitriol and bile. I had no idea what I had done to deserve this much hatred.

Then I noticed one of the figures, who had been eating standing at the end of the table. Merry stopped, embarrassed by her behaviour in front of a stranger. She blinked almost as if she was waking up. She looked around the room and at the nurse, who had come over. 'I'm very sorry if I disturbed your meal,' she said in a small voice.

Rather than joining either of our benches, the nurse pulled up a chair and sat at the end, gesturing to Merry to do the same. It was then I noticed she was a sister. Merry threw me a scared look. I knew what she was thinking – now we were really for it. I'd lost count of the number of times Matron had told us whatever problems we had they were nothing compared to what the men were caring for had endured.

'My two brothers signed up. They shipped out about a week ago. Every time we have new arrivals the first thing I do is scan each face to see if they are among the wounded. I don't want them to be wounded, but at least, if they were, they would be alive. Alive and home.'

Merry nodded. 'You do your work, but its like someone else is doing it, because you keep searching . . .'

'Who is it for you?'

'My husband,' said Merry and broke down weeping. This wasn't an angry bout of tears. This was a full out, head on the table, totally giving herself up to despair moment. Her sobs were neither loud nor dramatic, but seemed to come from deep within her. Her entire frame shook. The sister looked at me. 'I'll look after her. It's seeing the wounded that does it. We can't help thinking . . .' she trailed off.

'She's my best friend,' I said.

'Believe me, only someone who knows what she is going through can help.'

At that I turned on my heel and walked away without a word. Tears pricked like pins at the back of my eyes. I didn't let them fall. I pushed my emotions down. I had a mission to do. I didn't have time to weep for Bertram and Fitzroy. I didn't have time to open the door at the back of my mind where I kept my fears for their safety. I had a job to do. I had lives to save, and my own emotions had to be sacrificed for that. Finding the traitor and saving those lives was my duty. It might feel as if my heart was rending itself in two, but I would silently bear it. I would not acknowledge my torment let alone show it the world. Let Merry think me stone-hearted if she must. My feelings and I were unimportant compared to my mission.

My feet were leading me to the dorm. I touched the door handle and tiredness washed over me like a tidal wave. I pushed down to open the door and then I remembered. I needed Cuttle to send that cable for me. I sighed, and summoned up my last ounce of energy. On a nice night like this I was fairly certain I'd find him by the surgical ward's back door, smoking under the stars.

Chapter Twenty-two

Situation out of control

The next morning my body ached as if I had fought off six assassins. It had only seemed moments since I'd thrown myself down on my bed, and now everyone was hurrying off to breakfast. I was tempted to miss it, but I knew I'd regret that decision later. Merry's bed was empty, but it looked slept in. I stumbled my way through to the refectory to see her sitting amid a crowd of nurses, chatting happily.

I stayed at the back of the room, ate quickly, and went off to Ward D. I quickly fell into the ward's routine. There is something comforting about routine when one feels lost and alone inside. I made the early morning tea. I smiled and bantered with the patients as I delivered it. By now I didn't have to ask anyone how they liked their tea. I even left Hobson to the very last as I knew he liked his tea 'strong enough that a rat could stand on it', as he put it.

It was strange how simply remembering how they liked their tea seemed to cheer the men. Every time I handed over the right cup without enquiring I got a version of 'Oh, Nurse, you remembered' and a genuine smile. I wondered if it had something to do with being seen as individuals after being lost in the mass of war. But despite nursing so many men and seeing the awfulness of their injuries I couldn't properly imagine what being in the midst of the fighting had been like. None of the men spoke of their worst experiences. The most you ever heard them say was to comment on the personalities of those who had been alongside them. Or of the stories of home or bawdy jokes they'd been told. (Some of these were enough to make even me feel uncomfortable. They made the language I had complained about Fitzroy using seem akin to nursery rhymes. And despite my growing knowledge of biology, I didn't see how some of the things they spoke of were anatomically possible.)

After lunch, and this time I was asked to stay on the ward to help serve it and clear away, there was a bit of a commotion. I'd been asked if I wanted to scoot up to the refectory and catch the last of lunch or join the staff on the ward. I'd said I'd stay on the ward. A decision Sister was most pleased by. A lot of the nurses were also part of the surgical and operating teams. The new influx of patients had meant there were less nurses available to do general staffing, plus the new set of trainee nurses after us were apparently uncommonly 'dense' as Sister put it. 'I'm only glad none of them are eligible to work on this ward,' she said during lunch and away from the patients' hearing. 'I wouldn't trust them not to serve tea in a bedpan.'

I laughed at that. 'Honestly, Stapleford,' she responded, 'the things I've heard about them. One of them tried to force the door to the poisons cupboard because she thought it was where we kept the bandages.'

Dr Carlisle, who had also opted to say and eat the cold lunch, said, 'Really, they're sure that's what she thought she was doing?' Eating your way through a cheese sandwich it is hard to look suspicious, yet there was something in his tone that bothered me. He noticed me watching him and raised an eyebrow. 'What do you think, Stapleford?'

'I think it's very odd, but the missing morphine, if that's what you're thinking about, Doctor, went missing before she joined up.'

'True,' he said. 'But you have to bear in mind the quantity of drugs we have in this hospital has always been high and is only getting higher.'

'You mean that any gang or black marketeers or whatever you want to call them might send more than one person in to try and get the drugs? Or that more than one person might think this was a good way to make extra cash?'

'Either,' said Carlisle.

'Goodness,' said Sister, 'the way your minds work. I can't believe there are many – although I concede there may be some – people who would rob medication, painkillers, from our brave boys. Especially not those who have dedicated their lives to healing.'

'That's why all the trainees come under such scrutiny. Stapleford's lot are still under suspicion for the last theft. I believe a spot check on their quarters was done this morning.'

'That's rather rude,' I said. 'Shouldn't we have at least have been allowed to be present?'

'Something to hide, Stapleford?' said the ever irksome Carlisle. I ignored him.

'I'm afraid in these times some of our civil liberties may be curtailed for the sake of security and other measures,' said Sister. 'However, I can tell you nothing was found.'

'Of course not,' I said. 'Anyone clever enough to steal that amount of morphine wouldn't keep it with their possessions.'

'But they might dump it on someone else if they thought they couldn't get it off the hospital base,' said Carlisle. I must have frowned, because he continued. 'There's no passes for nurses for the next two weeks due to the influx of new patients. That can't be sustained. But it looks like we will get less and less time off as this situation progresses.'

'You mean the fighting,' I said. 'It's getting worse, not better? I don't like to ask the men what's happening and I haven't seen a newspaper in weeks.'

'That's deliberate,' said Sister. 'We don't want people worrying over their relatives. It's not like there is anything more we can do. But good on you for not bothering the men. If I had a penny for every time I'd had to forbid a nurse from doing that . . . Do you have anyone out there?'

'Two people, very dear to me,' I said.

Carlisle gave me an intense stare. I ignored him again.

'Well, I shall pray for them as I pray for all our boys here and abroad,' said Sister. 'Now, Stapleford, time to get back to the ward. I'll be through in a few minutes. I need to talk to Dr Carlisle. The other nurses will be back after refectory lunch. So it will be you and the cleaner. I'm having the ward scrubbed down again. Can't be too careful about infection. I'm sure you can hold the fort.'

If you've never had your insides suddenly turn to a gelatinous mess, you probably won't understand the feeling, but although I stood, smiled, and nodded, every step I took towards the ward felt like a pace towards the gallows. I wasn't even a fully qualified nurse and she was leaving me in charge? That couldn't be right. But I had learned that in an army hospital the only person who questions Sister is Matron or a brave doctor. (And as for who questions Matron, only senior or foolhardy doctors.)

Much of my fear was alleviated simply by stepping up to Sister's desk. 'Whatcha, Nurse!,' called Corporal Potter. 'Battlefield promotion is it?'

'Only if those are the temporary kind,' I said. 'Sister's talking to the doctor and the others are still eating lunch.'

'Oh, those six-course lunches you nurses get compared to the gruel and stale bread us poor men are given.'

'Exactly, Corporal Potter, that chicken pot pie, mashed potato, and gravy you were licking off your plate was nothing more than an illusion.'

He chuckled at me. 'You're all right, you are.'

This being the highest of complements one could receive from the men, I lowered my head to read the charts on the desk, so as not to show my blushes. I had every opportunity to read the charts at the end of the men's beds, but unless I was handing out medication (still always under supervision) I tended not to. To start with, this was because a lot of the terms were unfamiliar to me, and later because I saw the worried looks on the men's faces whenever anyone looked at them. Most of them knew exactly what was wrong with them, and what was likely to happen, but the ever-present fear of infection meant that all of them had a heightened state of anxiety over their well-being. Some showed it. Others didn't. But to survive the battlefield, the voyage back to Britain, and then to die in a hospital bed before you ever got to see your family, was the greatest fear. (Currently no visitors were allowed on base. I think this had a lot to do with the presence of Ward D).

Wilkins' file, a fuller account of his condition than the chart, lay on the top of Sister's paperwork. As much to give me something to do as anything else, now all the men were slipping into post-prandial lethargy, I opened the file. Less than five minutes later I closed it, blinking hard to stop my tears. Wilkins was technically out of danger, but the damage done by the fire meant that he would never walk again. But worse yet, his burns left him with a condition called 'Butterfly Skin'. This meant it was so thin that it tore almost all the time and put him at huge risk of infection. His prognosis was five years or less. The recommendation was that he should be sent to a nursing home, with no prospect of ever regaining his freedom or any kind of independent life. His recovery was ascribed to his youth and general fitness before the incident. There was a side note that if possible measures should be taken to keep him entertained as though of a naturally cheery disposition he was extremely bright for his class (and yes, that is what they wrote) and without mental occupation he might quickly sink into decline – especially when his long-term situation was fully explained to him.

It was the last part that hit me hardest. Wilkins probably had an inkling that his wounds would have a long-lasting effect, but that his recovery should be this limited had not yet been discussed. In other words the poor boy was living on groundless hope.

I had no impulse to tell him. I wanted the situation to be otherwise, but I agreed that telling him now could hinder the last section of his partial recovery. As I looked over, Hobson had pulled the edge of his screen back – the men often did this when they thought they could get away with it – and the two of them were sharing a joke. That Hobson, far from being the most sociable of men, bothered to do this suggested to me that he had sussed out the severity of Wilkins' dilemma. Thinking on it, he had always seemed something of a pet among the men here. I had put this down to his youth and boyish appearance, but it struck me as likely that the men understood on some level that he wasn't long for this earth.

I asked myself if I would want to live like Wilkins would have to do. I'd be a burden to my family and a constant source of grief. I had no fear of death, so I thought, on the whole, I'd rather I died a quick death. In such circumstances Fitzroy would probably shoot me, so I had that comfort.

'Sad reading, aren't they, ducks?' A cup of tea was slid onto my desk. 'Can't help seeing a bit of what's on their charts when I'm cleaning around the beds. Never mention it to the boys, of course. Everybody on this ward knows to keep their lips tight.' After this extraordinary statement the cleaner wandered off with a bucket and mop before I could reply. But then I supposed, like the nurses, she saw a lot of the patients day in and day out. The doctors always seemed to be rushing hither and thither. It fell to the nurses and the cleaners to deal with the dead. I didn't doubt the doctors cared for all their patients, but it was the others who saw more of them, and must necessarily feel their demise more keenly.

The tea had more sugar than I usually took, but short of finding some good black tea and a slice of lemon, nothing could have tasted nicer. I had been so surprised I hadn't even thanked the woman. However, it made me feel accepted as a member of staff and not simply someone passing through.

I shuffled the files back into neat order. Then, when I felt I could face the ward with composure, I sat back, sipping my tea and looked out over my charges.

While I had been undergoing emotional upheaval it appeared they had all still been sleeping. It is curious to watch a grown man sleep. Even the least appealing of them takes on a look of vulnerability when they rest, showing a shadow of the child they once were. I hadn't known I'd had maternal strings to be tugged upon, but it appeared I did. This raised a whole new range of spectres in my head. Fortunately, before I could tumble down that dark alley of thoughts and regrets, the ward door opened and a trainee nurse came in. Small, and particularly well-polished, she looked more military than some soldiers I had met. Her hair was neatly cropped for working in hygienic environments and she walked with a swift efficient gait.

'Good afternoon,' she said to me. I saw her lips about to add 'Sister',

189

but her eyes had flickered to my cap and I wore no such sign. However, she treated me with the courtesy of the nurse in charge. (Which rather puffed up my self-worth). 'I have a telegram for a patient. A Sergeant Hobson. It's not edged in black, so may I give it to him?'

'Of course.' I indicated the bed that Hobson lay in. His eyes were closed, but his breathing was light. 'He's not asleep,' I assured the nurse when she hesitated. 'He's resting. Let's hope it's good news for him.' I gave her a bright smile. To her credit she managed to repress any surprise at my comment. Nowadays, no one, but a fool, expected to receive good news.

I watched her walk over to Hobson's bed. Hobson sat up at once and opened the telegram. A wry smile twisted his face for a moment. He said something to the nurse, who left at once. I saw him pull back the screen cloth between him and Wilkins. He kept his voice low, but I heard Wilkins, squeak of happy delight. Cuttle had done his job. The news that their commanding officer was coming to pay a visit would shortly be all over the ward.

Chapter Twenty-three

Rory lays it out

I had hoped to see Rory again tonight, but Ward D kept me too late. There was a new energy in the room since the arrival of the telegram, which by now had been passed from bed to bed. Somehow this almost fever pitch of excitement had bled into the upper ward where the mentally unstable patients were kept. More than once I was left on my own to run the lower ward while doctors and nurses rushed to comfort or sedate the patients in the upper ward. Sister apologised for extending my shift, but said I was a 'Godsend'. Although my cooking skills are laughable, it has transpired I am adept at serving tea and dinners to military men with enough banter to cheer them, and enough dexterity to keep my person out of reach of their hands. I managed both the tea round and dinner on my own.

'You know why they like you, don't you?' said Corporal Potter to me.

'I'm female?'

Potter gave a rasping laugh. 'You don't mind the company of men.' He put his head on one side. 'You may even prefer it.'

I raised my eyebrows, waiting for some salty comment.

Potter shook his head. 'Oh no, not like that,' he said. 'I've heard you sit down and talk with a patient when they want to tell you some-thing about their war – not the worst bits, none of us will talk about them, but about the camaraderie in the trenches or which gun they preferred, or the strange tactics of the enemy.' He paused. 'You get it. The other women here, they try. They humour us, but you get it. I reckon you're the closest any of us will ever come to a female solider.'

'I'll take that as a compliment,' I said. 'Though there is no way you'd get me into the trenches.'

Potter smiled. 'Yeah, you get it alright.'

Eventually Sister appeared to relive me. 'Sterling effort, Stapleford. I'll make sure this goes down on your record.'

'Nothing of note happened,' I said. 'It was easy enough.'

'Nonsense,' she said, unconsciously echoing Potter, 'nothing happened because these men trust you. They're fighting men and they're vulnerable – not that dissimilar to a wounded animal. They relax when it's you in charge. They know you'll get them help if they need it. They're content to surrender control to you. That's no mean thing. Very rare ability in a nurse your age.'

I thanked her, but as I made my way up to the refectory in the hope of a late hot dinner (instead of the cold meal laid out on Ward D) and meeting Merry, I wondered if the men recognised a fellow combatant. I was no solider, but I had fought to defend myself. Even killed in self-defence and in defence of my partner. Fitzroy had always said that left a mark. Well, perhaps, it was a mark others who had done the same could unknowingly sense. It would be nice to have something good come of my prior actions other than my own survival and my modest contribution to the good of the nation.

I was in luck. Merry beckoned me over to her table as soon as I walked through the door. 'Thank goodness you did come,' she said. 'I convinced Cook to keep some hot food back for you. If you hadn't she'd have given me cold kippers for breakfast every morning for a week, I reckon.'

I sat down, and lifted the cover of the plate that waited for me. I smiled not only at the sight of the hearty hotpot with potatoes, but at Merry's friendly tone. My usually cheerful friend had become extremely unpredictable in her temperament of late. I ascribed this to her husband now presumably posted overseas. It still stung that I had two people of great importance to me over there, and I could not mention either.

'Eat up! We've got a meeting with Rory soon.'

It was late enough that lamps were being set on the tables as we spoke. Although the cook went off-duty for the night, the kitchen was currently leaving toast-making facilities available in recognition of the odd and long hours we were working with the new intake of patients. It might not sound like much, but hot buttered toast when you are dead on your feet and ravenously hungry is close to being the best food nature can provide. It is quick, hot, crispy, slippery with butter, and filling. It takes no time to . . .

'What? How are we meeting Rory?'

'Lower your voice,' said Merry, 'he's moved into the bed by the window. It's left ajar . . .'

'We are not climbing in the window to the men's ward!'

'Of course not, but we can speak to each other. We can go out the front door, and walk round the building. They only light up the road and the front door, so if we're careful no one can notice. Then we can whisper through the window.'

'Without anyone noticing anything?'

'The nurse gets her tea at eleven p.m. Rory says this one always has two sugars in hers. So he's hidden the sugar. He thinks she'll spend a while looking for it, and that that will give us enough time to outline our plan.'

'We have a plan?'

Merry nodded eagerly. 'Rory and I came up with it today. Rory's going to pretend his leg is worse than it is.'

'But it'll be on his chart at the end of the bed.'

'Yes, well, we're pretty sure it's not a doctor. Rory says they have to swear an oath "to do no harm" when they become doctors. And if anyone else picked up a chart and studied it, he'd notice. He admits he rarely notices anyone in a white coat. So as long as he looks unhappy and miserable it should work. I said this wasn't the same as the other chap, but he seems to think morbidly depressed is as good as physically maimed. Or at least in the killer's view.' She shoved the pudding towards me. 'Here, eat this. Hurry!'

Obediently, I started to spoon food into my mouth. I felt almost as hungry as I felt tired. Spending every moment wired and worried takes a greater toll than I had imagined. I missed having a partner. I missed having a superior officer I could lean on. I had no idea how Merry's plan would work, and I didn't particularly want to know. I wanted to go to bed.

'So as long as he makes it look as if he's bound for a life of misery it's almost certain the killer will come after him.'

At this point my usually reliable swallowing mechanism failed. Merry thumped me hard on the back until I exhaled two currents and reacquainted myself with breathing. 'The killer will what?' I said faintly.

'You know, try it on with Rory. Only he won't be low, miserable, and waiting to die. He'll give them a jolly good thump and catch them. Job done.' She sat back with her arms folded as if this sorted out the problem entirely.

I do try to be fair, and I realised that this was not a million miles away from what I was doing with Wilkins. However, my plan had Hobson as a back-up. It had been thought through. There was risk, but calculated risk. Whereas I found Merry's plan as idiotic as ironing a banana to stand it in a vase.

I pushed my plate away from me. The pudding, after almost killing me, had lost its attraction. 'How do you suppose the killer will attack Rory.'

'Oh, that's easy. They're going to inject him with morphine. You must have heard how much has gone missing.'

'Don't you think it would be a foolish killer who made his theft so obvious?'

Merry frowned at me and her eyes darkened.

'For example,' I continued, 'if I worked in a hospital and I was going to kill someone with morphine, I'd steal it a bit at a time, so it wasn't noticeable. A tiny bit here, a tiny bit there. I'd take it off injections I was told to give. Holding back a little at a time, until I'd built up enough to kill a man. Then I'd use it. I wouldn't shout about my plans by stealing a large bottle of the stuff.'

'Yes, but you're naturally devious and duplicitous,' said Merry. She didn't make it sound like a compliment as Fitzroy would have done. 'An ordinary person wouldn't think like that.'

'I'll agree,' I said, 'that killers are often ordinary people – ordinary people driven by some passion or cause or loss, or even greed – but that doesn't make them stupid.'

'Really?' said Merry, losing the frown and now wide eyed in fear. 'Killers are ordinary people – like you or me?'

'Can be,' I said. 'If someone harmed Michael, what would you do?'

'Gut them like a fish,' said Merry without hesitation.

'See? Everyone has pressure points.'

Merry shook her head. 'I don't like the way this conversation is going. Let's go and talk to Rory. He'll know what to do.'

I wasn't prepared for quite how offended I would feel when she said this. I bit my lip before I made some rash comment about having personal experience in killing (for the Crown). 'I know you work or worked with Major Fitzroy,' said Merry clearly reading my face, 'but it's men who know about killing, isn't it? It's not the kind of thing a woman can understand. You forget Rory's not a butler now. He's a soldier. He's seen action.'

I gave in. The sooner I spoke to him and scotched this ridiculous plan the better. 'Let's go,' I said.

We handed our dishes back into the kitchen. Merry made some unnecessary comments about how tired we both were and how we were about to head to the dorm. Fortunately there was no one present from our dorm to check. I insisted we took our dark cloaks to cover our white uniforms.

'I think that went well,' whispered Merry as we headed for the lobby. 'I could have been an actress.'

I smiled. 'Definitely,' I said. 'You would have been excellent in pantomime.' I speeded up so she had chance neither to reply nor punch my arm. The lobby was in half darkness, but the corridor beyond was bright with light. The telephone stood on the table, unattended once more. I was beginning to be sure it had been intended for me from the start. I took a rag I'd left from last time in the top drawer and opened the front door. I put the rag over the lock with a bit hanging out the front. Hopefully pulling on this would work again and open the door for us. It wasn't a sure-fire trick, but it was the best I could do. I didn't want to be climbing the ivy again tonight. Besides, I had no idea if Merry could climb.

Once we were outside, it was Merry who set the pace. She practically jogged off, she was so eager to have Rory explain things to me. I followed her, occasionally steering her by the shoulder into the more shadowy path. Then ahead I saw light spilling out from the ward. Merry was about to turn the corner, but I caught her and this time held her back.

'They'll see us,' I said. 'Even if the nurse is away one of the other patients may be asleep. We have to stay below the level of the window.'

'That would mean crawling in the mud,' said Merry.

'If you want to turn back now I have no objection.'

Merry's reply was no more than a huff. She knelt down on her hands and knees and crawled till she was under the open window. I put my cape inside–down on the ground, so only I would see the mud afterwards, and rolled myself up in it This kept my uniform clean and meant even when I wore the cape no one would see the stains on the inside. I was hoping that before they came around to cleaning capes, an outer garment not worn on the ward and low down the laundry lists, this would all be over.

The grass crumpled beneath my cape. Merry gave into the necessity of sitting, and in doing so showed grass stains across the front of her skirt. This was far worse than mud. Mud washes out easily. I sighed. We were going to have to get rid of that uniform and replace it.

The evening breeze carried the scent of jasmine, and in another time I might have enjoyed going into the park, lying on the grass and looking up at the stars.

Merry gave me an unfriendly glance. If she'd bothered to ask me I would have shown her what to do, but I hoped it might show her rushing in was not a good way of operating. 'Rory,' she hissed.

I didn't imagine he would hear her, but immediately the reply came. 'You're late. Is Euphemia with you?'

'Yes,' I said.

'Have you explained the plan?'

'Yes,' said Merry. 'She doesn't like it.'

'I think you're putting yourself in danger,' I said. 'We don't know this killer will use an injection. They might put poison in the tea. Or create some kind of medical situation you can't survive.'

'I'm not worried about the danger,' said Rory. 'I can handle myself.'

'You can handle poisoned tea? How would you detect that?'

'It would taste wrong,' said Merry. 'You're trying to look for flaws. Is it because it isn't your plan?'

'No,' I said taken aback. 'I don't want either of you to get hurt.'

'We can't do nothing,' said Rory. 'I've seen one man die needlessly in here. I won't see another. If I can stop just one death then maybe this – everything – has a purpose.'

I could hear the pain in his voice. 'I can't begin to imagine what you've see Rory, but –'

He cut me off. 'Don't patronise me, Euphemia. Since I left your husband's service I have acquired a great many skills, and I have changed. Changed in ways you could never understand.'

It was then I knew there would be no stopping them. Both Merry and Rory had cast me as the enemy in their plans before they'd even spoken to me. On some level they must know how desperate their action was, and the knowledge that a few wiser words could shatter their scheme made them unwilling to listen to anything from me. Another whiff of jasmine failed to console me. I heard the call of a night bird, and suddenly wished myself back at White Orchards away from all of this. I could do my job, but risking assets – assets that weren't even technically under my control – made me feel sick.

'Look,' I said, 'I realise you're going ahead regardless of what I think. What can I do to help make this as safe as possible for everyone?'

'I'm going to ensure I'm on the ward,' said Merry.

'But –' I stopped and swallowed the word. 'Didn't the last attack happen during the night? Would you consider asking to be swapped to nights? You could say you are realising this will be the career for

197

you for the rest of your life and you want to get as much experience as possible during training.'

'That's not a bad idea,' said Rory. 'But wouldn't night training be included later on?'

'I expect it would be,' I said, 'but I rather think in these times training might be rushed through and auxiliary nurses sent out to clearing hospitals.'

'You mean rather than let us finish training?' said Merry.

'I don't know,' I said truthfully. 'I have a gut feeling they're going to need a great many medical people in the near future – nurses in particular. Although right now they won't want females anywhere near the front lines. I expect they will call on the VADS eventually, but even that might not be enough. Besides, outside the army any-one can call themselves a nurse. You don't even have to pass an exam. Though no one in their right mind would hire someone who didn't have decent references.'

'Do you think we are some kind of experiment?' said Merry.

'All very interesting, girls,' said Rory, 'but not relevant. I can't think of anything Euphemia can do to help. She's not been available for most of our talks.'

I didn't rise to the challenge. I'd thought of something I could do that might help a bit.

'So we go forward as we planned,' said Merry.

'Yes,' said Rory. He sounded as definite as only an ex-butler can.

'Good luck,' I said. I knew they were going to need it.

I told Merry how to re-enter the building and leave the rag in the lock. I watched her close the door and the rag disappeared. I sighed. I didn't think she had done it deliberately, but it meant I'd have to climb in through the window. I needed to wake myself up.

I set off at a brisk pace, wearing my cape inside out so I didn't stain my uniform, and taking deep breaths of clear night air. By now I'd visited a number of countries and different towns, and with the exception of frosty Alpine air, I don't think there is anything more invigorating on this planet that a dose of fresh country air – especially if there are no cattle farms nearby. I hadn't noticed where the jasmine had been planted, but there had to be bushels of it somewhere. I seemed to recall there was a variety of jasmine that only flowered at night. Certainly the kind they had down here was almost intoxicating. Then I smelt something slightly different. That pungent tarry smell that catches you at the back of the throat, and speaks of home-made cigarettes made of brown threads rolled in paper. Our local shepherd, when I'd lived in the vicarage, had smoked them. They'd fascinated me. I used to sit and watch him roll them until my mother found out and sent him packing.

I diverted my path. I followed the smoke, ready to be indignant if necessary, but inside rather hopeful. It took me back round to the door by Rory's window. I kept away from those. I spotted the orange glow that meant someone else was hiding in the shadows tonight. Who it was and whether they were only having a noxious, but harmless, smoke, I couldn't tell. I slipped into the shadows. I stood still and closed my eyes for a few moments to accustom my sight to the darkness. Then I approached the figure as quietly as I could to get a better look. It didn't take me more than a moment to recognise Cuttle. I moved as close as him as I dared, and said, 'You've saved me a walk. I was . . .'

I got no further because he jumped in the air, tossing his cigarette away. He gave the small shrill cry of a six-year-old girl who has dropped her lolly. I clapped my hand over his mouth. (Fortunately, he was not a tall man) 'For heaven's sake, Cuttle, it's only me. What are you doing out here?'

I removed my hand. His mouth had left an unpleasant dampness on my palm. 'I were 'aving a smoke,' he squeaked in a slightly lower register. 'You damn near frightened the life out of me.'

'Guilty conscience?' I asked.

'Bleedin' hell, lady, you know I have.'

I came round in front of him. 'Actually I had no idea if you felt guilty about what you had done.'

'Yeah, well, I did. Anyways, your lot 'ave got me old mum sorted, so I'm grateful. What do you want me to do now?'

'I have a problem,' I said, 'that I think you can solve.'

'I don't know about that,' said Cuttle, his voice now almost back where it belonged, 'I ain't that smart. If I were you'd never have caught me.'

'I want you to keep an eye on Rory McLeod on Surgical Ward Six. Day and night. If you can't be there, get one of your fellow orderlies to do it. Someone you trust. Or at least have known for a while.'

'Why, what's this fellow going to do?'

'Oh, he's not going to do anything. He's quite safe.' I heard a small sigh of relief. 'It's the person who wants to kill him I want you to look out for.' This time I clapped my hand over his mouth before he squeaked. 'Calm?' I asked. He nodded and I released him.

'Look,' I said, 'as far as I am concerned you can make your observation as obvious as you like. If that puts the killer off from approaching him, all the better.'

'So if this villain sees me or a mate watching he'll clear off just like that?'

'Pretty much, Cuttle.'

'He can't want to kill this Rory much then.'

'And I very much don't want him to be killed. In fact, if he was I might become rather annoyed – and when I'm annoyed . . .' I trailed off to let Cuttle use his imagination (if he had one) to fill in the blanks.

Cuttle swallowed so loudly, even in the darkness I could tell. 'I'm guessing if anything happens to this Rory then things might go badly for me.'

'See, you are a smart bloke.'

'All right. Message received.'

I slipped back into the shadows, waiting until Cuttle was unsure if I had left, then slowly made my way back to the front of the building. Then, because I had no other option, I climbed up the dratted ivy again.

Chapter Twenty-four

Griffin

The morning came all too soon. Everyone else was enjoying a hearty breakfast in the refectory. I could barely eat. My brain was far too busy with plans and counter plans. There were so many unknowns and so many unpredictable factors in play that I felt quite dizzy trying to hold them in my head.

The first ploy to catch the traitor in the spotters was laid. Hobson had had the news that Major Fitzroy was on his way by telegram yesterday (sent by Cuttle. In reality we had no idea where Fitzroy was or even if he was still alive). I hoped this would have the traitor wriggling in his skin. Facing his old commander, who he had betrayed, should at least make the traitor twitchy. Today I had to set up the second phase of the entrapment. Wilkins knew something about who it was, but would only tell Fitzroy. Now I had made it look as if Fitzroy would shortly arrive it was my task today to ensure that I had 'salted the mine' enough and that the others also knew that Wilkins wanted to talk to Fitzroy. These two pieces of information together would, I hoped, push our traitor to action. I'd deliberately set the plays out in this order, so that the news Fitzroy was coming came first. This, I felt, made it seem less like a trap, but would still tighten the metaphorical thumbscrews on the traitor.

I'd forewarned Hobson and set him to guard the younger soldier. That he was in the next bed made him the best option. He was also savvy enough to know that if anything did happen to Wilkins I would be looking at him as the traitor. Although, if my gut was anything to go by, it wasn't him. He had a coldness about him, but even more than the others showed a warm-hearted compassion to the badly injured Wilkins.

What I feared most was the traitor was a coward. It might be that they would rather harm themselves than kill Wilkins. There is a great deal of difference between feeding information to the enemy and actually sticking the knife in one of your own. We needed the traitor alive. We needed to know who had set him to his task, to whom he had relayed their location and how.

And then while all this was brewing – a matter of national security no less – Merry and Rory were laying a trap for the killer they suspected worked in the hospital and was hastening the end of desperate and dying men. They had no proof other than one badly injured but recovering man had died in his sleep. That and Rory's gut feeling, which I felt was at least a little spawned from his old anger with me, and possibly even his intention to show he could do my job better than I. Although Merry knew I had worked with Fitzroy, it was only Rory who knew I had become an agent of the Crown. I could have left them to their games, but with a bottle of morphine having been stolen from the supplies of the hospital I couldn't discount their fears. As I couldn't be in two places at once, I had asked a black marketeer whom I was blackmailing into working for me to obviously watch Rory. Merry was also going to ask to be on night duty to help.

Everything felt extremely out of my control. I kept making plans and trying to shepherd people into their roles. However, rather like eels, every time I thought I had everything lined up, they somehow squirmed out of their assigned boxes and out of my control.

'I'm going to go and find Matron and ask about night duty,' said Merry to me, breaking in on my thoughts. 'Do you want to come with me? You're not due on shift for a little bit.'

I pushed my eggs to the side of my plate and left my cold toast lying in the middle of a puddle of cooling yolk. As I handed my dishes to the server I wondered how I had ever thought I could eat such foulness.

'I think she should be in her office, don't you?' said Merry, taking my arm and steering me towards the exit. 'She'll be teaching the new intake after breakfast, won't she? I suppose the fact they have another intake means we've done well.'

'Or they need them,' I said, only half listening as she prattled on. I understood Merry was nervous with authority figures. She'd been a serving maid when we had first met – but then so had I. But I had come down in the world then, and Merry was on the rise now. I only respected authorities who had earned my respect – although I knew how to keep my head down if required. Merry, on the other hand, was genuinely terrified of Matron. 'You'll be fine,' I said to her. 'You are excellent at nursing. I think it is worth considering whether you want to do this in the longer term – even after the war. You may have found your vocation.'

'Do you think so?' said Merry. She was looking pale and younger than her years. This was no way to ask Matron to let her look after a Ward on her own. It had daunted me, and I had had the benefit of field first aid training – enough to know that if something went wrong I could probably keep any of the men alive until help came. (Something of a necessity considering Fitzroy's recent proclivity to get injured.)

I stopped Merry by holding onto her elbow. 'What's wrong?'

'It's what you said about . . .' I didn't hear another word. Over her head, coming towards us, I saw a doctor in a white coat. Except this doctor was the double of Fitzroy's man Griffin. As he came close to us. He nodded to me. 'Euphemia,' he said and passed on by at a quick pace. My surprise made me far too slow to intercept him.

'Griffin,' I said almost under my breath.

'Oh, for heaven's sake,' said Merry. 'Why bother to ask me if you don't care!' Then she stormed off. I saw her rap hard on Matron's door. Then she opened the door and walked smartly in. I had no idea what I had done, but I suspected her anger would allow her to carry the day. She certainly seemed confident when it came to the door. All she had to do was carry that confidence on to face Matron.

I knew she would tell me later all about it.

I hurried down the corridor, not running, but moving as quickly as I could without actually doing so. Where had Griffin gone and what on Earth was he doing here? I could see no sign of him ahead. I stopped pole axed by the thought that Fitzroy might already be here. I turned and headed straight to Ward D. It would be just like the wretched man to turn up and spoil my entire plan. Just because I said he was coming in a telegram – did he have some kind of a watch over the postal services to see if his name was mentioned. I shook my head, drawing a few curious looks from a group of nurses heading towards the operating area. I was certain Fitzroy would love such a thing, but much though he valued his own importance and influence, there was no possible way he was that important and able to do such a thing. I was being paranoid.

I stepped outside into the still cool air of what promised to be a lovely day. As I came into sight of the door to Ward D, I saw the tail end of a white coat flicker as the person wearing it disappeared through the door. Could that be Griffin? I could feel my heart beginning to race. What was going on?

I walked into the ward, my gaze automatically going from side to side to see how the patients were doing. Wilkins winked at me from his bed. Hobson nodded. The other men observed me in the way they did any passing nurse. In other words, my identity mattered less than my form. The sister looked up and greeted me with a smile. It was the first time she had seemed genuinely pleased to see me. I tried to adjust my face to a similar expression. I clearly failed.

'What's wrong Stapleford? You look like you've seen a ghost,' she said in her usual speaking voice. Then she lowered it so that only the two of us could hear, 'You know how important it is we appear cheerful before the patients.'

'I'm so sorry, Sister,' I said. 'I thought I saw someone I knew, but by the time I got there they had gone. It was a bit of a surprise,' I finished vastly understating the matter.

It was at this moment that I saw Dr Carlisle and Griffin walk behind Sister's desk, their heads close in deep conversation. If Fitzroy hadn't drilled into me over and over again to block major emotions and assess them before I let them show, I'm pretty sure my jaw would have bounced off the floor. The tiny hope that Griffin might have a twin brother was squashed immediately by rationality. 'We seem to have a new doctor on staff?' I said brightly as if I was trying to talk of other things.

The reality was that I knew nothing of Griffin. As far as I knew he had appeared from nowhere. Fitzroy had never told me where he had acquired his batman/confidant. He had only said words to the effect that Griffin was deeply in debt to him. As I stood smiling at Sister, all my suspicions about Carlisle (which were really no more than a gut feeling he 'wasn't right') flooded back. Could Griffin, who had been with Fitzroy no more than a few months, be in league with the enemy? Could he know who the traitor was? Could he and Carlisle be planning the escape of the traitor?

I bit the inside of my cheek to pull my panic into check. Although all worthy questions, my mind was spiralling out of control. I needed information and Sister was talking.

'. . . worked in the same hospital briefly after they qualified,' she finished. I'd missed it all.

'I see,' I said. 'Do you want me to start with the morning teas?'

Sister checked her watch. 'Yes, at once. We've been chatting far too long. On you go, Stapleford.'

I walked briskly in the direction of the kitchen, then veered right behind her desk. Through the window I could see Griffin and Carlisle standing outside talking. Carlisle had his hands in his pockets and Griffin was gesturing expansively. Then he took a cigarette box out of his pocket and offered Carlisle one, who accepted. Now, my irrational mind jumped to him giving Carlisle a poisoned cigarette. Should I rush out and intervene? My breath was coming in bursts now. I was on the very edge of hyperventilating.

With a strong effort of will I stepped away from the window and went into the little kitchen. In there I ran my wrists under the cold water tap and splashed my face. I felt slightly nauseated. I recognised this as my body coming down from an adrenaline spike. I found a cup and poured myself some water. I turned the urn on and sipped the water while I waiting for it to boil. The cups and teapot was already set out on the tray. I'd started doing this when I brought the tea things back to wash, and whoever came after me had clearly adopted the habit.

I focused down on my concerns. I felt out of control. I wasn't thinking clearly. I needed to refocus. The best I could do for now was trust Fitzroy's judgement in employing Griffin. He'd been in this game a long time. Also, Griffin had acknowledged me by name, clearly meaning for me to notice him. He had signalled he was here, possibly in disguise, but he wasn't hiding from me. That also had to be a sign to the good. What I had to do was complete my mission and my next task was to ensure that all the spotters knew Wilkins was keen to talk to Fitzroy.

I made the tea in the pot, adjusted my smile, and rolled the trolley out onto the ward. As the cups clinked across the bumpy linoleum eyes opened and heads raised. Tea was an event on the ward. I started with the contained upper ward, which I usually did last, leaving cups for nurses to administer to the more confused patients. By the time I reached the spotters they were all sitting up in their beds as eager as dogs in a butcher's shop. ' 'Ere, Nurse, you better not have given all the good biscuits to 'em nutters!' called Potter.

'Enough, Corporal,' said Dwyer stiffly, 'let the good lady do her work in piece.' He then leered at me in his usual lewd manner, quite undermining his speech.

'All right, Algernon, all right,' said Potter.

'Don't you be calling him that,' interjected Lecky. 'He don't like people knowing he's called Algernon. Especially the ladies.'

'Understandable,' said Potter, 'I mean, if I were called *Algernon*, I wouldn't want people to know I was called *Algernon*.'

'Enough,' roared Dwyer, 'must I instruct you on how to address your superior officer?'

'Oh yes,' said Potter, 'I'm sorry. I'd forgotten you had a bit of a thing about rank.'

'Now you mention it,' said Lecky, 'I seem to recall that too. Didn't mean to stir up bad memories, *sir*.'

'If I could get out of this bed I'd thrash the pair of you,' said

Dwyer. 'Consider yourself on punishment duty the moment you get out of here.'

'I don't believe you're our commanding officer, sir,' said Lecky. 'Not sure you're anything to us at all.'

'I am a Major in the British Army and you are . . .'

I could see Sister rising from her desk. 'Wasn't Major Fitzroy your commanding officer? I heard from Hobson that he's coming to see you, is that right?'

The collapse of Dwyer was akin to all the air being let out of a balloon. 'Is it true?' he said in quiet another, and much fainter, voice. 'I thought Hobson was joking.'

I looked across the ward at Hobson and then back at Dwyer. 'I didn't think so,' I said uncertainly. 'Are you lads playing some kind of a joke? Only you should let Wilkins know. He seems really eager to see the Major – I mean Major Fitzroy again.'

'Yeah, he saved his life,' said Potter.

'Not sure he did him any favours,' said Lecky, sotto voce. 'The lad's not going to have much of a life.'

I pretended not to hear this, but I was surprised. From the expressions on the faces of both Dwyer and Potter they knew all too well what he was referring to. It appeared that Wilkins' condition was an open secret to everyone but Wilkins. How had such personal information become common knowledge?

I passed around the teas for this side of the ward. 'I'm sure you're right,' I said, slipping an extra nice biscuit onto Dwyer's saucer (though it pained me to do so), 'he's excited to tell the Major how well he's doing.' The men exchanged looks, which they sweetly thought I didn't notice. 'After all, I assume he thanked Major Fitzroy at the time. Or was there something else he'd want to tell the Major?' I moved away quickly to the other side of the ward. I've never been good at cooking, but I was fairly sure I'd over-egged that pudding. That was the problem when you had to rush things.

'Didn't realise you had such big feet, Nurse,' said Hobson quietly to me.

I acknowledged this with a small shrug. 'Time scale has moved forward,' I answered just as quietly. He raised an eyebrow at me, and I felt myself blushing slightly. I knew my performance wouldn't have passed muster at an infants' school nativity play, but I hoped the combination of illness and fear would prevent the real traitor seeing through me.

I went round to Wilkins. This time I didn't sit on the bed. Having read about his butterfly skin I thought I was lucky to have got away without hurting him before. Instead I glanced at Sister, who had her head down in notes, and pulled over a visitor's chair to use. (I had never seen one of them occupied and assumed they were here before the special restrictions were imposed on Ward D.)

'How are you doing, Wilkins?' I asked. 'I saved you some of those jammy biscuits you like.'

'Ah, miss, thanks.' With his good hand he took the biscuit off the saucer by his bed and bit into it. 'Ah, that's a right piece of home, that is. Now, if you could only convince Sister to let us have a nice bit of Battenberg or even a slice of the old fruit cake, I'd be a happy man.'

I smiled, 'I may not be much of a baker, but even I know you've picked two of the most labour-intensive cakes to make. The kitchen would never have time.'

'I'll trade down to the occasional tea cake, miss. Do you think if we put it to Sister like that I might get one?'

'I think I will talk to Sister about your desire for cake and see if anything can be down. I am not going to bargain with her. She's far too scary.'

'The ones with the faces of Angels are the toughest,' said Wilkins with a grin. 'They get advances from so many of the men they learn to protect themselves. I reckon you're one tough cookie, miss.'

I stood up. I couldn't bring myself to do anything else to make this young man a target. I felt bad enough about using him already. I vowed to myself that if someone did try to harm him I'd send him a bakery's worth of cakes. 'Stop the flattery,' I said pretending to chide him. 'I've already said I'll ask.'

'Thanks, miss. You're a good 'un.' Then he lowered his voice.

'I reckon you've the right of it too. I need to tell Major Fitzroy the truth. Tell the truth and shame the devil. That's what they say, isn't it?'

I hesitated. 'I don't suppose you would consider telling me?'

'I'd like to, miss, but if we're right and this chap is a rotter – and I never saw that coming, I swear. I mean it doesn't fit . . . makes no sense . . . I'm so sorry, miss, I don't know who here I can trust. But I know I can trust the Major. Hobson says he'll be here soon. I'll do my duty.'

I would have patted his arm, but I didn't dare. I smiled and nodded and started to wheel my trolley back up to the top of the ward so I could start collecting the used crockery. I didn't rush. I needed to ensure I'd given the nurses enough time to deal with the more difficult patients. No one had asked me to help with the men whose minds were more scarred than their bodies – and I was glad of this. There were always points in any mission when I wondered if I could stand the mental strain. I had, of course, but usually because Fitzroy was there supporting me. If things went wrong, if Wilkins or Rory died, I didn't know if I could bear it.

I felt a light tap on my shoulder. Griffin was walking past. He said softly, 'Our mutual friend sends his love.' Then he walked out the door. In the middle of tea duty I could hardly follow him. For some reason this thought seemed hilarious and I had to stifle a giggle.

'I was under the impression you were a married woman,' said Sister as I passed her desk.

'That doctor gave me a message from my husband,' I said, thinking quickly. 'He's seen him recently.'

Sister Evans smiled. 'Ah, that is quite different. I'm glad that he is well.'

After that I collected all the cups and saucers as fast as I could. I could feel a whirl of emotions inside me. Of course I was pleased that Fitzroy was safe – if that was even what Griffin was implying – but I still didn't know the fate of my actual husband. Keeping control of a fast-changing situation – oh, if I'm honest, I wasn't controlling things, all I could to do was try and keep on top of developments – doing this was draining.

As soon as I finished washing the dishes, Dr Carlisle came to find me to ask for my help. 'How's your ability to clean, dress and bandage a wound, Nurse? I know you're still training, but we're short-handed again. The surgeons have stolen half our nurses. Do you think you could manage?'

'Alone?'

'I'll watch you do the first. If you're all right then you can carry on alone. I'm only a shout away.'

I nodded. 'Thank you.'

'For what? Giving you more work? I'm aware you're one of our grafters. Always busy and you always have time for a cheery word with the men. I'm impressed.'

To my surprise he led me to the upper ward. 'Don't worry,' he said. 'I'm so short-handed I've had to sedate most of the upper ward. I won't ask you to work with anyone who isn't.'

The first patient had a leg wound that while not serious was threatening to suppurate. He was a large man, wearing blue-striped pyjamas that strained at the seams. Opening up the leg, which someone had sewn ties along the side of in a rather rough fashion, I quickly saw he was a heavily muscled individual. I imagined getting hit by him would be akin to being kicked by a horse. He gave a grumbling moan as I unwrapped the bandages, but he clearly was heavily sedated. Even through the bandages I could see the wound clearly needed cleaning. I washed it out thoroughly before gently applying salve, a cotton dressing, and then bandaging it so the patient couldn't get into it when he awoke. Carlisle stood over me waiting. It was mildly unnerving, but after I joined the Service I had had some fierce and intensive training – compared to that Carlisle was about as distracting as a pussy cat.

I was tidying everything and preparing the bandage for disposal. There was no way it could be reused.

'Excellent job, Nurse,' said Carlisle. I looked up at him, refocusing my attention. 'You forgot I was here!'

'The wound had obviously had necrotic tissue removed from it before, and I was concerned that it could start bleeding again if I didn't take care.'

'Indeed. You didn't seem at all squeamish.'

I looked at him blankly. 'Do you get squeamish nurses?' I asked.

'Squeamish trainees, yes. They usually leave. You're not one of them. Although Dr Griffin intimated you wouldn't be staying with us for that much longer?'

'I really couldn't say.'

'I appreciate you not lying to me. I should confess, now I have you alone, that I'm your Department's contact.'

I didn't reply.

He chuckled. 'That's all right. You don't have to believe me. I merely pass on anything any of the men say that might be relevant to the Department. It doesn't happen too often. I'm an asset, like you, rather than an agent like Griffin.'

Pride and caution warred within me. Pride won. 'You may have that the wrong way around.'

His eyebrows shot into his hairline. 'You're an agent. I didn't know they used women for anything other than, well, you know, using your charms to get gentlemen to say indiscreet things – and you don't seem that sort.' He blushed. 'Sorry, that was rude. Of course anything done in the name of King and Country is above reproach.'

'I don't *use my charms*, as you put it. I'm mainly sent in to observe.' That was my attempt to rein in my pride. I knew I shouldn't have said anything at all.

'I suppose that makes sense,' said Carlisle. 'People rarely suspect a woman – especially men. You must be very brave.'

I shook my head. 'I'm usually too busy to get scared. You don't realise what you've been doing generally until after you've done it. You do what is necessary.'

Carlisle nodded. He looked if anything more wary of me than before. 'Can I leave you to deal with the bandages or do you have something mission-specific you're meant to be doing?'

'No, I can do them,' I said.

I saw his mouth open slightly, but then he shut it again, nodded, and walked away. That he hadn't given in to temptation and asked me what my mission was made me inclined to believe he had had contact with the Department.

I worked the rest of the morning changing dressings. Carlisle hadn't exaggerated when he said they were understaffed. Sister repurposed me to deliver lunch to the patients. I happily did this, looking for one of them to show a sign of wariness or concern, but they all seemed much as before. Whoever this traitor was, if he existed, he was a cool customer.

I chose to have my lunch on the ward, and then went back to finishing the dressings. It was easier not to think of the patients when they were sedated and it meant I could concentrate on their wound. When wound and personality came together – as they had done for me with Wilkins – I tended to find myself caring, and that was distracting. I did my best and after a while I fell into a rhythm that allowed my mind to focus on other thoughts. The most intrusive was the realisation that no one, least of all me, was certain either Fitzroy's traitor or Rory and Merry's killer were real.

I stopped to do afternoon tea. Again, I tried to take the mood of the lower ward, but if someone was sweating under the collar they weren't showing it.

I was washing up the dishes, when Sister came to find me. 'Nurse Stapleford, you look as if you might drop to the floor any minute. I don't know what Dr Carlisle was thinking making you attend to those patients. Your work was excellent, but I am sure it was also exhausting. Working with those kinds of injuries demands a mental fortitude not everyone has. I'm happy to let you go for this evening. I suggest you find some supper and get an early night.'

I didn't protest. 'Thank you, Sister.'

As I walked out of the ward I nodded almost imperceptibly to Hobson, who returned the gesture. I had left a guard for Wilkins and it was the best I could do. Now, as long as Merry had actually managed to get on the night shift to watch over Rory, maybe I could actually get some sleep.

The night was cool after the intensity of the ward. I could still smell jasmine. The moon was half full, like a soft milky cheese. It had got much later than I realised. I started to walk round to the front of the building. This was the darkest part and the stars came alive with sparkly white fire above me. A figure stepped out in front of me.

'Hello, Euphemia, did you miss me?'

Chapter Twenty-five

A spot of dinner

I dropped my centre of gravity immediately, raised my guard, leaned forward slightly, and shifted my weight slightly onto the balls of my feet.

'Alice. Alice. Calm down. It's me.' Fitzroy stepped out of the shadows. I gasped. Although his arm was no longer in a sling, he was thinner and paler than when he had turned up at White Orchards. He wore casual country tweeds, and looked more than a little rustic. I could see the shadow of gingery-red growth on his chin.

'You look awful,' I said.

'It's nice to see you too.'

'Bertram?'

'Is safe.'

I felt as if the world had been lifted off my shoulders. I had an absurd impulse to burst into tears, but I controlled it.

'Fancy a spot of dinner? I know a nice little place down the coast. Or do you have things in play you can't leave?'

'No. But isn't it rather late?'

'Oh, they'll open for me. You hop to it and get out of that uniform – not that you don't wear it well – and I'll telephone ahead.'

Within half an hour I was sitting in the front seat of Fitzroy's new car. 'Do you like it?' he asked. 'I felt the old one never quite got over the Monaco race.'

'I hope that's not a stricture on my driving?'

I heard the laugh in his voice as he answered, 'As I recall, you only really drove on the way back, and I did say the race. More than

214

my life's worth to suggest your driving is anything other than,' he paused, 'adequate.'

My response was overtaken by our arrival in front of small inn that stood alone in its own grounds, with a sea view. It looked as if it had been the retirement home of some former admiral as at its centre was a tower rising two stories above the rest of the building. The top of the tower was glass-sided, and I could just make out what appeared to be a telescope. The building itself was chunky, grey stone, not particularly remarkable, but one of those that presents a narrow face and continues on and on behind the façade. A gravel drive swept up and around it, with trees outlining the edge of its small park.

For once Fitzroy came to help me down. But although I took his hand for balance and out of politeness, I didn't dare rest any weight on it, he looked so very frail. He grimaced slightly at that, but refrained from comment. As he saw me looking around, he said, 'Rather like a killing ground, isn't it?'

'Certainly no one could approach this place without being seen.'

'I think it's about a hundred years old,' he said, ringing the door bell, 'but it's always been sound practice to fortify yourself if you live on the coast.'

Our coats were taken and we shown through to an empty dining room by a gentleman so bland and discreet, it took all my concentration to notice his hair was brown and his eyes blue. He murmured encouragement as he led the way to a table, but I didn't catch a single word. He left after pulling out the chair for me.

'I'm afraid we'll be getting what we're given,' said Fitzroy. 'However, we will have the room to ourselves and I imagine the fare is better than you got at the hospital.'

'It wasn't bad. Hearty and plain, but they did a good job. Portions that would even satisfy you.'

'Goodness,' said Fitzroy, 'maybe you haven't been having as hard a time as I thought. Once we've got our entrée you can tell me all about it.'

After a rich chestnut soup accompanied by soft brown rolls and creamy country butter, we were both presented with steaks and a large variety of accompaniments in bowls, so we could help ourselves. Fitzroy politely waited for me to take a couple of carrots before he began piling his plate to most uncivilised heights. 'Tell me,' he said.

So I told him everything that had happened. I told him about enlisting Merry's help, but then finding she and Rory were scheming together, based on very little (if any) evidence. He grinned widely at my frustration. 'Reminds me of the time you and various assorted males of yours were assets of mine. Difficult doesn't even begin to cover how wayward you lot were.'

'I do appreciate that a bit more now.'

'It is also quite gratifying to hear how you are handling them. Some of my efforts must have rubbed off on you.'

Then I told him about the spotters, and in an emotionless tone commented on Wilkins' fate.

'Damn,' said Fitzroy, 'If I'd have known that would have been the outcome for the boy I might have put a bullet between his eyes myself.' He must have seen the shock on my face. 'I doubt I would have,' he said more gently. 'But there are some men I have known who would have asked for that fate rather than live as an invalid for the rest of their lives.'

'Would you?'

Fitzroy shook his head. 'Pretty sure I'll end my time by someone shooting me. I rather hope it's when I'm a hundred, and it's by a husband in his thirties.' He gave me a wink. 'But it will probably be another spy.'

'You want to go out in a blaze of glory?'

'Not especially,' said Fitzroy, 'but I don't want to die of something that will make my enemies laugh at my obituary. Like choking on a fish bone or tripping over a pot plant.'

I explained how I set up a watch with Hobson and my reasoning. He nodded. 'Sounds fair enough. Do you have a feeling who it is?'

'I don't think it's Hobson,' I said, 'or Wilkins himself.'

'Always consider all possibilities – and after what happened to him, I'd blame him less than the others.'

'But other than that, no, I don't. I find that puzzling.'

Fitzroy finished his steak and reached again for the potatoes. 'Spotters are an odd lot. They can seem cold to outsiders, but with their own kin they have a strong sense of camaraderie. It's not uncommon for them either to compartmentalise their work to the extent that outside of it they have an entirely different personality. Some of them will be the life of the party and others you couldn't trust with your grandmother's teeth. Hospital is a sort of halfway point, I imagine. They're neither on duty nor being themselves. None of them will feel that right in their skin. It would make them hard to read.' He paused to offer me the last two carrots. When I shook my head, he emptied the pot onto his plate, so all the butter in the dish emptied itself over his potatoes.

'I take it you've been back in the field,' I pushed gently.

'Hmm,' said Fitzroy. 'Got a bit short on rations. Have to make up for it now.' He grinned at me, but his eyes stayed cold.

'You're not going to tell me, are you?'

'Not now. When this operation is over – perhaps.'

'So are you here officially?' I asked.

Fitzroy continued to feast, but shook his head. Eventually he said, 'Medical leave,' before wrapping himself around the last of the potatoes.

'So anyway, Merry was describing her plan for catching a killer they had no real proof of, and at the same time as I was thinking how ridiculous it was . . .'

'You were thinking your plan was identically silly, and only based on my admittedly combat-weary words,' said Fitzroy briefly surfacing from a pile of peas.

I nodded. 'I agree the theft of the morphine is odd, but Rory had complained about unusual deaths before that happened. I suppose the killer could have been stealing morphine before and never been caught, but the hospital staff seemed too efficient for that.' Fitzroy nodded and waved the conversation on with his buttery knife to

217

which now adhered a number of peas. I paused, horrified and fascinated to see if he was going to eat off it. He caught my eye and carefully scraped his peas off and pushed them onto the back of his fork. Although all the time his gaze never left my face.

I found myself smiling. 'I've missed you,' I said. 'Weirdly, though, everyone seems to think I'm having an affair with you.'

Fitzroy swallowed. 'That's very emotional of you, Alice.' He beheaded a potato. 'Oh, and if you wouldn't mind writing the names of the people who said that down for me . . .'

'It's more difficult working alone, and when things start happening . . .' I said, hoping to distract him.

'It all goes at once,' said Fitzroy and for once I heard sympathy in his voice. 'Like a set of dominoes, even when nothing is related between operations.'

'Exactly,' I said. 'I had to make up a lot of it on the go – and I'm still not sure Cuttle was a good idea. Lacey was useless.'

Fitzroy shook his head. 'Very good in his own field, but I agree useless in our line of work. He's an investigator. Apparently extremely creative when it comes to persuasion.' He lingered on the last word to ensure I understood.

'Ugh, and he seemed such a happy soul.'

Fitzroy shrugged. 'That kind often is. Nothing to trouble their conscience about – because they don't have one. I'm surprised head office sent him to see you. On the other hand, he's only good when his subject is already caught and tried. I've no doubt you could take him in a fight.'

I paused. Fitzroy had admitted to training Cole, an assassin. I hadn't asked any questions because I hadn't wanted to know. But now he was talking about torture? 'Did you train Lacey?'

The spy's fork ceased being a blur of motion. He held it halfway towards his mouth, frozen. 'Did I what?'

'Did you train Lacey?' I repeated, although in what felt like a much smaller voice.

Fitzroy put his knife and fork down on his plate, and placed his forearms on the table. He leaned slightly towards me, tilting his face to directly line up with mine. 'Did I,' he said with a slowness I found painful, 'train Lacey in the arts of persuasion?'

'Yes,' I said, my voice becoming more mouselike.

'Of course I bloody didn't,' snapped Fitzroy loudly, throwing himself backward in his chair. 'What the hell do you take me for?'

'I'm sorry I felt the need to ask,' I said. 'But if I hadn't I would . . .'

'Always have wondered,' finished Fitzroy. 'Yes, I see that. Never ask another officer – well, anything like that. Either they'll be insulted, or if they have done what you expect it'll be beyond your pay grade to enquire. Asking those kinds of questions is an easy way to make enemies.'

'Are you angry with me.'

'Mildly insulted,' he said and resumed eating.

'There might be pudding?' I said.

Fitzroy's face softened. 'I hope so.'

'You can have it,' I offered.

This made him smile. 'You don't have to forsake your pudding to appease me. I'm not that cruel. Besides, for the first time operating alone you've done pretty damn well. A credit to me, of course. But I don't under-rate your efforts nor the strain you've been under. Hence this –' He indicated the meal. 'Pudding included.'

'And there was I simply thinking you were hungry.' I smiled and received a small ducking of the head, a minor admission on his part that I had said something slightly funny.

'That too.' He got up and went over to the doorway. 'Back in a min,' he said and disappeared.

He returned with the discreet gentleman, who began loading up our dishes. 'Trifle and lemon tart coming,' said Fitzroy. 'Odd combination, but I thought we'd better have both.' When the waiter had gone he plumped two sets of keys down on the table. 'It sounds to me as if you've left everything as controlled as it can be. I think we should stay here and get a decent night's sleep. It doesn't sound as if you've been getting much. Your operation is about to get to the critical stage and you're better to be bright for that. I'll even let you have the better room.'

'Is that what you would do?'

'Or is it because you're a frail female? When have I ever treated you like a normal female, Alice? You know me better than that. And yes, I probably would grab a night away if I could before going into action as it were. If it's safe to take a break, get some relaxation in then, you'll get yourself back up to full operating fitness.'

The waiter arrived with one of the biggest trifles I had ever seen and a large lemon torte. When he'd gone, Fitzroy continued. 'Of course, I might do other things than sleep,' he said with a slight smirk, 'but nothing appropriate for you to emulate.'

'Are you sure?'

'About the inappropriateness? Absolutely,' said Fitzroy taking a slice of torte and then piling it high with creamy trifle.

'No,' I said, blushing faintly.

The master spy looked up and gave me a very cheeky school boy grin. 'So you do follow me.'

'I meant about staying away from the hospital tonight.'

'Oh, that, I thought you'd seen Griffin? I'll give him a ring after dinner and check all is well. He should be able to hold the fort for a while.'

'He's an agent?'

Fitzroy shook his head. 'No, he was a doctor. A GP. Struck off. But he's highly intelligent and will give us a bell if there's a problem.'

'Struck off, and you let him . . .'

'He's hardly going to be operating,' said Fitzroy. 'Plus if anyone asks him anything medicinal he can answer correctly. I rather fancied wearing a white coat myself, but a moment's thought showed me that I could never pull it off. Besides, the old fellow has been missing his doctoring days. I'm sure the smell of blood and disinfectant will set up him right back up.'

'But . . .'

'Oh, and Jack is fine. He's staying in Matron's office. They seem to have taken to each other. Similar features, I suppose.'

He thrust a key into my hand. 'Off to bed, Alice. I'm going to finish off this morsel of trifle, give Griffin a ring, and then I'm up the stairs to bed myself. I'll get the maid to wake you for breakfast. Toodle-pip, old girl.'

There remained a great many questions in my mind, but the thought of a proper bed, with soft pillows, was too much for me. I took the key and left my training officer to his mountain of trifle. The room was lovely, but I barely noticed. I only just managed to get out of my clothes before falling into bed and a deep, comforting sleep.

Chapter Twenty-six

Cometh the hour

We were eating a breakfast that consisted of everything that could conceivably be fried. I rather suspected it had been cooked to the spymaster's order. Fitzroy had insisted I did not have to hurry back, and that he could always deal with Matron if necessary. I was rather looking forward to seeing this battle of wills, and was imagining the stand-off when he said,

'So how do you suggest we bring this all this to a climax?'

'I beg your pardon?' I said as I paused my fork, loaded with sausage, halfway to my mouth.

'Finish this thing off? Shall I show myself and force a denouement?'

'Oh, the mission,' I said exhaling.

Fitzroy raised an eyebrow at me. 'Why whatever did you think I was talking about, Alice?'

'We have to focus on the spotters,' I said. 'I realise Merry will be going off night duty, but finding a traitor in the Service has to rank higher than . . .'

'Rory McLeod's life?'

I swallowed. 'Yes.'

'I agree,' said Fitzroy, spearing a sausage. 'But I think we can ask Dr Griffin to hang around the ward while we do so. He was a junior doctor once, so he'll be used to long shifts. That way he can keep an eye on McLeod, and what's going on around him.'

I felt my shoulders drop from around my ears to a normal level. I hadn't realised I was so tense.

'Still,' said Fitzroy. 'It's good you were able to make that call. Not,' he added, reaching for a piece of bread and starting to mop his plate with it, 'because I don't like McLeod. I don't, as if happens, but that's immaterial. Finding the traitor has potential to save hundreds, possibly thousands, of lives.'

'Oh good,' I said. 'I feel absolutely no pressure now.'

The spy's face broke into the boyish grin that I so rarely saw. 'Welcome to the Service, Alice.'

'I suggest that I go back and let the ward know you're in the building. Hopefully by the time you come down the traitor will have made his move.'

'Why am I here? Solely visiting the men doesn't fit. They know how busy I am.'

'What if I say you'd come to talk to the chief surgeon and hope to pop down later.'

'Why?'

'Because the Service wants to look at the pattern of injuries coming back from the front, and demographically who is most likely to be seriously injured.'

'Bit of a desk jockey's job, that.'

'You look as if you're on medical leave,' I said. 'But if they know you at all, they'll know you would never sit on your hands.'

'I am on medical leave. But yes, I can work with that.'

'You certainly look bad enough . . .'

'Thank you. I admit I'd rather avoid a brawl at present. I have certain tendernesses about my person. However, should such a situation occur, I can, I assure you, still acquit myself favourably.'

We didn't speak on the way back to the hospital. Partly, this was due to that fact that speaking in the countryside while he maintained his usual style of driving meant one was liable to ingest a whole host of insects merely by opening one's mouth, and partly because we both knew we were going to have to play this one by ear. I imagine we were both hoping that each of us would be able to follow the other's lead. Fitzroy had made it clear this was my mission, but I knew if he felt it was all going wrong (he would use a cruder euphemism here) that he would feel bound to step in save the day if he could. I was grateful for this, but I still felt uncomfortable with how much he was letting me have my head.

On arrival I went into the hospital first to change, and Fitzroy disappeared off to speak to whomever. We'd agreed he'd come onto the ward in two hours. In the dorm I found a sleepy Merry, that minute off night shift, preparing for bed. 'How is Rory?'

'All quiet on the ward. There was an odd little man, who kept coming in and out. He always looked over to the corner Rory was in, but never went close. When I questioned him, he said he was an orderly who had lost his bucket. Can you believe that?' She yawned widely. 'I reported him, of course.'

Poor old Cuttle, I thought.

'Where have you been?'

'Major Fitzroy took me out on day release,' I said, getting into my uniform. 'Got a sit-down meal for once. It was odd to have time to chew one's food and not have to bolt it down.'

Merry gave me a frowning look, pulling her head back in and lifting a shoulder. She looked like a wary chicken. 'But you've been gone all night.'

'Separate rooms,' I said. 'With really comfy beds – or at least mine was. I had a glorious sleep.'

'I suppose you do look well rested. Is he staying around long?'

'We didn't discuss it, but I shouldn't think so.' It then dawned on me that if I completed my mission today I would be leaving to see Bertram. That had been the deal. I decided not to tell Merry. I didn't know what would be happening, so it was unfair to upset her unduly.

Merry stopped undressing. 'You know, if Major Fitzroy is around, I might not go to bed myself yet. I'd like to talk to him about what Rory and I think.'

'I did mention it,' I said, 'but he said our mission is critical.'

'Which is?'

I raised an eyebrow at her. 'Not you and Rory's phantom killer.'

Merry put her hands on her hips. 'Then I shall have to go and explain it to him properly,' she said. I almost felt sorry for the spy, such was the mulish expression on her face.

On Ward D everything seemed much as usual. Sister welcomed me back with the good news no one had died that night. She asked me to do the tea round. I noticed she hadn't mentioned cleaning the bedpans. She must have seen the curiousness in my face. 'We have a new trainee from the latest intake. Nurse Sutton. She is now the most junior on the ward and has taken over some of your chores. By rights she should probably do the tea too, but you have a camaraderie with the men, which cheers them but is not overly familiar. It will do her good to observe you. She's far too pretty by half to be on a men's ward.'

Sister was hardly unattractive, and I knew I could scrub up reasonably well, so I was very interested to see what 'almost too pretty to work on a men's ward' was when it was on two legs. I soon found out the answer. When I was filling the urn a young red-haired girl with porcelain skin and violet eyes came in carrying a bedpan. Most of us looked a little dumpy in our uniforms, but by some magic this girl's (she can't have been more than nineteen) uniform clung to her exquisite figure with a form-fitting grace that shouldn't be possible with mere cotton. She was carrying two bedpans. When she saw me and the urn, her mouth formed a little rosebud 'Oh' of distress.

'I'm in the wrong place, aren't I,' she said in a young, but melodious voice. I directed her to the sluice in my coldest tones. She blinked a couple of times, showing me dramatically long eyelashes and brimming tears. 'I'm so sorry,' she said, and half bobbed a curtsey to me, before rushing from the room.

She was, without a doubt, extraordinarily distracting to men and quite the last thing I needed when I was trying to get them to open up to me about their traitorous acts. I could only hope the bedpans from last night were dirty enough that they needed a thorough scrubbing. I found myself smiling at the thought. I then reflected that it was a thought unworthy of a vicar's daughter, but I couldn't quite extinguish it. I pushed my trolley onto the ward.

While Sutton was up to her elbows in suds and excrement I did a quick jaunty tea round, starting with Wilkins. I told him that I had heard Major Fitzroy had arrived in the hospital to speak to the Chief Surgeon. I said, bearing Hobson's letter in mind, he would probably be coming down later to see them on the ward. Hobson overheard me, as I'd intended, and without instruction shouted out to the rest of the ward. Then something completely unexpected happened.

'Sister! Sister!,' yelled Dwyer. 'Help me get up! I must get up! My commanding officer is coming and I'm not greeting him like a child in his cot.' Within moments the rest of lower Ward D were all shouting out the same request. Wilkins, being realistic, said to me he didn't need to get up, but could I find a couple of extra pillows?

The clamour over all became so loud that the patients in the upper ward joined in. Although their responses were less in words and more in shouts, yells and loud groans. Amidst all of this Sister stalked onto the ward.

'DO I NEED TO SUMMON MATRON?' she said very loudly in a voice that suggested that Matron was Beelzebub himself. I had a mental flash of some arcane sign chalked on the ward floor, surrounded by mirror-shine bedpans and an array of black candles.

The lower ward quieted at that, and I saw past Sister a flurry of staff attending to the patients in the upper ward. Clearly Sister had turned her attention first to the ones that were most disturbed by the noise.

'Nurse Stapleford! Can you kindly tell me precisely what is going on?' The implied following sentence *and why you allowed it to happen* hung heavily in the air.

'I believe the men's commanding officer is in the building and may be coming to visit the ward.'

'I don't see why that should cause such an uproar,' said Sister, 'I would expect the Captain –'

'Major,' corrected Hobson in a tight voice.'

'The Major, then,' said Sister not in the least bit cowed by Hobson's dark psychotic stare, 'would *expect* his men to behave in a more ruly fashion.'

226

'If I might add something, Sister. The men feel it is not appropriate for them to meet him lying down. They want to get on their own two feet.'

'I see,' said Sister. She turned on the spot passing a gimlet eye over the occupants of the ward.'

'All of them?'

'Me,' said Hobson, 'Dwyer, Lecky – and Wilkins wants another couple of pillows.'

'Private Wilkins can have his pillows. Nurse, fetch them now please. But as for the rest of you, we will have to see what Doctor thinks. He may permit you to sit in the seats beside your bed, but absolutely no standing. None of you are fit enough.'

I exited to the linen cupboard. How could I have been so stupid? If Sister was right, however much any of the men might have wanted to see off Wilkins, only Hobson would have been able to reach. I pulled down two plump pillows. Unless, of course, Hobson knew differently. Could it be that these men treated illness much as Fitzroy did? Being on medical leave had not stopped him working. He had admitted he'd rather not get into a hand-to-hand situation, but assured me he could still handle himself if necessary. They were all spotters, used to working in difficult and dangerous situations with little, if any, support. Could they have a better idea of how far they could push themselves than a ward sister, who was used to dealing with more standard soldiers?

I headed back to the ward telling myself I was fantasising, only to be greeted by Hobson standing by his bed and yelling loudly for his clothes. His skin was ghost white, but he stood sturdy as a rock. Dwyer likewise stood, but with one hand on the edge of his bed frame for support. The other patients in the ward were hooting and clapping their support. Lecky had sat up and was sitting with his legs over the side of the bed. He had gone beyond white to grey and without thinking I dropped the pillows on the chair by Wilkins' bed and hurried over.

'Lecky,' I said in my usual voice, rather than my friendly nursing one, 'Fitzroy will be unimpressed if you drop dead due to pride.'

Behind me Sister continued to argue with the spotters. I vaguely heard the voice of Dr Carlisle being added to the mix. It sounded like staff, from all areas of the ward, sluice, kitchen and duty room, were milling behind me. I focussed on the man in front of me. Waiting for him to do as I bid.

'You know the Major?'

I immediately realised my slip. 'I've worked for him, yes,' I said. Very slowly Lecky nodded. I helped him raise his feet back onto the bed. He lent back on his pillows and some of the colour returned to his face. He exhaled slowly.

'I feel a right dick,' he said.

I failed to suppress a slight chuckle.

'Reckon you do know him,' he said. 'Woman of your calibre wouldn't laugh at something like that unless she'd been exposed to the Major's much fruitier language.' He gave me a wink, much like his former self.

'He only swears badly when he's cross,' I said.

Lecky nodded. 'Yeah, I get that. He's very good at it, mind.'

'And often cross,' I said with a smile.

'Can't imagine he'd be cross with you often, ma'am,' said Lecky.

I realised my cover wasn't so much blown here, as utterly shredded. 'Be that as it may,' I said. 'He won't be happy to find you lot in a shouting match with the staff.'

'You might want to put your fingers in your ears, Ma'am.'

I saw him inhale deeply, and clapped my hands over my ears. The volume of his voice when it came was immense. The swearing was not quite on a par with Fitzroy's but a passable second. The gist of it was that they should stop wasting the staff's time and do what the doctor allowed. Then he stopped. I took my hands away from my ears. The sudden silence I encountered felt like we had all frozen in time. Then I head the unmistakable sound of the outer door opening and a familiar voice asking, 'Is there a problem here, gentlemen?'

As one all the men saluted. I turned to see Fitzroy standing at the edge of the ward. He was wearing military uniform. He was in the process of taking of his hat and tucking it, along with his swagger stick, under his arm. I went over under the pretence of taking them off him. 'They wanted to be on their feet to greet you,' I said very softly.

'Anything happening?'

'I think I overestimated their current condition.'

'I'll see what I can stir up,' said Fitzroy. 'Thank you, Nurse,' he said in a louder voice and walked into the middle of the lower ward. 'At ease. Shall we let these good people get back to their thankless task of healing you?' No one answered him. 'Well then, sit, lie, fall on the floor for all I care, but get out of the doctor's way.'

If I expected the men to be disappointed by Fitzroy's callousness I was to be disappointed. As meek as little lambs Dwyer and Hobson sat down in their chairs. The rest of the men in the ward lowered their chins to avoid Fitzroy's sweeping gaze, but the spotters were all smiling.

I went to put Fitzroy's hat and stick on Sister's desk. I was momentarily distracted by seeing tooth marks on it.

'Nurse, I need to pop to the latrine,' said Dwyer, coming up beside me. 'I'll take it slow, but I'm not asking for a bedpan now.'

I looked him in the eyes. The ward door was locked. If he was the traitor and looking for a way out there wasn't one. The men's facilities were at the top of the upper ward on the left side of the staff room. Dwyer's gaze became increasingly urgent. He shifted slightly from foot to foot. 'All right,' I said, 'but do take care. Sister will murder me if you fall over.'

'Thanks, Nurse,' he said and shuffled off.

I deposited Fitzroy's possessions on the desk and turned to find him in deep conversation with Dr Carlisle, who gestured around the ward, and then towards Sister. I hovered in the background. Sister caught sight of me out of the corner of her eye. 'Nurse, don't you have anything to do?'

Fitzroy smiled one of his most charming smiles, and said, 'Ah, I think she is waiting for me. Mrs Stapleford and I go back a long way.' He then walked up to be and much to my surprise kissed me on the

229

cheek. 'How are you finding nursing, my dear?' From behind him a number of patients cat-called. Fitzroy ignored them. I tried to do the same.

'It's most rewarding,' I said truthfully.

'If we are going to introduce the entire ward staff,' said Sister, sounding peeved, 'I should introduce Sutton.'

Carlisle must have only come down to the ward in the last few minutes as his eyes widened and his jaw slacken when he saw the Titian-haired vision before him. Fitzroy on the other hand merely glanced over and said, 'How d'you do?' He turned away before she could answer, signalling profound disinterest.

'Mind if I do the rounds, Sister?' he asked. 'I'd like to have a chat with the men I've fought alongside. Rally them on a bit, what?' He smiled again, dripping charm like butter off hot toast.

'Half look as if you should be in a bed yourself,' said Carlisle.

'Technically I'm on medical leave,' said the spy. 'But a quick chat with the men will do me as much good as it will do them.' He dropped his voice, 'They're all still with us then? Dwyer, Hobson, Wilkins and Lecky?'

'Wilkins is the only one giving us concern,' said Carlisle. 'He's in a very poorly state, poor lad.'

Fitzroy did a credible act of hearing this for the first time. 'I'll leave him to last then,' said Fitzroy, slightly louder.

'Fitzroy,' I interrupted. 'Dwyer has gone to the latrine. He'll return momentarily.'

'Hardly of bearing to Major Fitzroy,' said Sister, eyeing me in the same manner as she first had after my afternoon out with Lacey. I sigh inwardly as the remnants of my reputation fluttered to the floor around me once more. It didn't help that Fitzroy caught my eye and winked at me. His lips half curved in a mischievous smile.

Chapter Twenty-seven

Cometh the man

Fitzroy was sat chatting with Lecky, who contrary to his normal self was almost bashful in the spy's presence. I'd worked with Fitzroy in the field, but I'd never seen him command a group of men. I realised he must be rather good at it. The respect and even a rough kind of affection was clearly being displayed. The others in the ward, like Potter, who weren't spotters and whom he didn't know, also received a visit as he went from man to man, if not exactly spreading joy and light, certainly doing something that made his men, regardless of their wounds, perk up remarkably. While he did this I went around slowly collecting the long forgotten teacups and saucers.

Hobson saw me watching Fitzroy. 'He's good with people. Not a skill I've practised.'

I gave him a grin. 'I haven't noticed a problem.'

'Nah, I suspect you're like him in that way. Know how to get along with others.'

I shook my head. 'No, not like that. I can work out what people need or want easily enough and use that,' I said. 'But the Major can charm anything and anyone to do whatever he wants.'

Hobson nodded. 'You'd better watch out then.'

I frowned.

'He likes you,' explained Hobson. 'He likes you a lot. And if I know anything I know he's not the marrying kind.'

I smiled at that. 'I know – and please don't be like everyone else and think we're a couple. We never have been and never will be.'

'Never's an awfully long time,' said Hobson.

I shook my head in a scolding way and moved on. Beyond I could see on Wilkins' eager face his clear desire to speak to his rescuer. It was obvious that he didn't blame Fitzroy for what had happened to him. Something I had wondered. Instead he had a bad case of hero-worship. I decided to leave his teacup be and not disturb him. One way or another I'd be off this ward tonight, so what Sister liked or disliked no longer mattered to me.

I moved on to Sergeant Cobbs. We hadn't exchanged many words. He was one of the sleepiest men there. Even he was watching Fitzroy's progress and the wake of the reaction he left behind him. He ignored me as I remove the used crockery, which gave me time to look up towards as much as I could see of the top ward. Dwyer wasn't back yet. A sense of unease crawled up the back of my neck like a ten-legged spider. Something wasn't right. I looked back at Wilkins and to my astonishment I saw he'd fallen asleep. The excitement must have been too much for him. I crossed to the other side of the ward with my trolley and tried to get Fitzroy's attention.

He loaded a couple of cups on my tray. 'Wilkins has fallen asleep. You'll still speak to him, won't you? Sister doesn't like the patients to be woken.'

Fitzroy said, softly, 'If we don't manage to spook any other reaction it all rests on his word, doesn't it? So what Sister wants can be damned.'

We crossed paths with him moving onto the other side of the ward as I went to pick up Dwyer's empty cup. His empty bed lay there. Even if it was him, I told myself, he can't get out. My unease didn't die down. I had the unnerving prescience that someone was in mortal danger. Fitzroy was about to sit down on Hobson's bed. Hobson was sitting in the chair. His left arm dangled down by his side, on the opposite side to the spy. Unseen. His fist was clenched.

What happened next I saw as if everything moved at a fraction of normal speed. Fitzroy said something. A man on the other side of the ward called out, and as the spy turned his head to see, Hobson's fist rose.

I didn't wait. I half ran, half threw myself to the other side of the

232

room. I collided into Hobson's chair at an angle. Both Hobson and I went flying as it tipped and fell onto the floor. I land diagonally across his upper torso. My elbow was in his throat. My right hand griped that closed fist. Hobson was choking beneath me.

All hell broke loose as staff and patients converged in my direction. By some masterful display of command, which was invisible to me as I was staring into Hobson's face, my eyes two inches from his, Fitzroy quelled the riot and crouched down to open my right hand. Hobson released what he was holding into Fitzroy's hand. It took a moment for me to register what it was. A Saint Christopher medallion.

I removed my elbow at once. I scrabbled backwards for a moment before I felt myself lifted by my waist. 'Alice,' said a voice in my ear. I didn't struggle, but allowed Fitzroy pull me back. Dr Carlisle was on the floor beside Hobson, Sister knelt beside him.

'Back to your stations,' said Fitzroy in a stern voice. He still had hold of me, so people reluctantly obey.

'It's an ordinary medallion, isn't it,' I said.

'I'm afraid so,' said Fitzroy in the same whispering voice. 'I'd better keep hold of you as if you were my prisoner until we get this sorted out.'

'Is Dwyer back?'

Fitzroy glanced behind us. 'Yes. Sitting on the edge of his bed. I couldn't see how he could get out either. And he hasn't. Lecky showed not a hint of guilt. Nothing. He's good, but I'm better.'

'It's none of them?'

'Looks that way at the moment. Shall I say I'm taking you off to military jail?'

I slumped against him as if defeated. I felt him almost give, and moved my weight at once. 'Has she killed him?' said Fitzroy.

Carlisle helped Hobson to his feet. 'Shock and bruises,' replied the doctor. 'In his state that's more serious than it sounds.' He looked at me. 'What the hell did you think you were doing?'

I felt Fitzroy give a slight shake of his head. Carlisle backed down at once. 'Well, we all make mistakes.'

Unfortunately, Sister was in no mood to let this go. If I had thought she had been angry before she was incandescent now. 'I'll deal with this,' said Fitzroy still restraining me.

'With respect, Major, she is one of my nurses and I will –'

'Sister,' said Fitzroy in a tone filled with menace. 'I said I will –'

Only he too was cut off.

'Where are my men!'

Fitzroy and I turned as one, to see Major Cummings, who was meant to be strapped down, staggering into the ward. He had a scalpel in his right hand. He waved it at Sutton menacingly. She screamed and dropped into a dead faint on the spot. Carlisle rushed to her side. Cummings lashed out at him as he passed and a scarlet streak opened in the doctor's right cheek.

'Get in front of him,' Fitzroy commanded.

I ran in front of Cummings. I held up my hands in a gesture of peace. On his face was an expression of great sadness, but as I looked into his eyes I saw no sign of sanity. The sunlight streamed through the window, glinting in diamond points on the small and deadly blade. I concentrated my focus on that. Cummings lurched forward suddenly, thrusting the knife at me. I jumped backwards, raising my hands high and arching the middle of my body away from the scalpel.

'Was it you? Was it you killed my men?'

Drool ran down the side of his mouth, and the voice was hollow. I doubted it was even me he saw. Fitzroy attacked from behind. I moved in immediately and immobilised the hand with the blade.

In moments orderlies had appeared with a restraining jacket. I glimpsed Cuttle's anxious face. But Cummings sensed defeat. I tore the scalpel from his slackened fist. He sagged like a wet rag as the men pushed him into the jacket. Fitzroy stepped back, panting.

'Is it always this lively on your ward, Sister?' he said. I passed the scalpel to another orderly, who gave me an odd look.

The two men helped Cummings back to the upper ward. He was dragged between them like some sad lost thing, barely recognisable as human. I turned on the spot, surveying the ward.

'Where's Dwyer?' I said. 'His bed is empty. Where is Major Dwyer?'

'He is doubtless attending to matters of a personal nature, Nurse,' said Sister. 'Please calm down.'

But Fitzroy was already moving. I headed up the ward and he went downwards. Without speaking we had both realised that Dwyer had not visited the latrines, or if he did, had stopped on the way back to loosen Major Cummings' bonds.'

'Where the hell can he go?' yelled Fitzroy from the end of the ward. The staff also started to search. 'Be careful,' Fitzroy shouted. 'He's a dangerous man.'

Both of us pulled down screens and checked under beds. Sister was not happy. However, Dr Carlisle caught on this was serious and started to help. The cut on his cheek dripped blood, but he paid it no attention. Around then I noticed my hand was bleeding. I decided to ignore it.

I sat up on my heels as a thought struck me. 'You and Griffin were outside smoking,' I said to Carlisle. Neither of us paid any attention to Sister's lament. 'How did you get out?'

'There's a door at the back. Looks like a window. But it's locked.'

'Where's the key?' I asked.

Carlisle rummaged in his pocket and produced it.

'Is it the only one?' Fitzroy and I asked in union. He'd run up to us.

'Yes,' said Carlisle. 'Definitely, I use it for – for meetings with people like Dr Griffin.'

'How thick is the glass?' asked Fitzroy a moment before I was about to ask.

'Thicker than the windows.'

'He'll go for the lock first,' I said.

'Show us,' demanded Fitzroy.

The three of us ran through the ward, and the upper ward, towards a large picture window by the entrance to the kitchen. It had never occurred to me it might be a door. Dwyer stood by it. He had a metal jug in his hand and bashed frantically at the small nubbin of a lock I had never noticed before.

'It's over,' shouted Fitzroy. 'Don't make this harder than it needs to be.'

At this point I realised I hadn't asked him if he had brought a gun into the hospital. I thought it unlikely.

Dwyer looked at the three of us blocking his path. 'No,' he said. 'No. No. NO.' He gave the lock one last thump before he turned to face us. 'I won't go with you,' he said. 'I won't. He'll kill me before you ask your first question.'

'Who will kill you?' I shouted

I'd asked the wrong thing as with lightening reflexes he threw the jug at my head. It struck me on the temple. I felt a jagged pain and then my legs decided to fold up on themselves and I went down.

Fitzroy, in his first false move, knelt down next to me. 'I'm fine,' I said. 'Dizzy. I'm fine.'

'You're bleeding,' said Fitzroy.

'GO!' I shout.

Carlisle had already gone after him.

I opened my hand for Fitzroy to see. He nodded. 'I'll get him. He can't get out.'

I couldn't yet stand, so I watched from my position on the floor. Dwyer dodged and wove between staff. Potter stood and made a valiant effort to catch him, but got thrown back on his bed. Fitzroy didn't run. He stalked towards Dwyer. I could imagine the hatred in his eyes. I knew only the thought of finding out who Dwyer was reporting to stopped him from killing the traitor with his bare hands. A semi-circle of men closed in on Dwyer. I saw Sutton sit up, holding a hand to her head. No one paid her any attention.

Suddenly Dwyer uttered a loud cry and dived through the semi-circle, knocking two orderlies off their feet. He swiped a clean bedpan from the trolley Sutton had brought in. Then he turned again, holding the pan in front of him. I knew what he meant to do. I tried to sit up, but my vision swam.

Dwyer readied to rush the men once more. The orderlies scrambled to their feet, but were barely there before Dwyer charged again. This time he didn't stop. I saw him run full force at the window. I

236

heard the crash of the window as he went through. I couldn't see him from this angle, but I saw the fountain of red that arched high into the sky. I knew he was dead.

Fitzroy immediately forgot about our lost prize and demanded Carlisle attended to me. Still woozy, I was helped to the chair behind Sister's desk. Here against my protests my head was bandaged. The cut I had received when I clutched the scalpel needed to be stitched. When I saw the needle going into my flesh I felt extremely faint again. Fitzroy sat on the desk, knocking all the paperwork to the floor. He tapped my shoulder. 'Look at me,' he said. 'It's always worse watching yourself get patched up.'

For once I was glad to obey, so while Carlisle stitched my hand I looked at Fitzroy. He seemed more worried than cross. I managed to say, 'I'm sorry.'

Fitzroy shook his head. 'These things happen, Alice.'

Carlisle finished his work on my hand. 'She needs rest,' he said,

'I'll have her taken to her dorm,' said Sister. 'Orderlies . . .'

'No,' said Fitzroy. 'She comes with me.'

Sister started to protest, but Carlisle said, 'Don't you see, Susan, she works for him. She's been working for him all along.'

'Is this true, Nurse?' she asked.

I nodded and immediately felt giddy. Fitzroy put an arm around my waist and helped me to my feet. 'I don't believe we need to trouble you any longer with our presence,' he said. He picked up his stick and hat, and handed them to me.

'Did you know there are tooth marks on it,' I said. This seemed very important and I realised I might have concussion.

'Jack,' said Fitzroy. 'Let's go. Griffin can look after you.'

He started to help me across the ward. 'Wait,' I said. 'You should speak to Wilkins. He really wants to.'

Fitzroy turned slightly. 'Only a minute,' he said.

Then we saw Wilkins lying there still fast asleep. 'How could he have slept through all this?' I said.

'He couldn't have,' said Fitzroy darkly. He thrust me on to Carlisle for support and strode quickly to Wilkins' bedside. He stood there completely still for a moment, looking down at the young man. Then he spun on his heel. 'How many pillows were on this chair?' he demanded.

'Two,' I said.

I glanced around the room, but Fitzroy spotted her first. The cleaner – the one who had made me a cup of tea and been so kind when I first started – was heading towards the linen cupboard. In her arms she clutched a pillow.

Chapter Twenty-eight

Cruel to be kind

She started to run, but Fitzroy was on her in a moment. His grip was strong enough to make her cry out loud. Without reference to anyone else he dragged her up towards where Carlisle and I stood. 'Did you get that room ready that Griffin told you to?'

'The Cell? Yes.'

He pulled me towards him and thrust the now weeping cleaner at Carlisle. 'Lock her up. She's your hospital killer,' he said. 'She'll hang for this.'

'Why?' I asked.

Her face was already blotchy and raw from crying, but she answered me. 'Because they should have died. It's against nature. Against God and all that's right to keep them alive like that. None of them want it. None of them.' At this moment I recalled the conversation I had overheard on my first night here. Fatally, I had paid it no heed.

Carlisle didn't wait to hear any more. He took her away.

'C'mon, Alice,' said Fitzroy. 'Let's leave this place.'

I managed to walk with him as far as Matron's office before I collapsed. The last thing I remember was an excited Jack licking at my face.

When I woke up I was in a single hospital room, painted yellow, with blue gingham curtains that had been drawn to keep out the sun. I was lying, still dressed, on a bed that reminded me my dorm mattress was no more than a doormat. Fitzroy sat in a brown leather

239

chair in the corner. He put down the book he'd been reading and looked at me with a cold scrutiny. Jack was asleep on the foot of my bed. He whiffled slightly as I stirred, but fortunately didn't wake. I didn't think I could stand another face-licking. My whole head felt like a rotten tooth and hurt accordingly.

'Both Griffin and Matron say I can't take you out of here until you've improved,' said Fitzroy. His face became one enormous scowl. It took a moment, but I realised he was more angry at being thwarted than at me.

'I'm awake,' I said.

'Hmm,' said Fitzroy. 'You'll probably only collapse again if you get up and frankly, I'm not well enough to carry you. I take it you partook heartily of the food during your time here? You've obviously put on weight.'

'I tried your trick of eating instead of sleeping,' I said.

I got another 'Hmpf' that sounded not a million miles away from the snorts Jack was making in his dreams. I suppressed a smile.

'They want to feed you now,' said Fitzroy. 'If you manage not to be sick I believe it will be taken as a good sign.'

My stomach rolled over at the thought of food.

'And don't do that again,' said Fitzroy.

'What?'

'Get injured. You're going to have a scar. Bertram won't like it.' The scowl deepened. 'I don't like it. It's distracting.'

'I would have thought Nurse Sutton would have been more distracting for you?' I said, hoping he'd see the funny side.

The spy frowned. 'Sutton?'

'The incredibly beautiful redhead who fainted?'

He nodded. 'Ah, yes. Bit of a stunner.' He paused and half closed his eyes. 'I'm not saying I'd say no if she offered, but when it comes to longer-term relationships I am more interested in a woman's mind. Within reason, that is. Besides, she fainted. Most unattractive in a female.'

'Obviously within reason,' I said trying to keep the laughter out of my voice. 'You're outrageous.'

240

He shrugged slightly. 'I have that reputation.' He winked. Then his face relaxed into a genuine smile. 'Alice . . .'

The door opened. Fitzroy's mouth closed with an almost audible snap. His eyes blazed. Merry, totally unaware that she had interrupted something that Fitzroy obviously thought important, bounced in as much as the tray she carried would allow.

'I hear you're having all the fun,' she said. She cast a professional eye at my forehead. 'That will be as big as an egg by tomorrow.'

I groaned.

'How long will it take to go down?' said Fitzroy from the corner. Fortunately Merry had already set the tray, with the ubiquitous chicken hotpot, chipped potatoes, salads, and treacle tart on my lap, as she jumped a good few inches at the sound of his voice.

'Lord, Major Fitzroy. I had no idea you was here.'

Jack, now fully woken, squirmed towards my tray and the chicken. I eyed him warningly. Jack wagged his tail and stuck out his tongue at me. He made a gruff panting sound. 'Has he been fed?' I asked Fitzroy.

'Probably better than me,' said the spy, looking more surly than sinister for once.

'Do you want to share my pie?'

'Oh no,' said Merry. 'I'll go and fetch the Major another.'

'Make that two,' said Fitzroy, 'and don't forget the pudding.'

The door closed behind her. 'That was very ungracious of you,' I said.

Fitzroy stood up. He walked over to the bed and lifted Jack, gently, on to the floor. He sat down and helped himself to one of my chipped potatoes. 'These are the oddest thing,' he said. 'Now, Alice . . .'

The door opened again and Fitzroy swore loudly and retreated to his chair. Griffin came in. He wore a white coat and didn't seem at all ruffled by his greeting. His eyes widened slightly when he saw my face. 'Is it really that bad?' I asked.

'I'm sure it will be fine, ma'am, but it will look quite – er – spectacular for a while. Colours of an autumn sunset.'

'How long?' repeated Fitzroy.

241

'Two to three days for the swelling, sir and about a fortnight for the bruise to fade. Of course it depends on the person. I am aware Mrs Stapleford is in excellent health, so that may accelerate the process by a day or two.'

Fitzroy's face darkened. 'Damn and blast it!'

'She couldn't be removed from hospital tonight, anyway, sir. At least I wouldn't advise it.'

'Why not?'

'I could speak to you outside?'

'Oh, spit it out man. Alice has been training as a nurse for weeks.'

'I was only going to say,' said Griffin, stealing a look at me askance, 'that it appears Alice has not got a serious concussion, but that it would be preferable for her to be under observation for the next twenty-four hours.'

Fitzroy shrugged. 'So? You or I can watch her? And who told you to address her as Alice?' This last part was distinctly sharp.

'I did,' I said. 'And what Griffin means is that if I did have a concussion I might need treatment – such as an operation.'

Fitzroy paled slightly. 'Is that likely?'

I had the sense not to shake my head. 'No, I hope not. What Griffin doesn't want to say is that such operations, whether or not successful, do not always see the survival of the patient.'

Fitzroy was on his feet. 'What kind of a damned place is this?'

'It's a medical joke, sir. Not to be taken seriously.'

'An operation is only needed in the very worst of cases,' I said hurriedly. 'As I was hit by a flying jug it seems highly unlikely. However, my skull received quite a knock, so it is often better to say fairly still for twenty-four hours or so, to prevent from feeling much worse. Your brain actually sits in a – well, a lake of fluid – it's rather like having bad internal seasickness. I need the waves to calm. Also during that time, if anything is liable to have gone wrong, it should show up.'

Fitzroy addressed Griffin. 'So even with you around I shouldn't move her for twenty-four hours.'

'If at all possible, sir.'

'I'd really like that to be possible,' I said. 'But it's not as if you need to stay. The situation has resolved itself as well — or rather as badly — as it can. Merry's cheerful appearance suggests that no one tried to kill Rory last night.'

'Really? I would have thought his demise would cheer many people,' said Fitzroy.

'Not Merry,' I said, frowning at him, but also smiling.

'So what do you want, Griffin?' said Fitzroy focussing his attention once again on his unfortunate man.

'Doctor Carlisle reports that Margaret Love is calm enough to be questioned.'

'Who?' I asked.

'The cleaner,' said Fitzroy. 'One of the invisible hordes working here.'

'But she must have got clearance to work on Ward D!'

'One of the things I intend to ask her about.'

'I take it Wilkins is dead?' I asked.

Griffin nodded. 'She smothered him with a pillow. However, it appears she must have given him a sleeping draught as there are no signs of a struggle.'

I sat up sharply, rocking some chipped potatoes off my plate and onto the floor. I heard rather than saw Jack gobbling them up. My vision had turned entirely green and my aching head now flashed with pain. I felt the tray lifted off me. My pillows were gently removed and I heard Griffin say, 'Relax now, Miss Alice. You moved too suddenly. You'll be fine.'

I blinked several times. 'Deep breaths,' said Griffin. Gradually my sight came back and the pain receded once more to a dull ache.

'Could you help me sit up a little?' I asked. Griffin did so, and I saw Fitzroy with a knife and fork in his hands. My tray was on his lap. He caught my gaze, and went very slightly red, 'I was worried,' he said.

'Worried to the extent of half my pie and all my potatoes,' I said, 'but not concerned enough to eat the salad.' I looked at Griffin. 'I can't see the tray clearly. Has he eaten the pudding as well?'

'Yes, ma'am. He was clearly very worried.'

'Damn it, Alice. I'm no medical man. I had to trust Griffin to do the right thing. You know how I hate being helpless.'

'It doesn't matter,' I said. 'I'll eat yours when it arrives.' A look of pain crossed his face, and I lay back against my pillows and closed my eyes. Strangely enough I could understand Fitzroy eating my dinner when distressed. It was the kind of thing he would do, if there was nothing else to be done to help.

The door opened and I heard Merry's voice. 'Oh my Lord, she's not . . . she's not.'

'I'm fine,' I said. Griffin helped me sit up properly to take the tray. Strangely enough I did now feel hungry. 'But I think I've proved I'm not up to travelling.'

'No, you're not,' said Fitzroy. He thrust his empty tray at Merry. 'Griffin, stay and watch her. I'll be back later, Alice. I need to talk to you.' Then he got up and went to the door. Jack immediately followed. 'No, guard,' said his master. The dog gave a whine, but curled up again on the floor, watching me. It was quite unnerving.

Griffin took Fitzroy's chair and Merry sat down on the end of the bed. I began to pick at my dinner. Merry began to tell me in an excited manner how nothing had happened on Rory's ward last night. She plied me with questions, which I evaded, asking what had happened to me. Finally, I put down my cutlery and said, 'Merry, it happened on a ward where you need to be cleared and vetted by the government even to get through the door. Why on earth did you think I'd be able to tell you about it.'

'He seems to know all about it,' she said, pointing at Griffin.

'I don't believe Griffin is precisely what he appears,' I said.

'Are you a spy too?' said Merry in tones of awe. 'Like the Major and Euphemia?'

If I could have I would have buried my head in my hands, but since this would have involved a more intimate acquaintance with the pot pie than I intended I did not. Griffin smiled. It surprised me how open he was with his emotions, until I realised that I was used to the way Fitzroy expressed his.

'I am an aide to Major Fitzroy. My duties are various.'

Merry bounced on the end of my bed, much to my distress. 'He is! He is! You're all spies! Can I be a spy?'

'Perhaps,' I said aware of the acidity in my voice, 'that loudly talking about spies in a military hospital where one killer has already been caught is not the wisest notion.'

'You caught a killer!' said Mary.

I looked at Griffin. 'It's not common knowledge, ma'am. They thought it might unsettle the patients.'

'Of course,' I said sighing. 'Yes, Merry we caught a killer. I don't believe it had anything to do with your suspicions. This was an internal Ward D situation.'

'Oh.' Merry's face fell.

'Perhaps,' said Griffin kindly, 'you might like to tell me of your suspicions? I have some familiarity with hospital environments.'

Merry gave him a big grin. 'Well, Rory McLeod, he's the butler – or was the butler – at the Stapleford House where Euphemia and I met when we were maids. Or I suppose I should say we were there first. We had a selection of truly awful butlers. The name Harris still makes me run screaming from any room. But then Rory turned up and he was handsome, charming, and good at his job. He and Euphemia . . .'

'Does any of this have anything to do with what you're speaking of today?' I asked.

Merry turned round. 'I was trying to give Dr Griffin the full picture.'

'Just Griffin will be fine,' said Griffin.

'Oh,' said Merry looking from one to the other of us, 'it's secrets, is it? Oh, very well.' She told of Rory's observation that men in otherwise excellent health were dying and how the man in the next bed, although horribly mutilated, had been recovering, until suddenly he woke up dead. 'Or rather he didn't. If you see what I mean.'

'That can happen when someone has suffered bad injuries,' said Griffin. 'The body gives up. It's had enough.'

'I know,' said Merry, casting her eyes down. 'Both Euphemia and

I have seen that too many times, and we've hardly been here any time.'

'We've been training for months,' I said. 'Time goes quickly when you're busy.'

'Goodness,' said Merry. 'My sister wrote that Michael was trying to stand. I thought she was making it up. He must be so big by now.' This statement ended on a half hiccough, half sob. Griffin's eyebrows rose and he looked at me with wide eyes, clearly signalling 'help'. He was as frightened as any gentleman in the presence of a tearful woman.

'Tell him about Rory's dream,' I said. 'Maybe Griffin can make sense of it.'

Merry perked up a bit at this. 'He had this dream about being trapped underground in tunnels. With earth falling in on him.'

'Had he been working on any tunnels?'

'No, he said not,' said Merry, 'I can't imagine Rory ever digging. He was always so clean and presentable as a butler.'

I stared at her. Merry realised what she had said. 'Oh, I see what you mean. He'd hardly have been butler-ing in the trenches.'

'Did he say if it was a deep sleep he'd had?' asked Griffin.

Merry nodded.

'Were the eyes of the man who died bloodshot when they found him?'

Merry's jaw dropped. 'Yes!' she cried, bouncing on the bed. Pain shot through me head again. I felt very sick. Griffin stood and offered Merry his chair. She shook her head.

'I think Euphemia would appreciate it,' he said.

Merry looked at me holding my head again and moved. Griffin did not sit down. 'Well, ladies, if I accepted the idea there was a killer I would suggest the killer drugged your friend, and probably also the man who died, so they both slept deeply. Then it would be easy to smother the other man with a pillow. Of course his body would have still resisted. Even if he didn't wake, he would have thrashed around. Possibly through his dream your friend heard him and incorporated the sounds into his dream. On some level he knew it was someone being deprived of air.'

Merry swore. Then she said, 'However did you come up with that?'

Griffin shrugged. 'A combination of medicinal and criminal knowledge. I'm not only a pretty face.'

I gave him what I hoped was a stern look. Merry, on the other hand, smiled coyly.

'However,' said Griffin, 'I haven't heard any evidence that there is another killer. From what you've just said, this modus operandi would fit with the killing of Wilkins on Ward D. It could be we have already caught your killer. Or rather, Euphemia and the Major have.'

I raised my eyes to heaven. 'Griffin, she isn't cleared for this.'

'Ah,' said Griffin. 'But if it helps clarify the situation?'

'Why was this Wilkins killed?'

'That's exactly what the Major has gone to enquire of the killer. Once we understand her motivations we will be able to ascertain a lot more about the whole situation,' said Griffin.

'But we won't know anything until tomorrow, at least,' I said. 'Even if we do decide to tell you, Merry.'

'Oh well,' said Merry. 'I'm due on duty any minute. I'll come by at breakfast and say good morning. After that I'll be dead to the world for at least six hours.' She stood. 'Nice to meet you, Griffin,' she said, and I swear I saw her bat her eyelashes at him.

When she left I said to Griffin, 'You do know she's married, don't you?'

Griffin raised a single elegant eyebrow, 'I don't believe it is I who should be remembering that.' He gave a small bow from the neck. 'I'll ensure you are checked on regularly,' he said, 'but you should get some sleep now. It's almost certain there is no concussion, so the next thing you need is rest. If you have no objection, I will intercept the Major, and suggest he talks to you again in the morning rather than later tonight as he inferred.'

'Yes, I think that would be a good idea,' I said. 'My head aches terribly, and it is hard to concentrate.'

Griffin nodded at me, and left very quietly. I placed my head gingerly on the pillow and attempted to find a way to lie that didn't hurt. I couldn't, but I did manage to find a position that hurt less than the others. I closed my eyes, expecting to fall into sleep, but a growing feeling that I was missing something nagged at me. I tried to think, but my thoughts were hazy with dizziness and pain. Eventually I fell into a fitful sleep.

Chapter Twenty-nine

An old nightmare revisits

I was dreaming a dream I had had a long time ago at a lodge in the Highlands when still in service to Richard Stapleford, Bertram's villainous elder brother. In my mind's eye I saw rows and rows of men marching. As before, my first thought was they were marching to war, but a second look showed me their fish belly white faces and their black sightless eyes. Then I knew I was watching an army of the dead leaving this plane of existence. My dream, again, swooped in and focused on one face – it was Rory McLeod. I woke with a start to find myself drenched in sweat.

My hair clung stickily to my forehead, and the small of my back felt damp. I sat up with some difficulty. The light from the moon was all that lit the room. The curtains had unaccountably been left open and I could see out into the gardens beyond. Quiet and peaceful outside, inside there was only the low background hum of the hospital at night. Faint footsteps whispered in the distance from soft-soled shoes as doctors and nurses went about their business with brisk efficiency. No sounds of distress or emergency reached me.

My heart still pounded from the dream. I told myself that it was no more than a repeated nightmare. Rory had returned from the war and his injury was bad enough that I knew he would not be returning. It could not possibly come true. My dream consisted of nothing but old fears from the time we had been close friends. No doubt the dream itself was the fault of Fitzroy. He had doubtless mentioned something at the time – he had been an uninvited guest at the lodge, who had come to look into the accusation of murder that had been levelled against Rory. I must have overheard him speaking about the impending war to one of the other guests, and with Rory in danger of being hanged, I had put the two together in a dream. Albeit a dream so real and viscerally frightening that years later it could return to terrify me once more.

I ran my fingers through my hair, and took several long deep breaths in an attempt to slow my heart rate and quell the panic I felt. Maybe the dream had been shaken loose by the bang I had received to the head. Did powerful dreams remain with us, stored hidden deep within our brains, and could they be awoken by trauma?

Even this interesting thought could not distract me. I still felt scary, worried, panicky, and aware I had forgotten something. I wished Griffin had not told Fitzroy to stay away. I could have done with someone talking sense to me. I thought Fitzroy as liable to believe in omens as in my ability to fly.

I threw back the covers and swung my feet over the edge of the bed. My feet brushed something soft. A soft enquiring whiffle told me Jack was still here. I felt rather touched he had stayed. I bent down and picked him up. He was a middle-sized dog, but a diet of tidbits and treats alongside his regular meals had widened his girth. So I struggled slightly, but the good-natured beast was still sleepy. He clambered into my arms and gave my elbow a lick. His brown eyes looked up at me as if apologising for not standing to lick my face, but he was ever so tired. I found myself planting a kiss on the top of his head. Another whiffle, but, I thought, a happy one. He curled up on my lap and began to snore.

This had not been quite what I had intended, but having the warmth of Jack on my lap, and listening to his slow and deep breathing, calmed me much more than my thoughts had done. As my heart slowed and my fear ebbed, I was still left with a feeling that something was wrong. Try as I might, I could not shake this.

I looked around the room. I was in a hospital gown. Presumably put to bed by one of the nurses. However, Merry, or someone, had brought my dressing gown from the dorm. It hung on the back of the door. Carefully I transferred Jack onto the bed covers. Although

I rolled him more than lifted him. This brought an undoubtedly happy whiffle – Jack had a preference for human beds and a master who was determined to keep him out of them. He whiffled and wriggled, eyes closed, as he nested down on my bed.

I stood up slowly. It wasn't as bad as I had feared. I had a vague memory of someone offering me pills and some water. Whatever those painkillers had been, they had done their work. My head felt sore, but it was no longer so painful I felt nauseated. My body definitely felt it wanted to be in bed lying down, but I was able to force myself to stand. I spent a depressing amount of time getting into the dressing gown. My movements were slower than usual and less co-ordinated.

But I didn't give in to temptation, I knew something was wrong. I opened the door and went into the corridor. There was no sign of anyone in either direction. They had put me in a different part of the hospital, so I needed to re-orientate myself. I headed down the wider corridor. Once I reached an outside door I could determine if I was going to go out and knock on the window of Ward D to be let in. I didn't like to think of how Sister Evans would react if she was on duty tonight.

I walked on, far too slowly for the burning concern inside me. When I thought about Ward D I didn't feel any push to go there. Whatever was driving me on it was about Rory, I was sure now. Eventually I found myself in part of the hospital I recognised. I turned my shuffling steps towards Surgical Ward Six, where Rory now slept. At least Merry was on night duty there. She might laugh at me, but at least she wouldn't react like any of the other senior staff, who would send me back to bed and sedate me.

Finally I entered the surgical wards. Being female I would stand out like a sore thumb, but I hadn't accounted for the lull of the night. I passed three wards with no one noticing me. The night nurses within were either drowsily sifting through paperwork or moving quietly around the wards. No one was looking out into the main corridor, because no one expected anyone to be there. I might, after all, manage to peek in on Ward Six, content myself, and disappear off to bed without anyone noticing.

I had to hide behind a washing cart that absolutely should not have been left out to avoid the night nurse hovering over the nearest patient's bed on Ward Three. However, the night nurse in ward five was accommodating enough to have her head down on her desk and be fast asleep. I debated whether or not to wake her, and decided if she was still asleep when I came back this way, I would.

Finally, Ward Six. I peeked around the corner. Merry was wide awake, sitting at her desk and surveying her domain. I was about to wave slightly to attract her attention, when I saw our fellow trainee, Margaret Arden, walk up and greet Merry. I hung back. I saw Merry smile, nod and rise. Margaret, who Ruth had nicknamed Maggie in an attempt to rile the well-spoken woman, sat down in Merry's place. Merry headed towards the kitchen. There was nothing wrong with this scene. One nurse had come to allow her colleague to get a well earned cup of tea.

Except this wasn't done routinely. Sometimes nurses did manage to do this for their particular friends, especially if they had been assisting on another ward that had difficult patients who were now fully asleep. Except even when Merry had been cool to me and had been picked up by the others, I had never seen her exchange more than a few words with Margaret in all our time here. Margaret had struck me as a woman who thought herself too good for the rest of us. My mother would have said she was, 'probably a shopkeeper's daughter who married up. A real lady talks in a kind way to all, whether or not they are her social inferiors. In fact, particularly if they are.'

My mother was having a glorious time being a Bishop's wife.

I shook my head. My thoughts were everywhere. The movement made my vision swim, but as it refocused I saw that neither Margaret nor Merry were now at the desk. Surely I would have heard if a patient had called out for aid?

I walked quietly onto the ward. At once I felt eyes on my back, but when I turned all the patients appeared to be fast asleep. I padded quietly towards where I knew Rory lay. I had no reason to think Margaret wished him ill, but with her away the coast was clear for anyone to attack him. If I went to his bedside that would make anyone else who approached think twice about progressing with any nefarious plan.

Accordingly, I walked as swiftly as I could over to Rory's bed. He was in a bed by the window around which a screen had been placed for privacy. The thought crossed my mind that Margaret could be helping him with a bedpan. That would be embarrassing for both Rory and me. Although now I was married, and I was a nurse (technically a trainee), neither of us should be bothered about my appearance, I thought. I had helped other patients in such situations.

But no one I knew, an inner voice insisted. And certainly no one to whom I had been previously engaged. I hesitated. In that moment of hesitation the moon came out from behind a cloud and I saw a female figure crouching over Rory's bed.

I didn't wait long enough to even fully understand what I was seeing. I ran forward. I thought for a moment I'd heard Fitzroy's voice, but that had to be my mind playing tricks. I wanted him to be there.

I pushed the screen aside with my right hand. I used more force than I meant to as the screen fell onto its side. The scene I saw before me entered my mind in pieces as I made sense of it. I saw Margaret's face; her eyes blazed at me. Rory moved. He stirred but didn't wake. A tremendous frown descended on Margaret's face. 'What on earth do you think you are doing, Stapleford?' she said in a forceful whisper.

I stood frozen watching her. Rory slept on. 'What are you doing?' I countered.

'I heard Sergeant McLeod call out in his sleep. I came to see if he was in distress.'

'He didn't.'

'I beg your pardon?'

'He didn't cry out,' I said. 'I was standing watching you.'

Margaret stepped around the bed towards me. 'I think you are suffering from a worse concussion than the doctors thought. Come now. I'll help you back to bed.'

This was not unreasonable. I was behaving oddly. But yet, something was wrong. I knew it.

Margaret closed more of the gap between us.'

'Why do you have one hand behind your back?'

All my attention was on Margaret. Who suddenly revealed the syringe in her hand as she came hurtling towards me.

I was slow. Almost too slow. I caught her hand before the needle pierced my skin. The room swam. I couldn't remember any of my training. I felt dizzy and sick. All I knew was that I could not let that needle puncture me. It was almost there. I put up my other hand to help hold her back. But Margaret was forcing me backwards, off balance. I tripped on something behind me. My legs went from under me as I fell into an empty bed.

Finally I found the presence of mind to call out, 'Help! Help!' The first call was soft, but the second came louder. I heard a commotion outside. I grabbed her arm again by both wrists as she bent over me, holding her off. My eyes focused on the tip of the needle. It inched closer and closer. 'Help!' Why didn't Merry come? Why didn't someone come?'

I heard the sound of footsteps. 'Euphemia!' This time it was unquestionably Fitzroy's voice.

I turned my head. 'Help!' I said once more. My arms burned with pain, and suddenly gave. I saw Fitzroy running, but the needle had far less distance to go than he had left to run. He'd never make it.

I hoped whatever she had in that needle the death it would bring would not be painful. Everything slowed, as so often it does in these situations. I was acutely aware of the needle about to enter my skin, when a white blur passed over me. It resolved itself into the form of Jack as his jaws clamped over Margaret's arm.

She screamed and dropped the syringe. I rolled aside as it landed harmlessly on the bed. Margaret disappeared from my sight as the momentum of the charging dog threw her to the ground. I heard another scream followed by spine tingling growls. I sat up. 'Jack! Jack!' I called, worried that she would hurt the dog. I saw he still had her arm in his jaws and was pulling it from side to side, sinking his

254

teeth in further. Margaret desperately tried to fend him off with her other hand. The floor was turning red with her blood.

'Jack! Heel!' commanded Fitzroy. The dog at once let go and came to his side.

'That animal needs to be put down,' said Margaret. She struggled to sit on the floor. Blood poured from her arm. 'He's a menace to society.'

'Jack generally knows what he's doing,' said Fitzroy in a calm voice. 'May I ask what was in that syringe?'

'A sedative for Stapleford. She's clearly out of her wits. She needs to be in bed.' She rose shakily to her feet.

'Which you just happened to have on you?'

Griffin appeared from behind me and gently helped me to my feet. 'If you will allow me?' he said, and put an arm around my waist to support me. I would have objected, but my legs were most unreliable.

'She was going to inject Rory before I stopped her.'

'You're raving,' spat Margaret.

Fitzroy stood perfectly still watching her closely. 'It seems to me that McLeod is already sleeping soundly. Almost as if he has already been drugged. Isn't that your usual method of operating – and Love's?'

Margaret darted forward. She was unsteady on her feet, but she managed to stamp on the syringe before any of us could move. 'You've no proof.'

'We have Love,' said Fitzroy.

'An old servant I barely knew.'

'That's not how she tells it,' said Fitzroy, producing a gun from his pocket. 'For now I suggest you stay very still.'

'You won't shoot a woman.'

'I'd rather not, but I will. You tried to murder McLeod and when Euphemia caught you, you tried to kill her.'

'No jury would convict me. I am a member of the aristocracy.'

'Are you adding that to your list of crimes?' said Fitzroy.

Finally it clicked into place. 'The bottle of morphine. The stolen one. She has it.'

'Euphemia, sit,' said Fitzroy. 'Griffin, take her.'

This didn't seem to make sense. But then Griffin released me and stepped forward to tackle Margaret. She struggled against him, but I saw him use a hold I had seen other doctors use on Upper Ward D. It didn't hurt unless the subject struggled. Margaret struggled like blazes. Her long hair came out of its bun, and swung over her face as she cursed Griffin in the foulest language.

'Definitely a member of the aristocracy,' said Fitzroy coolly. 'Would you be so kind, Euphemia, as to search the pockets of this woman's clothing.'

At this Margaret stamped hard on Griffin's foot. He pulled a face. 'If you wouldn't mind hurrying, Miss Alice. She's a handful.'

'Stay still,' commanded Fitzroy. 'I can quite easily shoot you without harming Dr Griffin – and I am growing more inclined to do so by the second. Euphemia, don't come between the gun and her.'

Finally Margaret seemed to accept that she was in real danger. She spat in my hair as I searched her. Griffin responded by tightening his grip, causing her to cry out in pain.

I stepped back before Fitzroy could shoot her. (I knew he was feeling more and more like it). I held up the bottle. 'This is the stolen bottle,' I said. 'Or one identical to it. They're numbered so we will be able to check.'

'Can you manage to get her into the lock-up?' Fitzroy asked Griffin.

'Am I allowed to damage her?'

'As much as you need to to control her,' said Fitzroy.

'Boundaries?'

'Oh, none,' said Fitzroy putting away his gun. 'If she dies, she dies. It decreases my paperwork.'

I knew that to be a lie, but kept my mouth shut. Griffin dragged Margaret away. Fitzroy sat down beside me on the empty bed. 'You really are a lot of trouble,' he said. Jack jumped up next to us, and nuzzled under my arm.

'Where's Merry?' I asked.

Chapter Thirty

Fitzroy gives a warning

'She should be back by now.'

'Where did she go?' said Fitzroy rising.

'To make herself a cup of tea.'

Fitzroy stood and turned slowly on the spot. 'Does it strike you as odd none of these men have woken despite the disturbance?'

'You mean she drugged them all? But how?'

'The tea urn,' said Fitzroy. She must have put something in it after the last meal tonight, so their final tea of the day . . .'

I got up and went to the nearest patient. I checked his pulse at the wrist. 'Weak and thready,' I said.

'Stay here!' He ran off.

Less than a minute later Merry came out of the kitchen blowing on the top of her cup of tea. 'What are you –' she began.

'Don't drink that tea!' I cried, standing and swaying so badly I fell back down again. 'Margaret poisoned the tea.'

Merry put the tea down on her desk. 'I've been drinking tea all evening,' she said. 'I'm fine.'

'But look at the rest of them,' I said gesturing around the ward. 'Their pulses are thready and weak.'

Merry went to one patient and then another. 'Oh my God,' she said. 'You're right. What do I do?'

'Fitzroy has gone for help.'

'Why I am fine? Am I fine?'

'We think she put a sleeping draught in the urn earlier, but either

257

she got the dose wrong or she did mean to kill everyone. But then why try and inject Rory?'

Merry's eyes went very wide. 'What?' She started to tremble.

I hit my forehead. 'Think! Think! What's the antidote?'

'There isn't one,' said Merry in a faint voice. 'If she's overdosed them on sleeping pills . . .'

I stood up. 'Some of them will be hardier than others,' I said. 'Stomach lavage. It's the only thing.'

'Will it help?'

'It won't harm them,' I said.

'You need to make up the salt water.'

Merry looked around the ward. 'Enough for all of them. I don't know . . .'

'We have to try,' I said.

At this point we heard the sounds of people running. Within moments it seemed as if half the hospital staff were in here. Somehow Fitzroy, with Jack and Griffin at his side, found me in the mill of moving people.

'I need to help,' I said.

'You've done enough,' said Fitzroy. 'If you wouldn't mind, Griffin?'

Griffin swept me up into his arms. 'I'd carry you myself,' said Fitzroy gruffly, 'but not up to it at present.' He cast a dark look up at Griffin. 'Don't even think about enjoying this.'

'No, sir,' said Griffin meekly. When Fitzroy turned away he winked at me. I like to think I would have made some witty remark, but the evening's exertions caught up with me and I fainted completely away in Griffin's arms.

For the next seven days I wasn't allowed any visitors. The sole concession to this, I was later told, was to allow Jack in. Only with him settled at my side would I sink into a deep sleep. I remember very little of those days, but I do remember the warmth of Jack through the bedclothes, and the occasional whiffly nuzzle he gave my arm from time to time as if checking I was still alive.

I heard much later that most of the men had been saved. Rory was among these. Five died. Rather than committing a deliberate act of mass murder, it transpired that Margaret Arden had miscalculated the dose. About this she was inconsolable. Merry had been spared, because she hated the hissing and spitting of the tea urn with a passion and always used a small teapot when she made herself tea. Somehow she had found a small kettle that she brought down with her to night duty. I suspected that Cuttle Enterprises might have had a hand in its procurement. I never asked. The noise of it boiling had prevented her from hearing my struggle by Rory's bedside and my calls for help.

On the eighth day, I was told I should dress and collect my things from the dorm. I waited downstairs and around two o'clock Griffin arrived to collect me. 'Am I going home?' I asked.

'No, Miss Alice. The Major has rooms for us at a nearby billet. It seems there is something he must discuss with you before you head home.'

'Does he want me to go on another mission?' I asked as Griffin took my suitcase. 'I suppose I could. But I'm not feeling quite right yet.' In truth, although the dizziness and nausea had abated, the act of standing in itself was as exhausting as running full sprint.

'He hasn't mentioned anything,' said Griffin, handing me into the back of the car as if he was the chauffeur. Jack immediately jumped up beside me. 'Do you mind?' he asked.

'Jack?' I asked, gently stroking the dog's ear. 'Not at all. He's my hero.'

Griffin smiled. 'It's not far. I should in reference to your earlier question say that the Major remains on medical leave for some weeks yet. He had a bit of a setback after the events here. I shouldn't want his appearance to alarm you. He is on the mend even if he looks worse than when you last saw him.'

'Oh heavens,' I said. 'Poor Fitzroy. Is he very poorly?'

'More than he will admit, Miss Alice. Try not to be too hard on him.'

I lent back in the seat thinking this was an odd thing to say. Jack pushed his head under my arm and distracted me.

★

259

Fitzroy had acquired a small Manor House on the coast. It was clearly a family home. A neat house with seven bedrooms, three rather modern bathrooms, a drawing room, a fine dining room, a library, a billiards room, a smoking lounge, and presumably a kitchen. I was never allowed below stairs.

The spymaster came out to meet the car. Griffin pulled up directly in front of the door. Fitzroy came to help me out. He did indeed look awful. He was even thinner. The lines around his eyes had deepened and his cheeks were hollow. There was a touch of white in his hair. But his eyes twinkled as he looked up at me. 'I know I look as if I've been dead three weeks.'

I took his hand and climbed down. 'But on the positive side you don't smell as if you've been dead three weeks,' I said. He roared with laughter. Jack ran in circles around our legs, obviously ecstatic that we were all back together.

'Come in. I've not only let you have the best bedroom, there's already a fire lit in the grate. I may even allow you to keep Jack by your side a few more nights as long as you remember he's my dog.'

'I have a lot of questions,' I said.

'And I have a lot to talk to you about. You're not going to like some of it. So I'll start my apologies now.'

'What do you mean?'

'Go upstairs, Euphemia and rest until dinner. I'll explain everything after we've eaten.'

Griffin, whose skills appeared to be unlimited, cooked us a superb meal of venison. 'Did he shoot it too?' I asked.

Fitzroy shook his head. 'I doubt it. Game needs to be hung for some time before eating.' We had between us polished off an enormous meal ending with trifle, followed by coffee and petits fours. Griffin had not joined us. 'Really, Euphemia, did your mother have the help dine with her?' Fitzroy had said when I asked. He then relented slightly, 'I'll give him a game of billiards later. I might even let him score a point or two.'

But over coffee he became more serious. When Griffin had taken

260

the dishes away, he suggested we retired to the library to talk. Here too, despite it being the tail end of the summer weather, a fire had been lit. I didn't complain as I thought it was as much for Fitzroy, who remained painfully thin, as it was for me. Two wing backed chairs, upholstered in green leather had been drawn up to the hearth, and a small table set between them. The curtains were closed, and the atmosphere was one of peace and comfort. The only sound was the crackling of the logs as they burned and Jack's snores.

Fitzroy went over to a shelf and pulled open a section of books, which proved to be a false cupboard door with decanters behind. 'I will give you a brandy on one condition,' he said. 'That you promise to throw neither it nor your coffee over me.'

I laughed.

'Promise!'

'Really?' I said. 'Am I that bad a subordinate?'

'Humour me, Alice. Promise.'

'All right, I promise not to throw any drinks over you while I am in this house. Is it yours, by the way?'

Fitzroy shook his head, and passed me a glass. 'A generous promise. I'll hold you to it.'

'So, the murders?' I asked.

We were sat in the corner of the library, close to the fire. Most of the shelves faded into darkness, but one or two lamps were lit. The orange firelight reflected off Fitzroy's face, and I thought I saw relief in it when I asked my question.

'Apparently Margaret Arden is a member of a sect that believes modern medicine should not prolong life in certain circumstances. In fact, if I have it right they believe that prayer is the only medicine one should ever need.'

'My father believed in the power of prayer,' I said, 'but he believed in medicine too. He said God gave us brains for a reason.'

'Quite right,' said Fitzroy. 'I only wish he'd been more generous among the general populous.' He paused to sip his brandy. 'Now, this sect has never advocated more than protests and debate. It was when Arden's husband died that she broke away to form her own

261

sub-sect. Having seen her husband die without the aid of medicine, she decided, in her words not mine, 'to honour his devotion to God by saving those too unfortunate to save themselves.' In other words, patients who could not protest their treatment. But again this was a more in words than deeds sort of thing. However around this time she employed a servant, Margaret Love – notice the similar names – they decided their meeting was ordained in heaven. Love embraced her new mistress' philosophy, and when she left some years ago, to live with her mother, who was old, but not ill, she took up cleaning at the hospital. There she saw an opportunity to help a great many unfortunate souls.'

'She's been doing this for a while?'

Fitzroy nodded. 'Oh yes, years. Love may be the servant but she's the clever one. She chose her victims with great care. Now she's been caught she is only too happy to own up to what she did – on God's orders.'

'How awful.'

'Precisely. On the outbreak of war she wrote to her old employer, telling her of what she had been doing and begging to join her as a nurse. She knew Arden would never have accepted work as a cleaner, but the VAD offered her a perfect solution. Arden was delighted to answer the call, but Love presumed her old mistress would know how to be subtle. She didn't and made quite a hash of it from the start.'

'So her killing Wilkins was pure coincidence when it came to the mission?'

'I'm afraid so.' Fitzroy sighed. 'I am certain she has no knowledge of any traitor in the Service.'

'But she was cleared to work on Ward D!'

'Everywhere needs cleaners,' said Fitzroy getting up to pour himself a second drink. He held the decanter up to offer me one. I shook my head. 'Apparently, of the people they had to choose from she seemed the most harmless. She had no questionable contacts. In fact, apart from her mother she didn't associate with anyone else. That, in itself, should have been a warning sign if the vetter had done his job properly.' He shoved the decanter stopper back in with unnecessary force.

'And Dwyer?'

Fitzroy sat back down and stretched his legs out to the fire. 'I'm afraid there Love and Dwyer differ. I think Dwyer did know who the traitor in the upper ranks is and I think said traitor did order Dwyer to set us up for an ambush in the field.'

'But Dwyer's dead,' I said.

'I did notice,' said Fitzroy.

'So the knowledge has gone with him to the grave?'

'Yes and no,' said Fitzroy. 'His determination to flee, even at the cost of his own life, has caused me to think that this high-ranking traitor isn't a paranoid aspect of my imagination, but most solidly real. It has utterly convinced me we were ambushed on instructions that could only have come from London. This mission, your mission, has accomplished that at least – and that is a great deal. Now, we will have to start again trying to ferret the damned man out. Of course, it will all have to be under cover. We can hardly advertise to our superiors that we are seeking a miscreant among them.'

'I don't know any superiors, except you.'

'Hmpf,' said Fitzroy. 'I don't feel very superior at present. But I will introduce you to some others soon. If I do it all at once it will look odd, but we can work our way through possible traitors. Hopefully we will discover that a limited pool of suspects had access to the necessary files.'

'You have another mission for me? Maybe I will need that second drink.'

'Not for a while,' said the spy. 'You need to recover as much, if not more, than I do. It's a bad idea to go into the field when you're sub-par, as I should know.'

'You mean coming to my rescue?'

'No, I did another mission off book before that. It was more than . . .' he looked down into his glass for so long I thought I had lost him, 'a little difficult,' he finished.

'I'm sorry to hear that,' I said. 'I take it I can't know the details.'

Fitzroy upended his second glass down his throat. He looked over at the decanter as if debating internally whether to have another drink, but didn't get up. He turned to look at me this time, rather than gazing into the fire.

'Actually, I need to tell you about it in detail – and apologise. It's about your husband, Alice.'